BAHAMA CRISIS
DESMOND BAGLEY

"Desmond Bagley's writing is so fluid that his seemingly effortless style passes by almost unnoticed. It is the action that catches the eye, and makes page-turning compulsive."—*Financial Times*

D1289620

Also available in Perennial Library by Desmond Bagley:

The Freedom Trap
The Golden Keel
Running Blind
The Snow Tiger
The Tightrope Men
The Vivero Letter
Windfall

BAHAMA CRISIS

DESMOND BAGLEY

PERENNIAL LIBRARY
Harper & Row, Publishers
New York, Cambridge, Philadelphia, San Francisco
London, Mexico City, São Paulo, Singapore, Sydney

A hardcover edition of this book was published by William Collins Sons & Co., Ltd., in England and by Summit Books, a division of Simon & Schuster, Inc., in the United States. It is here reprinted by arrangement with Summit Books.

First PERENNIAL LIBRARY edition published 1985.

Library of Congress Cataloging in Publication Data

Bagley, Desmond, 1923–
    Bahama crisis.

    I. Title.
[PR6052.A315B3   1985]   823'.914   84-48575
ISBN 0-06-080755-5 (pbk.)

85 86 87 88 89   10 9 8 7 6 5 4 3 2 1

To Valerie and David Redhead
with much affection

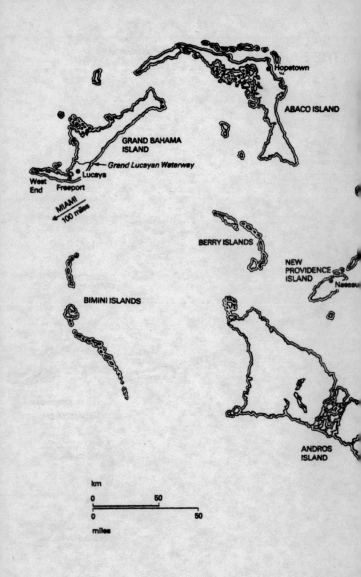

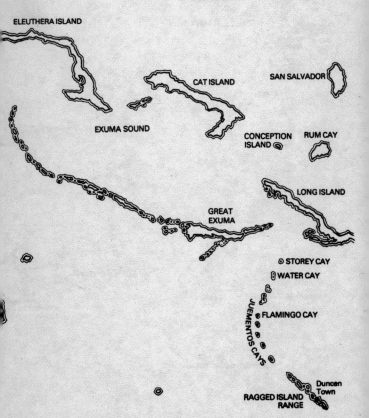

THE BAHAMA ISLANDS

N

ATLANTIC OCEAN

ELEUTHERA ISLAND

CAT ISLAND

SAN SALVADOR

EXUMA SOUND

CONCEPTION ISLAND

RUM CAY

LONG ISLAND

GREAT EXUMA

STOREY CAY

WATER CAY

JUEMENTOS CAYS

FLAMINGO CAY

Duncan Town

RAGGED ISLAND RANGE

PROLOGUE

MY NAME is Tom Mangan and I am a Bahamian—a resident of that chain of islands beginning about fifty miles off the coast of Florida and sweeping in an arc five hundred miles to the southeast to a similar distance off the coast of Cuba. The Bahamas consist of seven hundred islands (called cays locally, and pronounced "keys") and about two thousand lesser rocks. The name is derived from the Spanish *baja mar* which means "shallow sea."

I am descended from one of the families who fought on the side of the British in the American War of Independence. Life in the new United States was not comfortable for the erstwhile Tories. Reviled by their compatriots and abandoned by the British, many thought it prudent to leave, the northerners going mostly to Nova Scotia and the southerners to the Bahamas or to the sugar islands in the Caribbean beyond Cuba. So it was that in 1784 John Henry Mangan elected to settle with his family on the island of Abaco in the Bahamas.

There was not much to Abaco. Shaped something like a boomerang, Great and Little Abaco Islands stretch for about 130 miles surrounded by a cluster of lesser cays. Most of these smaller cays are of coral, but Abaco itself is of limestone and covered with thick, almost impenetrable, tropical bush. Sir Guy Carleton intended to settle 1,500 souls on Abaco, but they were a footloose and fractious crowd and not many stayed. By 1778 the total population was about 400, half of whom were black slaves.

It is not hard to see why Carleton's project collapsed. Abaco, like the rest of the Bahamian islands, has a thin, infertile soil, a natural drawback which has plagued the Bahamas throughout their history. Many cash crops have been

7

tried—tomatoes, pineapples, sugar, sisal, cotton—but all have failed as the fertility of the soil became exhausted. It is not by chance that three settlements in the Bahamas are called Hard Bargain.

Still, a man could survive if he did not expect too much; there were fish in the sea, and one could grow enough food for one's immediate family. Timber was readily available for building, the limestone was easily quarried, and palmetto leaf thatch made a good waterproof roof. John Henry Mangan not only survived but managed to flourish, along with the Sands, the Lowes, the Robertses and other families whose names are still common on Abaco today.

The Mangans are a thin line because, possibly due to a genetic quirk, they tend to run to girls, like the Dutch royal family. Thus they did not grow like a tree with many branches but in a single line. I am the last of the male Mangans and, as far as I know, there are no others of that name in the islands.

But they survived and prospered. One of my forebears was a shipbuilder at Hope Town on Elbow Cay; most of the local ships sailing the Bahamian waters were built on Abaco, and the Mangan family built not a few and so became moderately well-to-do. And then there was the wrecking. As the United States grew in power there was much maritime traffic and many ships were wrecked on the Islands of the Shallow Sea. The goods they contained contributed greatly to the wealth of many an island family, the Mangans not excepted. But the great turning point in the family fortunes came with the American Civil War.

The Confederate South was starved of supplies because of the northern blockade, and cotton rotted on the docks. Any ship putting into Charleston or Wilmington found a ready market for its cargo; quinine costing ten dollars in Nassau brought in excess of four hundred dollars in Charleston, while cotton costing four hundred dollars at the dockside was worth four thousand dollars in Liverpool. It was a most profitable, if risky, two-way trade and my great-grandfather saw his opportunity and made the family rich in half a decade.

It was his son, my grandfather, who moved the family from Abaco to Nassau on New Providence—Nassau being the capital of the Bahamas and the center of trade. Yet we still own land on Abaco and I have been building there recently.

If my great-grandfather made the family rich it was my father who made it really wealthy. He became a multimillionaire. Again, it was running an American blockade which provided the profit.

On January 15, 1920, the United States went dry and, as in the Civil War, the Bahamas became a distribution center for contraband goods. The Nassau merchants known as the Bay Street Boys, my father among them, soon got busy importing liquor. The profit margin was normally 100 percent and the business was totally risk-free; it was cash on the barrel and the actual blockade-running was done by the Americans themselves. It was said that there was so much booze stacked at West End on Grand Bahama that the island tipped by several degrees. And, for a Bahamian, the business was all legal.

All good things come to an end and the Eighteenth Amendment was repealed by Franklin Roosevelt in 1933, but by then my father was sitting pretty and had begun to diversify his interests. He saw with a keen eye that the advent of aircraft was going to have an impact on the tourist industry and would alter its structure. Already Pan-American was pioneering the Miami-Nassau route using Sikorsky seaplanes.

Bahamian tourism in the nineteenth and early twentieth centuries was confined to the American rich and the four-month winter season. An American millionaire would bring his family and perhaps a few friends to spend the whole season on New Providence. This, while being profitable to a few, was of little consequence to the Bahamian economy, millionaires not being all that plentiful. My father took the gamble that aircraft would bring the mass market and invested in hotels. He won his gamble, but died before he knew it, in 1949.

I was eleven years old then and had as much interest in money and business as any other boy of eleven, which is to say none. My mother told me that a trust fund had been set up for me and my two sisters and that I would come into my inheritance on my twenty-fifth birthday. She then continued to run the family affairs, which she was quite capable of doing.

I went to school in Nassau but spent my holidays on Abaco under the watchful eye of Pete Albury, a black Abaconian who I thought was old but, in fact, was about thirty at the time. He had worked for the family since he was a boy and looked after our property on Abaco. He had taught me to swim—a non-swimming Bahamian being as common as a wingless bird—and taught me to shoot, and we hunted the wild pig which is common on Abaco. He acted *in loco parentis* and tanned my hide when he thought I needed it. He stayed in my employ until his death not long ago.

Those early years were, I think, the most enjoyable of my life. In due course I went to England to study at Cambridge, and found England uncomfortably cold and wet; at least in the Bahamas the rain is warm. I took my degree and then went to the United States for a two-year course in business studies at Harvard to prepare myself for the administration of my inheritance. It was there I met Julie Pascoe who was to become my wife. In 1963 I was back in Nassau where, on my twenty-fifth birthday, there was much signing of documents in a lawyer's office and I took control of the estate.

Many things had changed in the Bahamas by then. My father's hunch had proved correct and the coming of the big jets brought the mass tourist market he had predicted. In 1949, the year he died, thirty-two thousand tourists came to the Islands; in 1963 there were over half a million. It is worth adding that next year the estimated total is over two million. My mother had looked after our interests well, but now she was getting old and a little frail and was glad to relinquish responsibility into my hands. I found that one of the things she had done was to become involved in the development of Grand Bahama. At the time that worried me very much because Grand Bahama was turning sour.

Wallace Groves was an American who had a dream and that dream was Freeport on the island of Grand Bahama. He persuaded Sir Stafford Sands, then Minister of Finance in the Bahamian Government, to sell him over two hundred square miles of government land on Grand Bahama upon which he would build a city—Freeport. His intention, not actually realized in his lifetime, was to create a duty-free area for the benefit of American corporations where they could avoid American taxes. In 1963 the scheme was not working; no immediate enthusiasm was being shown by any corporation anywhere. Groves switched the emphasis to tourism, recreation and residential housing, and twisted Sands's arm to allow the building of a casino to attract custom.

Sands was a quintessential Bay Street Boy who could catch a dollar on the fly no matter how fast it went. It was he who was primarily responsible for the vast increase of tourist traffic. Reasoning that the tourist needs much more than mere sun and sand he saw to it that the whole infrastructure of the tourist industry was built and maintained. He acceded to Groves's request and the casino opened in 1964.

It was the worst mistake Sands could have made. The shadowy figure supervising the running of the casino was Meyer Lansky, who used to run casinos in Havana until he was tossed out of Cuba by Castro. Having put out a contract on Castro for one million dollars, Lansky looked for somewhere else to operate and found Grand Bahama. The gangsters had moved in.

Politics and economics walk hand in hand, largely revolving around the question of who gets what, and the black Bahamians saw the wealth created by the tourist industry going into the pockets of the white Bay Street Boys who also controlled the House of Assembly and ran the country in the interest of the whites. Something had to give, and in 1967 the largely black Progressive Liberal Party led by Lynden Pindling squeaked into power with a two-seat majority. The following year Pindling unexpectedly held another election and the PLP got in with twenty-nine seats out of the thirty-eight.

This landslide came about because of the mistake made by Stafford Sands. As soon as Pindling came to power he decided to take a closer look at Freeport and, in particular, the casino. He found that Groves and Lansky were giving kickbacks to Sands and others in the form of dubious "consultancy fees" and that Sands himself was reputed to have taken over two million dollars. When this was disclosed all hell broke loose; Sands was discredited and fell, bringing his party down with him.

But Groves had been right—the casino had brought prosperity to Grand Bahama, and Freeport had boomed and was thriving. There were plans for vast residential developments; great areas were already laid out in streets, complete with sewerage and electricity. The streets even had names; all that was missing were the houses on the building plots.

But investors were wary. To them a Caribbean revolution had taken place and what would those crazy blacks do next? They ignored the fact that it had been a democratic election and that the composition of the Assembly now compared with the ethnic composition of the Bahamas; they just pulled out and took their money with them and the economy of Grand Bahama collapsed again and is only now recovering in the 1980s.

And what was I doing while this was going on? I was trying to keep things together by fast footwork and trying not to get my hands too dirty. To tell the truth I voted for Pindling. I could see that the rule of the Bay Street Boys' oligarchy was an anachronism in a fast changing world and that, unless the black Bahamian was given a share in what was going, there would be a revolution and not a peaceful election.

And among other things I got married.

Julie Pascoe was the daugher of an American doctor and lived in Maryland. When I left Harvard we kept up a correspondence. In 1966 she visited the Bahamas with her parents and I took them around the Islands; showing off, I suppose. We married in 1967 and Susan was born in 1969. Karen came along in 1971. The propensity of the Mangans to breed daughters had not failed.

Although I had been worried about the investments on Grand Bahama, recently I decided that an upswing was due. I floated a company, the West End Securities Corporation, a holding company which I control and of which I am president. More importantly I moved my base of operations from Nassau to Freeport, and built a house at Lucaya on Grand Bahama. Nassau is an old town, a little stuffy and set in its ways. Brave new ideas do not sprout in an environment like that so I left for Grand Bahama where Wally Groves's dream seems about to come true.

I suppose I could have been pictured as a very lucky man—not worrying where my next dollar was coming from, happily married to a beautiful wife with two fine children, and with a flourishing business. I *was* a lucky man, and I thought nothing could go wrong until the events I am about to recount took place.

Where shall I begin? I think with Billy Cunningham who was around when it happened just before the Christmas before last. It was the worst Christmas of my life.

Bahama
Crisis

1

BILLY CUNNINGHAM was a scion of the Cunningham clan; his father, uncle, brother and assorted cousins jointly owned a fair slice of Texas—they ran cattle, drilled for oil, were into shipping, newspapers, radio and television, hotels, supermarkets and other real estate, and owned moderate tracts of downtown Dallas and Houston. The Cunningham Corporation was a power to be reckoned with in Texas, and Prince Billy was in the Bahamas to see what he could see.

I had first met him at Harvard Business School where, like me, he was being groomed for participation in the family business, and we had kept in touch, meeting at irregular intervals. When he telephoned just before Christmas asking to meet me on my own ground I said, "Sure. You'll be my guest."

"I want to pick your brains," he said. "I might have a proposition for you."

That sounded interesting. The Cunningham Corporation was the kind of thing I was trying to build West End Securities into, though I had a long way to go. I had a notion that the Cunninghams were in mind for expansion and Billy was coming to look over the chosen ground. I would rather cooperate than have them as competitors because they were a tough crowd, and I hoped that was what Billy was thinking about. We fixed a date.

I met him at Freeport International Airport where he arrived in a company jet decked in the Cunningham colors. He had not changed much; he was tall, broad-shouldered and blond, with a deep tan and gleaming teeth. The Cunninghams seemed to run to film star good looks, those of them I had met. There was nothing about him to indicate he was American, no eccentricity of style which might reasonably be expected. If he ever wore them, then Billy had left his ten-gallon hat, string tie and high-heeled boots at home, and was dressed in a lightweight suit of obviously English cut. Being a Cunningham he would probably order them casually by the half-dozen from Huntsman of Savile Row.

"How's the boy?" he said as we shook hands. "I don't think you've met Debbie—this is my little cousin."

Deborah Cunningham was as beautiful as the Cunningham menfolk were handsome; a tall, cool blonde. "Pleased to meet you, Miss Cunningham."

She smiled. "Debbie, please."

"Tell me," said Billy. "How long is the runway?"

That was a typical Billy Cunningham question; he had an insatiable curiosity and his questions, while sometimes apparently irrelevant, always had a bearing on his current train of thought. I said, "The last time I measured it came to eleven thousand feet."

"That should just about take any airplane," he commented. He turned and watched the Cunningham JetStar take off, then said, "Let's move."

I drove them through Freeport on my way to the Royal Palm Hotel. I was proud of the Royal Palm; for my money it was the best hotel in the Bahamas. Of course, it had been my money that had built it, and I was looking forward to seeing Billy's reaction. On the way I said, "Is this your first time in the Bahamas, Debbie?"

"Yes."

"Mine, too," said Billy. That surprised me, and I said so. "Just never gotten around to it." He twisted in his seat. "Which way is Freeport?"

"Right here. You're in downtown Freeport." He grunted in surprise, and I knew why. The spacious streets, lawns and widely separated low-slung buildings were like no other city center he had seen. "It shows what you can do when you build a city from scratch. Twenty years ago this was all scrubland."

"Oh, look!" said Debbie. "Isn't that a London bus?"

I laughed. "The genuine article. There seems to be a mystique about those all over the English-speaking world—I've seen them at Niagara, too. I think the London Transport Board makes quite a profit out of selling junk buses as far-flung tourist attractions."

In the foyer of the Royal Palm Billy looked around with an experienced eye. The Cunningham Corporation ran its own hotels and knew how they ticked. He glanced upwards and gave a long, slow whistle. The foyer rose the entire height of the hotel, a clear eight stories with the bedrooms circling it on balconies. "Wow!" he said. "Isn't that a lot of wasted space?"

I smiled; even the Cunninghams had a lot to learn. "It might be in a city hotel, but this is a resort hotel. There's a difference."

Jack Fletcher, the hotel manager, was standing by and I introduced him to the Cunninghams. He booked them in with as few formalities as possible, then said, "Here are your room keys—Mr. Cunningham, Miss Cunningham." He gave Billy another key. "Your car's in the garage."

I said, "Find another car for Miss Cunningham; she might like to do some sightseeing by herself."

"Hey!" said Billy. "No need for that."

I shrugged. "No sweat; we run a car rental company and the season hasn't topped out yet. We have a few cars to spare."

He took me by the elbow and led me to one side. "I'd like to talk with you as soon as possible.

"You always were in a hurry."

"Why not? I get things done that way. Say, fifteen minutes?"

"I'll be in the bar." He nodded in satisfaction.

He was down in ten minutes and strode into the bar at a quick clip. After ordering him a drink I said, "Where's Debbie?"

Billy smiled crookedly. "You know women; she'll take a while to prettify herself." He accepted the bourbon on the rocks. "Thanks."

"Your room all right?"

"Fine." He frowned. "But I still say you're wasting a hell of a lot of space."

"You're thinking in terms of city downtown hotels. Space is cheap here and the clientele is different." I decided to push. "What are you here for, Billy? You mentioned a proposition."

"Well, we have a few dollars to spare and we're looking for somewhere to invest. What's your idea of the future of the Bahamas?"

"My God, Billy, but you have a nerve! You want to come in here as a competitor and you're asking my advice?"

He laughed. "You won't lose out on it. You've already said a couple of things that have set me thinking. We think we know how to run hotels back home, but it might be different here. Maybe we could set up a partnership of sorts and use your local expertise."

"A consortium?" He nodded, and I said contemplatively, "A few dollars. How few would they be?"

"About forty million few."

The bartender was standing close by, polishing an already overpolished glass. I said, "Let's go and sit at that corner table." We took our drinks and sat down. "I think the future of the Bahamas is pretty good. Do you know much of our recent history?"

"I've done my homework." He gave me a swift and concise rundown.

I nodded. "That's about it. You Americans are now coming to the realization that Pindling isn't an ogre and that he runs a fairly stable and conservative government. He's safe. Now, let's come to your hotels and the way you run them. Your clientele consists of businessmen and oil men, fast on their feet and on the move. They want fast service and good service, and they're here today and gone tomorrow. Because your land values in the city are so enormous you pack them in tight and charge them the earth because you have to. If you didn't, the operation wouldn't pay; it would be more profitable to sell up and move into some other business. Have I got it right?"

"Just about. Those guys can pay, anyway; we don't get many complaints."

I waved my arm. "What do you think of this place?"

"Very luxurious."

I smiled. "It's intended to look that way; I'm glad you think it succeeds. Look, Billy; your average tourist here isn't a jetsetter and he doesn't have all that many dollars to spend. He's a man and his wife, and maybe his kids, from Cleveland, Ohio. Perhaps he's done one trip to Europe, but he can't go again because Europe is too damned expensive these days. So he comes here because he's going foreign and economizing at the same time. Big deal."

"What about Europeans? Lots of those around here." Billy jerked his thumb toward the lobby. "Out there I heard German, French and Spanish."

"The Spanish would be coming from the Argentinians," I said. "We get lots of those. They, and the Europeans, come for the same reason—because it's cheaper here. But they don't come first class or even tourist. They come on charter flights in package deals organized by the travel agents—mostly German and Swiss. Neither the Americans nor the Europeans, with few exceptions, have a lot of money to throw around. So how do we handle the operation?"

"You tell me."

"Okay." I spread my hands. "We give them the semblance of luxury—stuff they can't get at home. Palm trees are cheap to buy, easy to plant and grow quickly; and you don't get many of those in Cleveland or Hamburg. And they look damned good. We have a few bars dotted about the place; one on the beach, one by the pool, a couple inside. We hire a local guitarist and a singer to give the live mood music—Bahamian and Caribbean calypso stuff—very romantic. We have a discothèque. We have a place to serve junk food and another for gourmet dining—both are equally profitable. We have shops in the lobby; jewelry, clothing, local handicrafts, a newsstand and so on. So far those have been concessions, but now we're tending to operate them ourselves; I've just started a merchandising division. And, as I said, we run a car rental outfit; that's part of the tours division. On the beach we have a few sailboats and wind-surfing boards, and we hire a beach bum to act as lifeguard and to show the clients how to use the stuff. That's free. So are the tennis courts. There's also use of an eighteen-hole golf course for a concessionary fee. There's a marina linked to the hotel so we also pull in the boating crowd."

"It seems a customer can get most of what he wants on his vacation without ever leaving the hotel," Billy hazarded.

"That's it," I said. "That's why they're called resort hotels. But what we *don't* have in the lobby is a liquor store; if a tourist wants his booze he pays bar prices. We want to squeeze as many dollars and cents out of these people as we can while they're in our tender care. And they *are* in our care, you know; they have a good time and they're not cold-decked. We have a nursery and a children's playground—that's more to keep the kids out of people's hair than for anything else—and we have a doctor and a nurse. And there's no drill or razzmatazz—they're just left alone to do as they please which seems to be mostly roasting in the sun."

Billy grimaced. "Not the kind of vacation I'd go for."

"Neither would I, but we're not tourists. So what happens when our man goes home? His friends look at that deep tan and ask him about it. 'Gee!' he says. 'I had the greatest time. Free sailboating, free tennis, cheap golf on the most superb course you can imagine. It was marvelous.' Then he does a hip shimmy around the office. 'And, man, that calypso beat!' That's what he tells his friends when the snow is two feet deep in the street outside the office, and they like the idea, so they come too, Maybe the year after."

Billy mused. "Fast turnover and small margins."

"That's the name of the game," I said. "That's why room occupancy is critical; we keep filled up or go broke."

"Any trouble in that direction?"

I smiled. "We're doing just fine," I said lightly.

He grunted. "I'd like to see your P and L and your balance sheet."

"If you come up with a firm offer I might give you a quick

look." I thought for a moment. "I'll introduce you to a few people and you can get a feel of the place. David Butler is a good man to talk to; he's top man in the Ministry of Tourism here on Grand Bahama." I hesitated. "There might be a problem there."

"What problem?"

"Well, you're a Southerner. Would you have any problem dealing with a black on equal terms?"

"Not me," said Billy. "Billy One might, and Jack certainly would; but they won't be involved out here." Billy One was Billy's father, so called to distinguish him from Billy. Jack was his uncle and head of the Cunningham clan. "Is this guy Butler black?"

"He is. There's another thing. Any hotels you build here must be Bahamian-built and Bahamian-staffed."

"The Bahamas for the Bahamians—is that it?"

"Something like that. No one else can hold down a job here if it can be done by a Bahamian."

Billy jerked his head towards the lobby. "Your hotel manager—Fletcher; he's white."

"So am I," I said evenly. "We're both white Bahamians. But the manager of the Sea Gardens—that's our hotel on New Providence—is black."

Billy shrugged. "It doesn't worry me as long as we have an efficient operation."

"Oh, we're efficient." I looked up and saw Debbie Cunningham coming into the bar. "Here's your cousin."

She was wearing a halter top and a pair of short shorts—a long-stemmed American beauty. "I hope this is okay," she said, and looked down at herself. "I mean, do you have *rules*?"

"Not so as you'd notice. Our visitors can dress pretty much as they like—up to a point." I inspected her. "I don't think you've reached the point yet, though. Will you have a drink?"

"Something soft; a Coke, maybe." I signaled a waiter and she sat down. "This is quite a place. Have you seen the pool, Billy?"

"Not yet."

I checked the time. "I'm going to be busy for the next hour. Why don't you give the place the once-over lightly and I'll meet you at the desk. We'll have lunch at home. If you need to know anything ask Jack Fletcher."

"That's fine," said Billy. "You've told me enough already so I know what to look for."

I left them and went to my office to do some hard thinking. When Billy had told me the size of his proposed investment it had given me quite a jolt, although I had tried not to show it. Forty million dollars is a hell of a lot of money and that much injected into West End Securities could provide for a lot of expansion. The problem would be to avoid being swamped by it, and it was going to be quite a puzzle to put together a suitable package which would keep both me and the Cunningham Corporation happy.

If Billy had been surprised by the Royal Palm Hotel he was equally surprised by my home and he showed it. I took him through into the atrium where the swimming pool was. He looked around and said, "My God!"

I laughed. "Ever been in Rome in August?"

"Who goes to Rome in August?" He shrugged. "But yes, I have—once," and added feelingly, "Goddamn hot. I got out of there fast."

"And humid—just like here. When I built this place I had an architect dig into the plans of Roman villas; the ancient Romans, I mean. I had a feeling they'd be building for the climate. This is not a reproduction of a villa—more an adaptation. With modern conveniences, of course; air conditioning included. But my air conditioning costs less to run than any of my neighbors' because the building design helps. We used some of that know-how when we built the Royal Palm; that big, tall lobby is a natural cooling tower."

Billy was about to say something when Julie walked out of the house. I said, "Here's Julie now. Julie, you've met Billy, but I don't think you know Debbie, his cousin."

"Hi, Billy, welcome to Grand Bahama. Glad to meet you, Debbie."

"You have a beautiful home," said Debbie.

"We like to think so." Julie turned and called, "Come out of there, Sue. We have guests; come and meet them."

My elder daughter emerged from the pool as sinuously as an otter. "Say 'hello' to Mr. Cunningham," commanded Julie.

"To Billy," I amended.

Sue shook hands gravely. She had an impish look as she said, "Hello, Mr. Billy Cunningham."

"And this is Debbie." Sue curtsied, something that would have looked better done in a crinoline instead of a minimal bathing suit.

"How old are you, Sue?" asked Debbie.

"Eleven years, two months, three weeks and six days," said Sue promptly.

"You swim very well," said Debbie. "I bet you swim better in I do."

ulie looked pleased—Debbie had said exactly the right ig. "Yes, she swims well. She came second in the Mara- n in her class."

said, "It's a two-mile course in the open sea."

Debbie was visibly startled and looked at my daughter th new respect. "That's really something; I doubt if I can im a quarter-mile."

"Oh, it's nothing," said Sue airily.

"All right, fish," I said. "Back into your natural element." I turned to Julie. "Where's Karen?"

"She's running a temperature. I put her to bed."

"Nothing serious?"

"Oh, no." Julie looked at Debbie. "She's been having school problems and might even be faking it. Come and see her; it might buck her up."

The women went into the house, and I said to Billy, "I think drinks are indicated."

"Yeah, something long and cold."

"A rum punch, but easy on the rum." As I mixed the drinks I said, "Air conditioning in hotels is important if we're to have a year-round season. We don't want the tourists frying even if it is good for the bar trade."

Billy took off his jacket and sat in a recliner. "Hey, I know about heat. You know what Sherman said about Texas?" I shook my head. "He said, 'If I owned Hell and Texas, I'd rent out Texas and live in Hell.' "

I laughed. "Then you'll see the problems, although we're not as bad as Texas. There's always a sea breeze to cut the heat."

We chatted while Luke Bailey, my general factotum, laid the table for lunch. Presently the women came back and accepted cold drinks. "You have two very nice girls," said Debbie.

"Julie must take the praise for that," I said. "I get any of the blame that's due."

Talk became general over lunch and I was pleased to see that Julie and Debbie got on well together. If the womenfolk of business associates are bitchy it can upset things all round, and I have known several sweet deals fall down because of that.

At one point Julie said, "You know Mom and Pop are coming for Christmas."

"Yes." It was an arrangement that had been made earlier in the year.

"I thought I'd do my Christmas shopping in Miami and meet them there."

I said, "Why don't you give them a sea trip? Take *Lucayan Girl* and bring them back by way of Bimini. I'm sure they'd enjoy it."

She said, "That's a good idea. Will you come?"

"Afraid not, I'll be too busy. But I'll have a word with Pete; he'll need an extra hand for that trip."

"Still a good idea," said Julie meditatively. "I think I'll take Sue—and Karen, if she's better."

"Take me where?" Sue had joined us draped in a towel. She helped herself to ice cream.

"How would you like to go to Miami to meet Grandma and Grandpop? We'd be going in the *Girl*."

Ice cream went flying and Sue's squeal of delight was an adequate answer.

After lunch Julie took Sue back to school and Debbie went along because Julie said she would show her the International Bazaar where you can walk from France to China in one stride. When they had gone Billy said, "How big is your boat?"

"Fifty-two feet. Come and look at her."

His eyebrows lifted. "You have her here?"

"Sure. This way." I led him through the house to the lagoon on the other side where *Lucayan Girl* was moored at the dockside. Pete Albury was on board and when he heard us talking he appeared on deck. "Come and meet Pete," I said. "He's skipper, but sometimes he thinks he's the owner."

"Tom, I heard that," called Pete, his face cracking into a grin. "But I'll allow you on board anyway."

We went aboard. "Pete, this is Billy Cunningham, an old friend from the States."

Pete stuck out his hand. "Glad to know you, Mr. Cunningham."

I was watching Billy carefully. He did not know it, but this was a minor test; if he had hesitated, even fractionally, in spite of what he had said I would have been worried, because no one who is a racist, even in a minor way, can get along successfully in the Bahamas. Billy grasped Pete's hand firmly. "Glad to know you, Mr . . ."

"Albury," said Pete. "But I'm just Pete."

"I'm Billy."

I said, "Julie wants to go to Miami next week to do the Christmas shopping and to pick up her parents. She'll be taking Sue and maybe Karen, and you'll be touching in at Bimini on the way home. Is everything okay for that?"

"Sure," said Pete. "Are you comin'?"

"Sorry. I can't make it."

"Then I'll need a hand. Don't worry; there's always

youngsters around the marinas. I'll pick a good one who'll be glad of the ride for a few dollars."

"That's it, then," I said.

Billy was looking at the lagoon. "This is man-made," he said abruptly.

"I hoped you'd notice." I pointed. "The channel out to sea is there—by the Lucayan Beach Hotel. That's where the BASRA Marathon begins."

"BASRA?"

"The Bahamas Air-Sea Rescue Association. The Marathon is run by and for BASRA to raise funds. It's a voluntary organization—a good crowd. If you're coming in here it wouldn't do you any harm to donate a few dollars or offer facilities."

"Do you do that?"

"Yes. We have the company planes—" I broke off and laughed. "Not big jets like yours, but we have four Piper Navajos—seven-seaters we use to take tourists to the Out Islands, part of our tours division. And they're used on other company business, of course. But if a boat is lost and BASRA wants an air search the planes are available."

"Good public relations." He nodded back toward the lagoon. "So this has been dredged out?"

"That's it. This lagoon, and others like it, stretches for about three miles up the coast."

Billy looked at the lagoon and then back at the house. "Not bad," he said, "having a house with a water frontage. And it's protected, too; no big waves."

"You've got it. Now I'll show you something weird. Let's take a drive." We said farewell to Pete, left the house, and I drove about four miles east into Lucaya. "Notice anything?"

Billy looked around. "Just trees—and the traffic is light."

That was an understatement; there was no traffic. I had not seen a car for the last two miles. But there were many trees. I pointed. "That's a street. See the name plate? Now keep your eyes open."

I drove on and presently the trees thinned out and we came on to a plain dotted with mounds of limestone. I said,

"We're coming to the Casuarina Bridge. It crosses the Great Lucayan Waterway."

"So?"

"So we're going to cross it."

"I don't get it," said Billy.

I said, "We've been passing streets, all named and paved. Those poles carry power lines. Now, I don't know how it is in the States where any wide place in the road can call itself a city, but to me a road is something that goes from one place to another, and a street *is* a place, but it usually has houses on it."

Billy was momentarily startled. "Houses!" he said blankly. "No goddamn houses! Nary a one."

"That's it. But I've more to show you or, rather, not show you. We'll get a better view from Dover Sound." I drove on to Dover Sound and Observation Hill. It is not really a hill—just a man-made mound with the road leading up and a turning circle at the top. I stopped the car, took a map from the glove compartment, and we got out. "What do you think of that?"

Billy looked at the view with a lack of comprehension. I knew why because I had been baffled by the sight when first I saw it. There was land and there was water and it was not easy to see where one stopped and the other began. It was a maze of water channels. Billy shrugged helplessly. "I don't know. What am I supposed to think?"

I said, "Think of my house and the lagoon. This is the Grand Lucayan Waterway—it cuts right across Grand Bahama, nearly eight miles from coast to coast. But it has forty-five miles of water frontage." I flapped open the map I held. "Look at this. You can see where the streets and waterways fit together like fingers in a glove."

Billy studied the map, then took out a calculator and began punching buttons. "At a hundred feet of water frontage to a house that's nearly twenty-five hundred houses. Where the hell are they?"

"There's more. Look at the map." I swept my hand over an area. "Twenty square miles of land all laid out in paved streets with utilities already installed—the unfleshed skeleton of a city of fifty thousand people."

"So what happened?"

"An election happened. Pindling got in and the investors ran scared. But they're coming back. Take a man who runs his own business in Birmingham, Alabama, or Birmingham, England, for that matter. He sells out to a bigger company at, say, the age of fifty-five when he's still young enough to enjoy life and now has the money to indulge himself. He can build his house on the canal and keep his fishing boat handy, or he can take one of the dry land plots. There's sun and sea, swimming and golf, enough to keep a man happy for the rest of his life. And the beauty of it is that the infrastructure already exists; the power station in Freeport is only working to a tenth of its capacity."

Billy looked over the expanse of land and water. "You say the investors are coming back. I don't see any sign of 'em."

"Don't be fooled." I pointed back the way we had come. "You can see the landscaping has begun—tree planting and flower beds. And that big parking lot, all neatly laid out. It looks a bit silly, but it's probably earmarked for a supermarket. There are houses being built right now, but you don't see them because they're scattered over twenty square miles. Give this place a few years and we'll have a thriving community. That's one answer to a question you asked—what's the future of the Bahamas?"

He rubbed his jaw. "Yeah, I see what you mean."

"Don't take my word for it—look for yourself. I'll lend you a plane and my chief pilot, Bobby Bowen, and you can do some island hopping. Go to Abaco; we have a hotel there—the Abaco Sands at Marsh Harbor. Go on to Eleuthera where we're building a hotel. Have a look at some of the other islands and don't leave out New Providence. I'll give you a list of people you can talk to. Then come back and tell me what you think."

"Okay," he said. "I'll do just that."

2

BILLY WENT on his tour a couple of days later after looking around Grand Bahama, but Debbie stayed on at the Royal Palm. Billy confided in me that he had brought her along in an attempt to cure a fit of the blues; apparently Debbie had been having man trouble—an affair had turned sour. Anyway, she got into the habit of going to the house and using the pool, and she and the children became friends in no time. Debbie would pick up the kids from school and take them home and then stay on to lunch with Julie. Julie must have liked her because she put off her trip to Florida until Billy came back.

As for me, I was damned busy. I roused Jamieson, the chief accountant, who nearly burned out the computer as we figured the net worth of the company as of the end of that month. I wanted to have all my ammunition ready and dry for Billy when he came back because I had the notion he would be ready to talk turkey.

One evening after Julie had put the girls to bed I told her about Billy's proposition and asked what she thought of it. She was ambivalent. She saw the possibilities for expansion, but on the other hand she said, "I don't know if it would be good for you—you're too independent."

I knew what she meant. "I know I like to run my own show and that's my problem—how to extract forty million bucks from the Cunninghams without losing control. I have a few ideas about that and I might be able to swing it."

She laughed at me. "I always knew I married a genius. All right, if you can do that then it won't be a bad thing."

I had to consult my sisters, Peggy and Grace. Both had stock in the West End Securities Corporation, enough for them to have a say in any decision as big as this. Peggy lived on Abaco with her son and daughter and her husband, Bob Fisher, who ran the Abaco Sands Hotel for the corporation. Grace had married an American called Peters and lived in Orlando, Florida, with their three sons. It seemed that the tendency of the Mangans to produce girls was confined to the males. It meant some flying around because this was not something that could be settled on the telephone, but I had written agreements by the time Billy came back.

He returned to Grand Bahama after eight days, having gone through the Bahamas like a whirlwind. He was armed with so many facts, figures and statistics that I wondered how he had assembled them all in the time, but that was like Billy—he was a quick student.

"You were right," he said. "The Bahamas have potential, more than I thought. You didn't tell me about the Hotels Encouragement Act."

I laughed. "I left you to find out yourself. I knew you would."

"My God, it's like falling over a gold mine." He ticked the points off on his fingers. "No customs duty on anything imported to build or equip a hotel; no property taxes for the first ten years; no company taxes for the first twenty years. And that applies to hotels, marinas, golf courses, landscaping—anything you can damn near think of. It's incredible."

"That's why we're going to have two million tourists next year."

He grunted. "I've been thinking about that. I was talking to that tourism guy, Butler. He told me that eighty percent of your economy and two-thirds of your population are supported by tourism. That's a hell of a lot of eggs in one basket, Tom." His voice was serious. "What if something happens— like a war breaking out?"

Something told me I had better come up with a fast answer. I said lightly, "If World War III breaks out everybody's eggs get broken."

"I guess you're right at that."

"Are you ready to talk business yet?"

"No. I'll be speaking to Billy One and Jack today. I'll let you know the decision tomorrow."

I grinned. "I promise I won't bug the switchboard. I won't be coming in to the office tomorrow. Julie is leaving for Miami and I like to see them off. Why don't you come to the house and bring Debbie along?"

"I'll do that."

So Billy and Debbie arrived at the house next morning at about ten o'clock. Debbie joined the girls in the pool and I winked at Julie and took Billy into my study. He said, "I think we're in business."

"You may think so, but I'm not so sure. I don't want to lose control."

He stared at me. "Oh, come on, Tom! We're talking about forty million bucks. You don't want us busting in as competitors, do you?"

"I'm not afraid of competition. I have plenty of that, anyway."

"Well, you can't expect us to put up all that dough and not have control. That's ridiculous. Are you joking or something?"

"I'm not joking," I said. "I'm perfectly serious. But I'd like to point out that there are different kinds of control."

Billy looked at me speculatively. "Okay, I'll buy that. What's on your mind?"

"I take it you'd be setting up a corporation here."

"That's right, we would. I've been talking to some of your corporate lawyers over in Nassau and they've come up with some great ideas, even though they'd be illegal back in the States. This sure is a free-wheeling place."

"Rest easy," I said. "As an offshore tax haven we're positively respectable, not like some others I could mention. What would you call your corporation?"

"How would I know? Something innocuous, I guess. Let's call it the Theta Corporation."

I said, "I run three hotels with a fourth building for a total of six hundred fifty rooms. That's a lot of bed linen, a lot of crockery and cutlery, a lot of kitchenware and ashtrays and anything else you care to name. Now, if the Theta Corporation is going to build and equip hotels it would be better to consolidate and keep the economy of scale. You get bed sheets a damn sight cheaper if you order by the five thousand pair rather than the five hundred pair, and that applies right down the line."

"Sure, I know that." Billy flapped his hand impatiently. "Come to the point."

"What I'm suggesting is that the Theta Corporation take over West End Securities in return for stock."

"Ha!" he said. "Now you're talking. How much stock?" "One-fifth."

"We put in forty million dollars, you put in West End and take a fifth of the stock. That makes it a fifty-million-dollar corporation, so you estimate West End as being worth ten million dollars. Is it? What's the book value?"

I said, "Jamieson and I have been working it out. I put it at eight million."

"So you put in eight million and take stock worth ten million. What kind of a deal is that? What do we get for the other two million bucks?"

"Me," I said evenly.

Billy burst out laughing. "Come on, Tom! Do you really think you're worth that?"

"You're forgetting quite a few things," I said. "If you come in here on your own, you come in cold. I know you've picked up your facts and statistics and so on, but you don't know the score—you don't know the way things get done here. But if you come in with me you begin with a firm base ready for expansion, eager for expansion. And you don't only get me, but you get my staff, all loyal to me personally. And don't forget the Bahamas for the Bahamians bit. Call it goodwill, call it know-how, call it what you like, but I reckon it's worth two million."

Billy was silent for a long time, thinking hard. "Maybe you're right," he said at last.

I gave him another jolt. "And I get to be president of the Theta Corporation," I said calmly.

He nearly choked. "Jesus, you don't want much! Why don't you just pick my pocket of forty million bucks and be done with it?"

"I told you. I don't want to lose control. Look, Billy; you'll be chairman and I'll be president—the Cunninghams retain financial control but I have operational control. That's the only way it can work. And I want a five-year contract of service; not a cast-iron contract—that breaks too easily—an armor-plate contract."

Billy looked glum, but nodded. "Billy One might go for it, but I don't know about Jack." He drummed his fingers on the desk and said cautiously, "If we take over West End we get everything? Not just the hotels part of it?"

"You get all the trimmings," I assured him. "Tours division, car rental fleet, merchandising division—the lot."

"Before we go any further into this," he said, "I'd like to have your ideas about expansion. Have you given it any thought?"

I pushed a folder across the desk. "There are a few ideas here. Just a beginning."

He studied the papers I had put together and we discussed them for a while. At last he said, "You've obviously been thinking hard. I like your idea of a construction division." He checked the time. "I need the telephone. Will you give me half an hour? I might have to do some tough talking."

I pushed the telephone towards him. "Best of luck."

I found Julie holding Karen in her arms and looking faintly worried. Karen was sniffling and wailing. "But I *want* to go!"

"What's the matter?"

"Oh, Karen's not well," said Julie. "I don't think she should come with us. Her head cold is worse and she's got a fever."

"It's not *fair!*" cried Karen. "Sue's going."

I put out my hand and felt her forehead; Julie was right

about the rise in temperature, but it was not much. "Maybe we should cancel the trip," said Julie.

"Put her to bed and we'll talk about it." I looked around. "Where's Sue?"

"On *Lucayan Girl* helping Pete or, rather, getting in his way. I'll be back soon." Julie walked into the house carrying Karen who had burst into tears.

I found Debbie relaxing by the pool and dropped into a chair next to her. "Poor kid," she said. "She's so disappointed. How sick is she?"

"Not very. You know how kids are; their temperature goes up and down for no apparent reason. She'll probably be all right in a couple of days. But Julie is thinking of canceling the trip."

"If Julie wants someone to look after Karen, I could do that," Debbie said.

"It's a kindly thought," I said. "But if it comes to that I'll take Karen to the Royal Palm. We have a very efficient and charming young nurse there whom Karen knows very well. I've done it before when Julie has been away."

"Then talk Julie out of canceling. It would disappoint Sue so much."

"I'll do my best." Presently Julie came out of the house, and I asked, "How is she?"

"Rebellious."

"You don't have to cancel the trip. I don't want *two* gloomy kids sulking about the house. Debbie has offered to look after Karen, and there's always Kitty Symonette at the hotel."

"Thanks, Debbie." Julie thought for a moment. "Very well—we'll go." She looked at Debbie. "Don't let Karen take advantage of you. That little kid is full of tricks."

I stood up. "If everything's aboard I'll come and see you off."

Just then Billy came striding out of the house and beckoned me with a jerk of his head. He said, "There'll be a squad of lawyers and auditors flying in to look at your books.

If everything checks out we have a deal." He laughed and put out his hand.

So it was with a light heart that I saw Julie and Sue away on *Lucayan Girl.* I told Julie about the deal and she was delighted, and then we went out to the lagoon where the *Girl* was ready to cast off, her engines already ticking over. Sue was running about taking photographs with the camera I had given her for her birthday; her teacher had set her the exercise of a photo-essay as her homework for the Christmas vacation. By the look of her both she and her stock of film would be exhausted before the voyage began.

I had a word with Pete who was coiling the rope in the bows. "Got a crewman?"

"Sure."

"How is he?"

"He'll do," said Pete laconically. Knowing Pete, that meant the young fellow was pretty good.

"Where is he?"

"Below—greasing the shafts." Pete raised his voice. "All right, then; all aboard that's goin' aboard."

Sue scampered aboard and Julie kissed me and followed more sedately. "Cast off the after line, Miss Mate," said Pete. He cast off the forward line and quickly went to the helm on the flying bridge. The engines growled and *Lucayan Girl* moved slowly away.

We watched as the *Girl* went down the lagoon and turned into the channel which led to the open sea and so out of sight. I said to Billy, "I think we have work to do." I stooped to pick up Sue's camera which she had left on a chair. "Sue will be mad enough to bust. When Julie rings tonight I'll tell her to buy another one. We mustn't let the teacher down."

3

It was late in the day when it went bad—an hour from midnight. Billy and I had worked late, sorting out the details of the proposed merger and outlining future plans, and were having a final drink before he went back to the Royal Palm. Suddenly he broke off what he was saying in midsentence. "What's the matter? You got ants in your pants? That's the third time you've checked your watch in five minutes. I hope I haven't overstayed my welcome."

"Julie hasn't phoned," I said shortly. "That's not like her."

I picked up the telephone and rang the Fontainebleau in Miami where she usually stayed. The call took an annoyingly long time to connect and Billy occupied himself with shuffling his papers together and putting them into his briefcase. Finally I got through and said, "I'd like to speak to Mrs. Mangan."

There was a pause. "Do you know the room number, sir?"

"No."

Another pause. "There's no one of that name in the hotel, sir."

"Put me through to the desk clerk, please." Again that took a bit of time but I finally got him. I said, "My name is Mangan. Has my wife checked in yet?"

A rustle of papers. "No, sir."

"But she did make a reservation?"

"Yes, sir; two rooms. Mrs. Mangan and Miss Mangan, and Mr. and Mrs. Pascoe."

"Have the Pascoes checked in?"

"No, sir."

"Thank you." I put down the telephone and said blankly, "She's not there."

"What time was she supposed to get into Miami?" asked Billy.

"Before dark; say, eight o'clock. Pete has standing instructions from me to get into port in daylight if possible, especially with the family aboard. She's a fast boat for her type and he'd have no trouble about that."

"She's only three hours overdue, Tom. Anything could have happened. Engine trouble, perhaps."

"Boats with Pete aboard don't have engine trouble," I said sharply. "Besides, the *Girl* has two engines."

"If one was knocked out it would slow her down."

"Not by a lot—not by three hours." I picked up the telephone again. "I'll ring the marina in Miami." Ten minutes later I knew that *Lucayan Girl* had not arrived. I said to Billy, "I've got a feeling about this. I'm going over to BASRA—they can raise the US Coast Guard."

"How long will you be?"

"Fifteen—twenty minutes. It's quite close."

"I'll stick around until you get back. Julie might call."

BASRA headquarters on Grand Bahama are in the building which also holds the Underwater Exploration Society. Five minutes later I was climbing the stairs to the Tide's Inn, a tavern which supports both the Society and BASRA. The place was noisy with vacationers and I found Joe Kimble of BASRA employed in his favorite occupation—chatting with a couple of nubile females. I crossed to his table. "Sorry to interrupt, Joe, but *Lucayan Girl* is overdue in Miami."

He looked up. "How much overdue?"

"Over three hours now." I met his eye. "Julie and Sue are aboard."

"Oh!" He stood up. "Sorry, girls, but business comes first."

We went down to the BASRA office and I said, "What's the weather like in the Florida Straits?"

"Calm—no problems there." He sat behind a desk and took a pen. "When did she leave?"

"Dead on eleven this morning."

"Give me the number of the marina in Miami." He scribbled it down, then said, "You'd better go home, Tom, and stick by your telephone. But don't use it. I'll do any telephoning that's necessary—you keep an open line. I'll ring the marina and tell them to notify BASRA if she comes in."

"What about the Coast Guard?"

"I'll radio them but there's not much they can do at night—you know that."

"Can I use the phone here?" At Joe's nod I picked it up and rang Bobby Bowen at his home. I outlined the situation, then said, "There may be nothing in it, but if there's no report in the next few hours I'll need planes in the air at first light. How many can we raise?"

"Just two here," said Bowen. "There's one in Nassau and the other has its engine stripped for the hundred-hour check."

"Get that plane back from Nassau as fast as you can. You'll liaise with Joe Kimble of BASRA who will be coordinator. Unless the order is canceled you'll rendezvous at . . ." I twitched an eyebrow at Joe who said, "Lucayan Beach Air Services."

I passed that on, and added, ". . . at five-thirty A.M." I put down the phone. "I'm going home, Joe. Julie might ring."

He nodded. "If I'm going to fly tomorrow I'll need some shuteye. I'll get one of the groundlings to stand by here as soon as I've raised the Coast Guard."

I had an argument with Billy which he won. "I'll stay by the telephone," he said. "You've got to sleep. If anything comes through I'll wake you." He raided the kitchen and made me warm milk laced with brandy. Afterward he told me that he had roused Luke Bailey who found Julie's sleeping pills and he dissolved one into the milk.

So it was that when he woke me at five in the morning I felt doped and fuzzy. At first I did not know what he was doing there in my bedroom, but then the knowledge hit me. "Any news?" I demanded.

He shook his head. "Just a call from BASRA; the Coast Guard are putting helicopters out of Miami as soon as it's light enough to see."

I got up and found Debbie in the living room; Billy had rung her and she had immediately come from the hotel. None of us did much talking because there was nothing much to say, but Debbie insisted that she was going to stay to look after Karen. Luke Bailey made an early breakfast and I drove to the airport feeling like hell.

Joe Kimble was in the office of Lucayan Beach Air Services, allocating areas on a map. Bobby Bowen was there, and Bill Pinder, another Corporation pilot, and there were three other pilots, volunteers from BASRA. Joe said, "Now, remember we're tying in with the US Coast Guard on this. Stick to your own areas and watch your altitude. And watch for the choppers—we don't want a midair collision to complicate things."

We walked out to the tie-down lines and the sky was just lightening in the east as we took off. I flew with Bobby Bowen and, as we flew west and gained altitude, the panorama in the rising sun was achingly beautiful.

Lucayan Girl was of a type which the Americans call a trawler. Because of recurrent oil crises a demand has arisen for a boat not particularly fast but with range and sea-keeping qualities, and light on fuel. These boats, no matter who the designer, all look pretty much alike because they were all trying to solve the same problems and inevitably came up with the same results. And our problem was that in Florida and Bahamian waters they are as thick as fleas on a dog.

Not many people make night passages in power boats in the Islands but we spotted our first twenty miles out and heading our way. We were flying at twenty-five hundred feet, adhering strictly to regulations for the course we were on, and Bowen dropped us one thousand feet, again going by the book. I looked at the boat through the glasses as we went by and shook my head. Bowen took us up again.

It was a long and futile search. We found six boats but not

Lucayan Girl. From the intermittent chatter on the radio no one else was having any luck either. Visibility so early in the morning was generally good, but as the sun rose, clouds began to form. Presently Bowen said, "Got to go back." He tapped the fuel gauge.

So we went back, the engine coughing as we landed, and found that the others had already returned. No one had seen the *Girl* and neither had the US Coast Guard. Joe Kimble reamed out Bobby Bowen. "You cut that too damn fine."

Bowen managed a tired smile. "No problem; I emptied my cigarette lighter into the tank."

"I sure as hell don't want to go out there looking for plane wreckage because some damn fool has run out of gas. Don't do it again."

I said, "Refuel, Bobby."

One of the BASRA pilots stirred. "I'll take you out again, Mr. Mangan. I'm fueled up."

So I went out again. They all went out again. They were a good crowd. And we all came back, but not *Lucayan Girl.*

The next few days were grim. People pussyfooted around me, not knowing what to do or say, and work went to hell. I felt as numb as though I had been mentally anesthetized and I suppose I acted like a zombie, one of the walking dead. I wished I was dead.

Billy said, "This is no time to talk business, Tom. Let me know when we can get together again." He went back to Houston, but Debbie refused to go home and stayed on to look after Karen. I was in no mood to argue.

Looking back I can see that this was worse than a normal death in the family. There was no funeral, no assuaging ceremony—nothing to do. There was the ever-present expectation of a telephone call which would magically solve everything and restore my wife and daughter to me and bring back my old friend, Pete Albury. I jerked every time a phone rang—anywhere.

The house was haunted. Although the pool was mirrorlike

in its quietness there was still held in the mind's eye the image of a lithe young body, sleek as an otter, breaking the surface with a shout of joy, and I expected, on turning a corner, to find at any moment the dark beauty of Julie, perhaps going about some domestic chore like watering the roses.

I suppose I was a haunted man.

Debbie was very good. At first she sought to cheer me up, but I was impervious so she desisted and contented herself with acting as a barrier between me and the world of the newspapers. And she saw that I ate regularly and did not drink too much or, at least, drink alone. She need not have worried about that; I have never considered that diving into a bottle could solve any problems.

She looked after Karen and played with her and stopped my little daughter from worrying me too much in those awful first days.

Karen had not been told, but sooner or later I would have to tell her that her mother and sister were dead. I sweated at the thought.

And then there were Julie's parents, Mike and Ellen Pascoe. I did not know how to contact them because they were on the move, driving from Maryland to Miami where they expected to meet Julie at the Fontainebleau. I left a message at the Fontainebleau asking that they ring me immediately on arrival.

The call came two days later and Ellen was on the line. "Julie isn't here," she said. "Has she been held up?"

"Can I speak to Mike?"

"Of course." Her voice sharpened. "Is anything wrong, Tom?"

"Just let me talk to Mike for a moment." Mike came on and I told him what had happened, and I heard his breath hiss in my ear.

He said, "Is there no . . . hope?"

"Oh, God! Hope is the only thing that's been keeping me going. But it's been nearly three days, and every hour that goes by . . . Look, I'll send a plane for you. It'll be there this afternoon. Just wait at the hotel for Bobby Bowen. Okay?"

"All right," he said heavily.

Half an hour after that telephone call Debbie came into my study. "There are two men to see you. Policemen."

I jerked around. "With news?" She shook her head sadly and I sighed. "All right; show them in."

Debbie led them into the study and then left. I stood up and looked at them in some perplexity. Deputy-Commissioner Perigord, a black Bahamian, was the top-ranking police officer on Grand Bahama and I knew him slightly, having met him at social functions. His companion was also black but unknown to me. Both were in uniform.

Perigord said, "I'm sorry to have to intrude at this time, Mr. Mangan; I assure you I wish it were otherwise. I put it off for as long as possible but. . . ." He shrugged.

"I know," I said. "Won't you sit down?"

He took off his uniform cap and laid it on my desk together with his swagger stick. "This is Inspector Hepburn."

I nodded in acknowledgment and sat down. Perigord said, "I knew Mrs. Mangan slightly; we met at PTA meetings— our daughters attend the same school. If there is anything my wife and I can do to help then please call on us. However, I am here on a different errand. You must know that in circumstances like this there are questions to be asked."

"Yes," I said. "Just get on with it."

He took out a notebook. "The name of your boat is *Lucayan Girl*?"

"Yes."

"Where did she sail from?"

"Here." I pointed through the window toward the atrium. "Her mooring is just through that archway."

"Would you mind if Inspector Hepburn looks at the mooring?"

"No—but what does he expect to find?"

"I don't know. Police work consists of looking at a lot of things, most of which turn out to be useless in the end. But sometimes we get lucky." He nodded to Hepburn who got up and left the room.

"I don't see how the police come into it." I saw Hepburn walk by the pool and disappear through the arch.

"There is more to police work than crime; we fulfill many social functions. Were you present when *Lucayan Girl* sailed?"

"Yes."

"Who was on board?"

"Julie, my wife; my daughter, Susan; Pete Albury, the skipper; and a crewman."

"What is the crewman's name?"

"I don't know."

Perigord frowned. "You don't know!" he said with a tinge of perplexity in his voice.

"Pete Albury hired him. I didn't want my wife and daughter to sail with only Pete aboard so I asked Pete to hire a hand just for this trip."

"I see. But if you hired him you were obviously going to pay him. Was it to be by cash or check?"

"I don't know," I said to Perigord's obvious bafflement. As he made a disapproving clicking sound with his tongue I said, "That was Pete's business. He ran *Lucayan Girl*; he had a bank account from which to draw funds, and I checked the account monthly. He'd have paid, but whether in cash or by check I wouldn't know."

"You must have trusted Mr. Albury," said Perigord.

"I did," I said evenly.

"Now, then, what did this man—this crewman—look like?"

"I don't know; I didn't see him."

Perigord defintely lost his composure. "You mean you hired a man you didn't even *see*!"

"I didn't hire him," I said. "Pete did. I had every confidence in Pete to pick a good man. Look, I run a business. I don't hire personally everyone who works for me, neither do I necessarily know them by name or sight. That's known as delegation of authority."

"And so you bring your business practices into your household."

"I trusted Pete," I said stubbornly.

"How do you know that this ... this stranger was on board when the boat sailed?"

"Pete told me. I asked him and he said the crewman was below greasing the shafts."

"But you don't know it of your own knowledge."

"I can't say that I do."

Perigord pondered for a moment, then asked, "Is there anyone else to whom I can refer who would know it from his own knowledge?"

I thought about that, casting my mind back to the scene by the lagoon. Billy, Debbie and I had walked through the archway together and if I had not seen the crewman then neither could they. I shook my head. "No, I don't think so."

Inspector Hepburn came back and Perigord glanced at him. "So what it comes to is this—we have a man, probably dead, whose name we don't know and whom we can't describe. We don't even know his color. In fact, Mr. Mangan, we might even be wrong about the sex—this crew member *could* be a woman for all we know."

"No," I said definitely. "I asked Pete about him, and Pete said, '*He*'ll do.'"

"Well, that's something," said Perigord. "Where does Mr. Albury live?"

"Here," I said. "There are some workrooms and storerooms for ship's chandlery with an apartment over. Pete moved in here when his wife died last year."

"There may be something in the apartment to give us a lead. Do you mind if Inspector Hepburn looks?"

"Of course not." I opened the wall safe and took out the key to Pete's rooms and gave it to Hepburn, then rang for Luke who appeared with suspicious alacrity. "Show the Inspector where Pete's rooms are."

They left and I turned to Perigord. "There's something here which may possibly be useful." I took a small book from the safe. "I record the serial numbers of any important equipment I own, and there's a section for *Lucayan Girl* in here—her engine numbers, radar, radio and so on. Even the binoculars and the cameras we routinely carry aboard."

"Ah, that's better!" Perigord took the book and flicked through it. "And the numbers carried on certain documents, I see. Is the boat insured?"

"Of course."

"And you, Mr. Mangan, do you carry life insurance?"

"Certainly."

"And Mrs. Mangan? Was her life insured?"

I stared at him. "I'm a rich enough man not to want to benefit by my wife's death. What the hell are you getting at?"

He held up his hand in a conciliatory gesture. "I'm sorry; in my work we are forced to intrude at inopportune moments with questions which may be construed as tactless—tactless but necessary. I did not wish to offend, sir."

"I'm sorry," I said. "No apology is necessary."

There were more questions, the answers to most of which appeared to satisfy him, and presently Hepburn came back and Perigord picked up his cap and swagger stick. "That will be all for now, sir. There'll be an inquiry; I'll let you know where and when it will be held. May I offer my profound sorrow and my . . . condolences. I did like Mrs. Mangan."

"Condolences?" I said in a choked voice.

"It *has* been two and a half days," said Perigord gravely.

I took a grip on myself. "Commissioner, what do you think happened?"

"I doubt if we'll ever know. Perhaps a gas leak in the bilges leading to an explosion—that's rather common. Or the boat could have been run down by a supertanker."

"In daylight!"

"We don't know that it was daylight," he pointed out, and shrugged. "And those ships are so big they could run down a moderately small craft and no one would feel a thing. A ship carrying three hundred thousand tons of oil has a lot of momentum. We'll do our best to find out what happened, but I offer no certainties." With that he and Hepburn left.

He had not been gone two minutes when Luke Bailey came

in wearing a worried frown. "I'd like to tell you something."
He jerked his head at the door. "That policeman . . ."

"Who—Perigord?"

"No, the other one—the Inspector. He's on the Narcotics
Squad. I thought you'd like to know."

4

THAT EVENING I had to cope with the Pascoes who, oddly enough, were more philosophical about it than I. I was in a cold, helpless, miserable rage; wanting to strike out at something but finding nothing to hit—no target. The Pascoes were more equable. They were nearing the end of their own days and I suppose that death was a not unexpected figure lurking over the horizon, something with which they had come to terms on a personal level. Besides, Mike was a doctor and death had been a factor in his professional life. They did their best to comfort me.

I had a long talk with Mike after Ellen had gone to bed. "I know how you feel," he said. "I lost a boy—killed in Vietnam. Did Julie ever tell you about that?" I nodded. "It hit me hard. Allen was a good boy." He wagged his head sagely. "But it wears off, Tom; you can't grieve forever."

"I suppose so," I said moodily. Deep in my heart I knew he was wrong; I would grieve for Julie and Sue for the rest of my life.

"What are you going to do now?" he asked.

"I don't know."

"For God's sake, wake up! You can't just let everything slide. You're running a corporation and you have people depending on you. You're still a young man, too. How old? Forty what?"

"Forty-two."

"You can get married again," he said.

"Let's not talk about that now," I said sharply. "Julie's not been gone three days. And maybe. . . ."

"Maybe she'll come back? Don't set your heart on that, Tom, or you'll drive yourself nuts." I said nothing to that and there was a long silence. After a while Mike stirred. "What are you going to do about Karen?"

"I haven't thought about it yet."

"Then you'd better put your mind to it. Debbie Cunningham's a good girl from what I've seen of her, but she won't be around forever. You'll have to make some arrangements. Bringing up a daughter aged nine *and* running a corporation could be a mite tough—tough on Karen, I mean."

"I'll get a woman in to look after her, I suppose."

"Humph!" Evidently he did not think much of that idea. I did not think much of it myself. He said, "Ellen and I have been talking. We'd like to take Karen until you've got things settled in your mind."

"That's generous of you."

"No, just plain horse sense. Karen should be with her own kin." He smiled slowly. "But I thought I'd gotten past the age of child-raising."

"I agree," I said. "I had a call from my sister Peggy this morning. She wants to take Karen to Abaco, at least until I get settled and can make other arrangements. She has two kids of her own, and that might be better for Karen."

Mike looked a shade relieved. "It would be better," he said positively. "Children brought up by old folks sometimes turn out funny. You're starting to think, Tom."

We talked about it some more and then I changed the subject. "There's something I can't understand. I don't see why Perigord should be conducting this investigation personally. He's a deputy-commissioner, the top cop on the island. I shouldn't have thought this would warrant it."

"You're running yourself down," said Mike. "You're a prominent citizen on Grand Bahama. And you say he knew Julie?"

"So he says. He says he met her at the school, at PTA meetings. I didn't go to many of those."

"Maybe he feels he has a personal obligation."

"Perhaps. But then there's Hepburn. Luke Bailey tells me Hepburn is a narcotics officer, and he did give Pete's rooms a good shakedown. There's something behind all this, Mike."

"Imagination!" he scoffed. "Probably Hepburn was the

only officer handy in the precinct house at the time." He got up and stretched. "I'm going to bed; I'm not as young as I was." He looked down at me. "Tom, I've been a doctor all my life until I retired three years ago. I've seen a lot of people die and a lot of grief in families. Tell me, have you shed one single tear since Julie went?"

"No," I said flatly.

He walked to the corner cupboard, poured four fingers of brandy into a glass, and brought it back to me. "Drink that, relax, and let yourself go. There's nothing wrong with a man crying, and bottling it up can harm you." He turned and walked out of the room.

Mike was a kindly man and a good man. He had once said that being a doctor made a man a fair jackleg psychologist and he was right about this. I sat for a long time holding the glass and just looking into its brown depths. Then I swallowed the lot in two gulps. The brandy burned going down and I gasped. Fifteen minutes later I was sprawled on the settee and crying my heart out. I cried myself to sleep, awoke in the early hours of the morning and went to bed after turning out the lights.

It was acceptance that Julie and Sue were dead; and Pete and an unknown man. The acceptance brought a curious kind of peace; I still felt numbed in my mind, but I felt better and was a functioning man. Mike had known what he was doing.

Four days later I took Karen to Abaco, and Debbie came with us. It was then, in the presence of Peggy and Bob, that I told Karen that her mother and sister were dead and that she would be staying with her aunt and uncle for a while. She looked at me, wide-eyed, and said, "They won't be coming home? Ever?"

"I'm afraid not. You remember when Timmy died?" Timmy was a pet kitten who had been run over by a car, and Karen nodded. "Well, it's something like that."

Tears welled in her eyes and she blinked them away.

"Timmy didn't come back," she agreed. "Does that mean I won't see Mommy and Susie—not ever?" She burst into tears and tore herself away. "I don't believe you," she cried, and began to wail, "I want my mommy. I want my mommy."

Peggy caught her up in her arms and comforted her, then said over her shoulder to me, "I think a mild sedative and bed is the best thing now." She took Karen away.

Bob said awkwardly, "It's hard to know what to say."

"I know—but the world goes round as usual. It'll take me a bit of time to get used to this, but I'll pull through. Where's Debbie?"

"On the patio."

I looked at my watch. "We'll have to get back; the plane is needed. I'll come across as often as I can—at least once a week."

Debbie and I did not talk much at first on the flight back to Grand Bahama; both of us were immersed in our private thoughts. It was a long time before I said, "I suppose you'll be going back to Houston."

"Yes," she said tonelessly. Presently she said, "And I thought I had troubles."

"What happened?"

She laughed shortly. "Do you really want to know?"

"Why not? We can cry on each other's shoulder."

"A man happened—or I thought he was a man. I thought he loved me, but he really loved my money. I happened to pick up a telephone at the wrong time and I heard a really interesting conversation about the big deals he was going to make and the life he was going to lead as soon as he'd married me. The trouble was that he was talking to another woman, and she was included in his plans."

"That's bad," I said.

"I was a damned fool," she said. "You see, I'd been warned. Billy was against it all along because he didn't trust the guy and he made that very clear. But would I listen? Not me. I was grown up—a woman of the world—and I knew it all."

"How old are you, Debbie?"

"The ripe old age of twenty-five."

"I had my fingers burned, too, when I was your age," I said. "That was before I met Julie. You'll get over it."

"You think so? But, God, it's taught me something and I don't think I like what it's taught me. Here I am—a poor little rich girl—and from now to eternity I'll be looking at every guy I meet and wondering if he wants me or all that lovely dough. That's no way to have to go through life."

"Other rich people cope," I said.

"Yes?" she said challengingly. "Examined the divorce statistics lately?"

Her voice was bitter and I could see that she had been badly hurt. And coming to Grand Bahama and seeing how happily Julie and I were married could not have helped much. Presently she said quietly, "But you don't want to be burdened with my problems even though you do seem to have got over the worst of your blues. Was it the talk you had with Mike Pascoe the other day?"

"Yes," I said. "He dutch-uncled me, and it helped. It could help you."

"All right, Tom," she said. "What would you do if you were me? I know you can't possibly put yourself in my position, but I've told you enough to know about me. I'd like your advice. You know, Billy thinks a lot of you and I respect Billy's judgment—now."

I scratched the angle of my jaw and thought about it. "Well, I wouldn't get rid of your money, if that's what you're thinking about. It's too useful; you can do a lot of good if you have enough dollars."

"Buying my way out?"

"Not exactly. Are you thinking of being a missionary in Calcutta or something like that?"

Her laugh was rueful. "You know more about me than I thought."

"Forget it," I said. "It doesn't work. Besides, charity begins at home. Now, you're a Texan. I'll bet there are poor black kids in Texas who have never even seen the sea."

"That's a thought. What are you getting at?"

"I'm working it out," I said slowly. "Starting from the fact that we're in the Bahamas with plenty of black faces around. Your black Texan kids wouldn't stand out if you brought them here, and we've no color bar to speak of. Teach them to swim, scuba dive, sail a boat—things they've only been able to dream about back home. If you brought them out of season I could give you cheap rates in the hotels. They could go to Abaco and Eleuthera; real desert island stuff."

"My God!" she said. "What a marvelous idea. And there are poor white kids, too."

"All right, mix 'em up." I saw she was caught up in enthusiasm, and warned, "But you'll have to do more than pay for it, Deb, if it's going to work—I mean for you personally. You'll have to participate and bring the kids yourself, with perhaps a couple of assistants. It's something to think about."

"It surely is."

My eye was caught by Bill Pinder, the pilot, who was waving at me. I leaned forward and took the piece of paper he held. It was a message that had been radioed through Freeport air control and told me that Perigord wanted to see me urgently in his office.

I took Debbie along to the police station which was on the corner of Pioneer's Way and East Mall. I suppose I could have driven her to the Royal Palm and then gone back, but there was something about Perigord's message which made me want to see him fast, so I asked Debbie if she minded stopping off. It was a hot day and I did not want to leave her sitting in the car so I took her inside with me.

I happened to catch Perigord walking through the entrance hall so I introduced them, and added, "Miss Cunningham and her brother were present when *Lucayan Girl* left for Miami."

Perigord looked at her thoughtfully. "You'd better come into my office—both of you," he said abruptly, and led the way. In his office he turned to Debbie and asked without preamble, "Are you a good friend of Mr. Mangan?"

She was startled and shot me a swift look. "I would say so."

I said, "I haven't known Miss Cunningham long but I would certainly consider her my friend. Her cousin and I have been friends for many years."

For a moment Perigord looked undecided, then he waved at a chair. "Please sit down." He sat opposite us and said, "I am not certain that Miss Cunningham should be here at this point, but you might need some support from a friend."

"You've found them," I said with certainty.

He took a deep breath. "A fisherman found the body of a small, female child on a beach on Cat Island."

"Cat Island!" I said increduously. "But that's impossible! *Lucayan Girl* was going southwest to Miami—Cat Island is two hundred miles southeast. It *can't* be Sue!"

"I'm sorry, Mr. Mangan, but there is no doubt."

"I don't believe it. I want to see her."

"I would advise against it." Perigord shook his head. "You wouldn't recognize her."

"Why not?"

Perigord was unhappy. "I don't have to explain to a fellow Bahamian what happens to a body in our seas in a very short time."

"If I wouldn't recognize her how in hell can *you* be so sure?" I was becoming angry at the impossibility of all this. "How could Sue have got to Cat Island?"

Perigord took a card from his desk drawer and laid it flat. "This is your daughter's dental record; we obtained it from the school. Dr. Miller, your daughter's dentist, has done a comparison and it fits in every respect. We took no chances; we had another evaluation from a dentist who does not know your daughter. He confirmed Dr. Miller's identification."

I suddenly felt sick and a little dizzy. It must have shown in my color because Debbie put her hand on my arm. "Are you all right, Tom?"

"Yes," I said thickly. I raised my head and looked at Perigord. "And Julie? And the others?"

"Nothing, I'm afraid." He cleared his throat. "There'll be an inquest, of course."

"How do you explain Cat Island? You know it's bloody impossible. Anything abandoned in the Florida Straits would be swept northeast in the Gulf Stream."

"I can't explain it; at least, not to your satisfaction." He held up his hand as I opened my mouth. "It might help if you could identify the crewman."

I said dully, "I didn't see him."

Perigord said, "We have asked questions at the marinas with no luck at all. The trouble is that the marinas have, literally, a floating population." He repeated that, appreciating the double edge. "Yes, a floating population—here today and gone tomorrow. Nobody has been reported missing because everybody is missing, sooner or later. It makes police work difficult. We have also checked from the other end by asking Mr. Albury's friends if he had been seen talking to a stranger. Again, no luck."

Debbie said, "He might not have been a stranger."

"Oh, yes, I think he was," said Perigord confidently. "I think he was a beach bum, one of the young Americans who hitchhike around the islands on the cheap and are willing to crew for anyone if it gives them a leg further. I think this one was going home."

"Then he might be on an American missing persons list," she remarked.

"Why should he be?" asked Perigord. "He's only been gone a week, and he's probably a footloose young man, a social dropout. In any case, in which American city do we ask? And with no name and no face how do we operate?"

My brain started to work creakily. Perigord had said

something which aroused my ire. "You said you couldn't explain how Sue came to be on Cat Island *to my satisfaction.* Does that mean that you are satisfied?" I was becoming enraged at Perigord because I knew he was holding something back.

That got to him. "By God, Mr. Mangan, I am not satisfied. It gives me no satisfaction to sit here and pass on bad news, sir."

"Then what's all the bloody mystery? Is it because I am a suspect? If I am then say so. Am I to be accused of blowing up my own boat?"

My voice had risen to a shout and I found myself shaking. Again Debbie held my arm and said, "Take it easy, Tom."

"Take it easy? There's been something damn funny going on right from the start." I stabbed a finger at Perigord. "No one can tell me that a deputy-commissioner of police does his own legwork when a boat goes missing. Especially when he brings a narcotics officer with him. Perigord, I'm well known in Government circles, and if you don't come across I'll be over in Nassau talking to Deane, your boss, and a few other people and you won't know what hit you."

Perigord made a curious gesture as though to brush away an irritating fly. "I assure you that the police are treating this with the utmost seriousness. Further, the Government is serious. And alarmed, I might add. The Attorney General, acting under direct instruction from the Prime Minister, is putting very heavy pressure on me—as much as I can stand—and I don't need any more from you."

"But you'll damn well get it," I said. "Good Christ, this is my family we're talking about!"

He stopped being impervious and his voice softened. "I know—I know." He stood up and went to the window, looking out on to East Mall in silence and with his hands clasped tightly behind his back. He stood there for a long time evidently having difficulty in making up his mind about something.

Presently he turned and said quietly, "I suppose if I were

in your position I would feel and act as you do. That's why I'm going to tell you something of what is happening in the Bahamas. But I'll want your discretion. I don't want you going off half-cocked and, above all, I want your silence. You must not talk about what I'm about to tell you."

Debbie rose to her feet. "I'll leave."

"No," said Perigord. "Stay, Miss Cunningham." He smiled. "Mr. Mangan will want to talk to someone about this; he wouldn't be human if he didn't, and his confidante might as well be you. But I'll need the same assurance of your silence."

Debbie said, "You have it."

"Mr. Mangan?"

I thought Perigord was every bit as good an amateur psychologist as Mike Pascoe. "All right."

He returned to his seat at the desk. "It is not normal for a well-found boat to vanish in a calm sea, and the inquiries made before I took over the case gave us the assurance that *Lucayan Girl* was a very well-found boat with more than the usual complement of safety equipment."

"I made it so," I said.

Perigord examined the backs of his hands. "There have been too many boats going missing these past few years. There has been much ill-informed and mischievous talk about the so-called Bermuda Triangle of which we are in the center. The Bahamian Government, however, does not believe in spooks—neither do the insurance companies. The Government is becoming most worried about it."

"Are you talking about piracy?" said Debbie unbelievingly.

"Just that."

I had heard the rumors, as I suppose every other Bahamian had, and it had been a topic in some of the American yachting magazines. I said, "I know there was piracy around here in the old days, but these boats aren't treasure ships— they're not carrying gold to Spain. I suppose you could sell off bits and pieces—radar, radio, engines, perhaps—but that's chicken feed, and dangerous, too. Easy to detect."

"You're right. Your boat is probably on the sea bed by now, with all its equipment intact. These people are not going to risk selling a few items for a few dollars. Mr. Mangan, I think we're dealing with coke smugglers, and I don't mean Coca-Cola—I mean cocaine. It comes through here from South America and goes to the States. Some heroin, too, but not much because we're not on that route. Some marijuana, also, but again not much because it's too bulky."

He nodded and gestured toward the large map of the Bahamas on the wall. "Look at that—one hundred thousand square miles of which only five percent is land. If the land were conveniently in one place our task would be easier, but there are thousands of cays. An area the size of the British Isles with a population of two hundred and twenty thousand. That's what we have to police."

He walked over to the map. "Take only one small group." His arms slashed in an arc. "The Ragged Island Range and the Jumentos Cays—one hundred and twenty miles long with a total population of two hundred, mostly concentrated in Duncan town in the south. Anyone could bring a boat in there with a ninety-nine certainty of not being seen even in daylight. They could land on Flamingo Cay, Water Cay, Stoney Cay—or any one of a hundred others, most of which don't even have names. And that's just one small chain of islands among many. We could turn our whole population into police officers and still not have enough men to cover."

Debbie said, "How does piracy come into this?"

"It's not called piracy anymore, although it is," said Perigord tiredly. "It's become prevalent enough to have acquired its own name—yacht-jacking. They grab a boat and sail it out of the local area, fast. A quick paint spray job of the upperworks takes care of easy identification. They head for the cay where the cocaine is hidden and then run it to the States. Once the cocaine is ashore they usually sink the boat; sometimes they may use it for a second run, but not often. And you know how many we've caught?" He held up a single finger.

"And for that they murder the crew?" I demanded.

"Do you know what the profits are, Mr. Mangan? But normally the boats are stolen from a marina and there are no deaths. That's easy enough, considering the informality of most boat owners and the laxity of the average marina."

"*Lucayan Girl* wasn't stolen from a marina."

Perigord said deliberately, "When a man like you sends his wife and small daughter to sea with a crewman he has never seen and whose name he doesn't know he's asking for trouble."

He had not come right out and said it, but he was implying that I was a damn fool and I was inclined to agree with him. I said weakly, "But who could have known?"

Perigord sighed. "We hand out circulars, put posters in marinas—watch your boat—know your crew—use your keys—and no one apparently takes a damn bit of notice." He paused. "I wouldn't say that the case of *Lucayan Girl* is the norm. Boats *are* lost at sea for other than criminal reasons; storm damage, fire, explosions, run down, and so on. But if they're taken by piracy and then sunk who's to know the difference? That's our problem; we don't *know* how many acts of piracy are occurring. All we know is that too many boats are being lost."

Debbie said, "Are you implying that the crewman on *Lucayan Girl* might be alive?"

Perigord spread his hands. "Miss Cunningham, if this is a simple matter of sinking, which we can't discount, then he's probably dead. If it is piracy, which is more than likely because of what we found on Cat Island, then he is probably alive. And that's why I want your silence. If he's still here I don't want him to know he's being looked for." He pursed his lips in a dubious manner. "But without a name or description he's going to be difficult to find."

I said, "Commissioner, find the bastard. If it's a matter of a reward to be offered I'll put it up, no matter how much."

"I mentioned discretion," said Perigord softly. "Offering a public reward is hardly being discreet." He clasped his hands in front of him. "This is a professional matter, Mr.

Mangan; a matter for the police. I don't want you butting in, and you did give me your word."

"He's right, Tom," said Debbie.

"I know." I stood up and said to Perigord, "I'm sorry if I blew my top."

"No apology is necessary. I understand."

"You'll keep me informed of developments?"

"Insofar as I can. You must understand that I may not be able to tell all I know, even to you. Discretion also applies to the police when in the public interest."

He stood up and we shook hands, and with that I had to be satisfied. But as Perigord had warned, it was not to my entire satisfaction.

5

AND SO there was a funeral after all, but before that, the inquest. I attended, but before the proceedings began Perigord had a word with me. "Regardless of the findings of this inquest we're treating this as a murder case."

I looked at him sharply. "New evidence?"

"Not really. But your daughter didn't die by drowning; there was no salt water in the lungs. Of course, in the event of an explosion on the boat she could have struck her head hard enough to kill her before entering the water. The head injuries are consistent with that." He paused. "It might help you to know that, in the opinion of the forensic pathologist, death was instantaneous."

Debbie sat with me at the inquest—she was staying until after the funeral. The inquest was beautifully stage-managed; by Perigord, I suspect. The coroner had obviously been briefed and knew all the questions he was not supposed to ask, and he guided witnesses skillfully. As I gave my evidence it occurred to me that one of the factors in Perigord's decision to tell me what he had was to prevent any awkward questions coming from me at the inquest.

The verdict was death by unknown causes.

The family was at the funeral, of course. Grace came from Florida, and Peggy and Bob from Abaco, bringing Karen with them. Karen had regained most of her spirits but the funeral subdued her a little. Also present were some of my Bahamian friends and a surprising number of Corporation employees.

It was sad to see the pathetically small coffin being lowered into the sandy earth. Karen cried, so I picked her up and held her close during the brief ceremony. A few last words were said and then it was all over and the crowd drifted away.

Debbie left for Houston the next day to be home for Christmas and I drove her to the airport. I picked her up at the Royal Palm, and on the way she asked me to stop at the International Bazaar as there was something she wanted to pick up. I parked outside, and she said, "Don't bother to come in; I won't be long." So I sat in the car and waited, and she was back in five minutes.

At the airport we had coffee after we had got rid of her luggage and were waiting for her flight announcement. I said, "You can tell Billy I'm willing to talk business as soon as he's ready."

She looked at me closely. "You're sure?"

"Mike was right," I said. "Life goes on, and the Corporation doesn't run itself. Yes, I'm sure."

"I've been thinking of what you suggested when we were coming back from Abaco. You know, when I think of it I've lived a pretty useless life." She smiled wryly. "The Cunningham family doesn't believe in women in business. They're supposed to be ornamental, be good in bed and make babies—preferably boys to carry on the line. Damned misplaced southern chivalry. So I've been decorative and that's about all."

I smiled. "What about the bed bit?"

"You won't believe this, but I was a virgin until I met that bastard back in Houston." She shook the thought from her. "Anyway, I think all that's going to change, and it's going to give a hell of a shock to my father—me mixing with black kids and poor white trash. I think I can get it past Billy One though."

"Stick at it. It's time the Cunninghams made something besides money. Making people happy isn't a bad aim."

We talked about it some more, and then she excused herself and walked across the concourse to the toilets. When she came back she was hurrying, her heels clicking rapidly on the hard floor. She stopped in front of me and said, "There's something I have to show you, Tom. I wasn't going to, but . . ." She stopped and bit her lip nervously, then thrust an envelope into my hand. "Here!"

"What is it?"

"You remember Sue left her camera behind. Well, I took out the film and had it developed. I just picked up the prints at the International Bazaar and I went into the john to have a look at them."

"I see," I said slowly. I was not sure I wanted to see them. There would be too many memories of that last day.

"I think you ought to look at them," Debbie urged. "It's important."

I took the prints out of the envelope and shuffled through them. There were a couple of pictures of the *Girl* in one of which Pete posed in the bows, striking a mock-heroic attitude; three pictures of Sue herself, probably taken by Julie, which damn near broke my heart to see; and the rest were of Julie herself in various locations—by the pool, by the boat, and on board supervising the loading of luggage. There was one picture of Debbie and also four duds, out of focus and blurred. Sue had not yet got the hang of the camera—and now never would. I got a lump in my throat and coughed.

Debbie was watching me closely. "Look again."

I went through the pictures again and suddenly Debbie said, "Stop! That one." In the picture where Pete was in the bows there was a dim figure in the stern—a man just coming on deck from below. He was in the shade and his face was indistinct.

"Well, I'll be damned!" I put down the print and took out the negative. A 110 film negative is damned small—it will just about cover your thumbnail—and the bit which showed the man was about as big as a pinhead. "The crewman!" I said softly.

"Yes. You'll have something to show Perigord."

"But I'll have it enlarged first. I'm not letting this into Perigord's hands without having a few copies for myself. His ideas of discretion might get in my way. I have a shrewd idea that once he gets this I'll never see it again."

Debbie's flight was announced, garbled by bad acoustics, and I accompanied her to the barrier where we said our goodbyes. "I'll write to you about our scheme," she said. "Take care of yourself, Tom." She kissed me, a chaste peck on the cheek.

Then she was gone and I went back into Freeport to find a photographer. I left the film and then accompanied Peggy and Bob back to Abaco to spend a sad, subdued Christmas with Karen.

Two days later I had what I wanted. I sat in my office and examined the duplicate negative, the copies of the color print, and the six glossy black-and-white blowups of the pinhead-sized area of the negative which was the head of the crewman. The darkroom technician had done a good job considering the size of the image he had to work with. It could not be said to be a good portrait, being very grainy and slightly out of focus, but it was not all that bad.

The man was youngish—I would say under thirty—and he appeared to be blond. He had a broadish forehead and narrow chin, and his eyes were deepset and shadowed. One hand was up by his face as though he intended to hide it, and the head was slightly blurred as though it was in motion when the picture was taken. On the color print it looked as though he was emerging from below, and perhaps he had suddenly been aware that he was on candid camera. If so, he had not beaten the speed of a camera shutter and a fast film.

I studied the face for a very long time. Was this a callous murderer? What did a murderer look like? Like anyone else, I suppose.

I was about to ring Perigord when the intercom buzzed so I flicked the switch. "Yes, Jessie?"

"Mr. Ford to see you."

I had forgotten about Sam Ford. I pushed the photographs to one side of my desk, and said, "Shoot him in."

Sam Ford was a black Bahamian, and manager of the marina which was attached to the Sea Gardens Hotel on New Providence. He was an efficient manager, a good sailor, and did a lot for the branch of BASRA over there. Ever since the talk in Perigord's office and his expressed views on marina security I had been thinking about ours, and I had a job for Sam.

He came in. "Morning, Mr. Mangan."

"Morning, Sam. Take a chair."

As he sat down he said, "I was real sorry to hear about what happened. I'd have come to the funeral, but we had problems that day at the marina."

There had been a wreath from Sam and his family. "Thanks, Sam. But it's over now." He nodded and I leaned back in my chair. "I've been reviewing our policy on marinas. We have three, and soon we'll have another when the hotel is finished on Eleuthera. If things turn out as I hope we'll have more. So far the marinas have been attached to the hotels with the marina manager being responsible to the hotel manager. It's worked well enough, but there's been a certain amount of friction, wouldn't you say?"

"I've had trouble," said Sam. "I don't know about the other marinas but my boss, Archie Bain, knows damn all about boats. The times he's asked me to put a quart in a pint pot I swear he thinks boats are collapsible."

I had heard similar comments from other marina managers. "All right, we're going to change things. We're going to set up a marinas division with the marina managers responsible to the divisional manager, not to the hotel managers. He'd be running the lot with the centralized buying of ship's chandlery and so on. How would you like the job?"

His eyebrows rose. "Divisional manager?"

"Yes. You'd get the pay that goes with the job."

Sam took a deep breath. "Mr. Mangan, that's a job I've been praying for."

I smiled. "It's yours from the first of the month—that's two weeks from now. And as divisional manager you get to call me Tom." We talked about his new job for some time, settling lines of demarcation, his salary, and other details. Then I said, "And I want you to beef up on security in the marinas. How many boats have you had stolen, Sam?"

"From the Sea Gardens?" He scratched his head. "One

this year, two last year, and two the year before. The one this year was recovered on Andros, found abandoned. I think someone just took it for a joyride."

Five in three years did not sound many out of all the boats Sam had handled, but multiply that by the number of marinas in the Bahamas and it was a hell of a lot. I began to appreciate Perigord's point of view. I said, "Go back over the records of all our marinas for the last five years. I want to know how many boats went missing. And, Sam, we don't want to lose any more."

"I don't see we're responsible," said Sam. "And there's a clause in the marina agreement which says so. You know boat people. They reckon they've gotten the freedom of the seas. Maybe they have because no one has gotten around to licensing them yet, but some are downright irresponsible."

I winced because Sam had hit a raw nerve; I had been a boat owner. "Nevertheless, beef up security."

"It'll cost," Sam warned. "That means watchmen."

"Do it."

Sam shrugged. "Anything more, Mr . . . er . . . Tom?"

"I think that's all."

He stood up, then hesitated. "Excuse me, but I've been wondering. What are you doing with those pictures of Jack Kayles?"

"Who?"

Sam pointed to the black-and-white photographs. "There. That's Jack Kayles."

"You know this man?"

"Not to say know like being friends, but he's been in and out of the marina."

"Sam, you've just earned yourself a bonus." I pushed a photograph across the desk. "Now, sit down and tell me everything you know about him."

Sam picked it up. "Not a good picture," he commented. "But it's Kayles, all right. He's a yacht bum; got a sloop—a twenty-seven-footer, British-built and glass fiber. Usually sails single-handed."

"Where does he keep her?"

"Nowhere and everywhere. She's usually where he happens to be at the time. Kayles can pitch up anywhere, I reckon. He was in New Providence two years ago and told me he'd come up from the Galapagos, through the Panama Canal, and had worked his way through the islands. He was going on to look at the Florida keys. He's pretty handy with a boat."

"What's she called?"

Sam frowned. "Now that's a funny thing—he changed her name, which is mighty unusual. Most folk are superstitious about that. Two years go she was called *Seaglow*, but when I saw her last she was *Green Wave*."

"Maybe a different boat," I suggested.

"Same boat," said Sam firmly.

I accepted that; Sam knew his boats. "When was he last in your marina?"

"About three months ago."

"How does Kayles earn his living?"

Sam shrugged. "I don't know. Maybe he crews for pay. I told you; he's a yacht bum. There's plenty like Kayles about. They live on their boats and scratch a living somehow." He thought for a moment. "Come to think of it, Kayles never seemed short of cash. He paid on the nail for everything. A few bits of chandlery from the shop, fuel, marina fees and all that."

"Credit card?"

"No. Always in cash. Always in American dollars, too."

"He's an American?"

"I'd say so. Could be Canadian, but I don't think so. What's all this about, Tom?"

"I have an interest in him," I said uninformatively. "Any more you can tell me?"

"Not much to tell," said Sam. "I just put diesel oil in his boat and took his money. Not much of that, either. He has a pint-sized diesel engine which he doesn't use much; he's one of those guys who prefers the wind—a good sailor, like I said."

"Anything at all about Kayles will be useful," I said. "Think hard, Sam."

Sam ruminated. "I did hear he was awful quick-tempered, but he was always civil to me and that's all I cared about. He never made trouble in the marina but I heard he got into a fight in Nassau. Like all yachtsmen he carries a knife, and he used it—he cut a guy."

"Were the police in on that?"

Sam shook his head. "It was a private fight," he said dryly. "No one wanted police trouble."

I was disappointed; it would be useful if Kayles already had a police record. "Did he have any particular friends that you know of?"

"No, I'd say Kayles is a loner."

"When he left your marina three months ago did he say where he was going?"

"No." Sam suddenly snapped his fingers. "But when I met him last month in the International Bazaar he said he was going to Florida. I forgot about that." Then he added, "The International Bazaar here—not the one in Nassau."

I stared at Sam. "Are you telling me you saw Kayles here on Grand Bahama a month ago?"

"Not a month ago," corrected Sam. "Last month. It would be a little over two weeks ago. I'd brought a boat over for a client to give to Joe Cartwright here." Sam tugged his ear. "Chances are that Kayles had his boat here, too. I didn't see her, but I wasn't looking. He knew about the discount."

We had a system whereby a yachtsman using one of our marinas got a ten percent discount in any of the others; it helped keep the money in the family. I rang my secretary. "Jessie, get Joe Cartwright up here fast. I don't care what he's doing but I want him here." I turned back to Sam. "Did Kayles say how he was going to Florida?"

"He didn't tell me and I didn't ask. I assumed he'd be going in *Green Wave*."

I hammered at Sam for quite a while, but could get nothing more out of him. Presently Joe Cartwright arrived. He was the marina manager for the Royal Palm. "You wanted me, Mr. Mangan?" He flicked his hand in a brief salute. "Hi, Sam!"

I pushed forward the photograph. "Did this man bring a boat into the marina about two weeks ago?"

Sam said, "His name is Kayles."

"The face and the name mean nothing to me," said Joe. "I'd have to look at the records."

I pointed to the telephone. "Call your office and have someone do it now."

As Joe spoke into the mouthpiece I drummed my fingers restlessly on the desk. As least I had something for Perigord and I hoped it would prove to be a firm lead.

Joe put down the telephone. "He was here, but I didn't see him. He came in a British sloop with a red hull."

"Green," said Sam.

"No, it was red. Her name was *Bahama Mama.*"

"He changed the name again," said Sam in wonder. "Now why would a man do that?"

My upraised hand silenced him. I said to Joe, "Is the boat still here?"

"I'll find out." Joe picked up the telephone again and I held my breath. If the boat was still here than Kayles, in all likelihood, was dead with Julie, Sue and Pete. If not . . . ? Joe said, "She left on the twenty-fifth—Christmas Day."

I let out my breath with a sigh. That was six days after *Lucayan Girl* had disappeared. Joe said, "No one saw her leave; suddenly she wasn't there." He shrugged. "It didn't bother anyone; the marina fee had been paid in advance to the end of the month. We made a profit on that one."

I said, "I want both of you to wait in the outer office until you're wanted." They left and I called Perigord. "I've got a name and a face for you. That crewman."

He did not sound surprised. All he said was "Who?"

I told him.

"Where are you?"

"My office at the Royal Palm."

"Ten minutes," he said, and hung up.

6

PERIGORD PUT Sam Ford and Joe Cartwright through the wringer, but did not get much more out of them than I had, then he took the negative and photographs and departed. But he did not take all of them; I had retained some, locked in the office safe. I spoke to Sam and Joe. "If you see or hear of this man I want to know, but don't alarm him—just contact me."

Sam said, "What's all this about, Tom?"

I hesitated, half inclined to tell him, but said briefly, "You don't have to know. It's a police matter." I changed the subject. "We're organizing the marinas into a division, Joe; and Sam will be boss. Spread the word that we're expanding. There'll be no firings and a lot of hirings. Sam will tell you all about it. All right, that's it."

And that was that.

Jack Kayles did not come to the surface, not then, but Billy Cunningham arrived a couple of weeks later with a platoon of lawyers and accountants and they started to go through the books of West End Securities, finding not much wrong and a lot that was right. After a few days Billy came to me and said with a crooked smile, "You underestimated your value by about a quarter-million—but you're still not going to get more than a fifth of Theta stock."

"Suits me."

"The Corporation will be set up by the end of the week; I've had the Nassau lawyers working on it. Then we can sign papers."

"You'd have done better to have consulted me on that," I said.

"Perhaps, but I thought that maybe you weren't in any condition to think straight."

71

"You could have been right," I admitted.

He stood up and stretched. "It's been a hard week. I could do with a drink. Where do you keep your office bottle?"

I opened the cabinet, poured drinks, and handed him a glass. "Here's to the Theta Corporation."

We drank the toast, and Billy said, "You sure put a burr under Debbie's saddle. What the hell did you do?"

"Just a bit of fatherly advice."

Billy's lips quirked. "Fatherly!" He sat down. "My revered uncle, Jack Cunningham, chairman of the Cunningham Corporation and something of a prime bastard, thinks you're some kind of subversive nut. He says you've been putting leftist ideas into his daughter's head."

"What do you think?"

"I think it's the best thing that ever happened to her," he said frankly. "She's been spoiled silly all her life and it's time she thought of something other than herself. Maybe this will do it."

"I hope so."

He hesitated. "She told me about Sue, and the funeral. Why didn't you let me know?"

"Not your problem." I tasted the whiskey. "Did she tell you about the photograph?"

"What photograph?"

So Debbie was keeping her promise to Perigord; she had not even told her family. I was not as honorable. "I'll tell you about it, but keep it under your hat."

So I told him and when I had finished he said, "Jesus, I've never heard of anything like that!" He picked up the photograph I had taken from the safe. "You mean this son of a bitch killed your family?"

"That's the general theory. If he's still alive he did, and if he's dead who took his boat from the marina here?"

"This is a crummy picture," said Billy. "I think we can do better than this?"

"How?"

"You know we have the Space Center in Houston. I know

a lot of the guys there because we do business with NASA. When they shoot pictures back from space they're pretty blurred so they put them through a computer which sharpens them up; makes a computer-enhanced image, as they call it." He tapped the photograph. "I think they could do the same with this, and if they can't you're no worse off. Mind if I take this back to Houston?"

I thought it was a good idea. "Take it."

Three days later we signed the papers and I was president of a fifty-million-dollar corporation.

Time passed.

I had a heavy workload as I buckled down to making the Theta Corporation work. I began by activating some of the suggestions I had outlined to Billy, beginning with the construction division. Jack Foster was a childless widower who ran a construction company based in Nassau. He was past sixty and wanted to get out, not seeing the point of working himself into the grave when he had no one to leave the company to, so I flew to Nassau and we did a deal, and I got the company for a quarter-million less than I expected to pay. Since this was the company that was building the hotel on Eleuthera things started to move faster there because I saw to it that the Theta Corporation got first choice of materials and manpower. The sooner the hotel was completed the sooner the cash flow would turn from negative to positive.

The quarter-million I saved I put into a geographical and economic survey of the Bahamas, hiring an American outfit to do it. I did not expect them to come up with anything that would surprise me, but what they found would buttress my ideas with the Cunninghams.

I flew to Abaco at least once a week to see Karen, even if only to stay an hour. She seemed to have settled down completely and seemed none the worse for her bereavement. I wished I had her resilience; I stopped myself from brooding only by hard work and keeping occupied. But there were times in the small hours. . . .

I discussed the question of taking Karen home but Peggy counseled against it. "Tom, you're working all the hours God sends. How do you expect to look after a little girl? Let her stay here until things ease off for you. She's no trouble."

Peggy and Bob were thrilled because I was funding them to a golf course to compete with the one at Treasure Cay. I also told them I was having joint meetings with the Ministry of Finance, the Ministry of Tourism and the Department of Public Works to see if anything could be done about the God-awful road between Marsh Harbor and Treasure Cay. I told them I had produced the Pilot's Bahamas Aviation Guide—the bit where it says that if anyone wants to get from Treasure Cay to Marsh Harbor they'd better fly. "I asked them, 'What sort of tourist advertising is that?' I think we'll get our improved road."

"It would help our lunch trade a lot," said Bob. "People coming on day tours from Treasure Cay."

"The hell with lunch. You'll be running a car rental."

So I was keeping busy and the time passed a little less painfully.

I made a point of dropping in to see Perigord from time to time. The computer-enhanced pictures of Kayles came back from NASA and I gave them to him. Perigord took one look at them and blinked. "How did you do this?" he demanded.

"Ask no questions," I said. "Remember discretion."

There was no sign of Kayles. "If he's still alive he could be anywhere," said Perigord. "Yachtsmen are mobile and there's no control over them at all. For all I know he's in Cape Town right now."

"And he'll have changed the name of his boat again."

"And perhaps his own," said Perigord.

"He'd surely have passport difficulties there."

Perigord looked at me a little sorrowfully. "It may come as a surprise to you to know that the skipper of a boat, no matter how small the boat, doesn't need a passport; all he needs are ship's papers and those are easily forged. In any case, getting a passport is easy enough if you know where to look."

Perigord was stymied.

Three months passed and Debbie came back bringing with her two young black American women about her own age. She blew into my office like a refreshing breeze and introduced them. "This is Cora Brown and Addy Williams; they're both teachers, and Addy has nursing qualifications. We're an advance scouting party."

"Then I'd better fix you up with rooms." I stretched for the telephone.

"No need," she said airily. "I made reservations."

I made a mental note to tell Jack Fletcher to inform me any time Debbie Cunningham made a reservation. "So you're going ahead."

They told me about it, extensively and in detail. They were going to bring twenty children each month for a two-week stay. "I had a bit of trouble with the school boards about that," said Debbie. "But I pointed out that both Cora and Addy are teachers and the whole thing is one big geography lesson, anyway—with sports thrown in. They went for it."

Cora and Addy were to give the kids lessons in basic arithmetic and English, and they were to learn the history of the Bahamas in relationship to the United States. That took care of the education bit. Debbie said tentatively, "You said something about the Family Islands. I thought a week here and a week on one of those. . . ."

"Sure," I said. "That's easy. While they're here those kids who can swim can go along to the Underwater Exploration Society and learn scuba diving. They'll give you a low rate. Those who can't swim can have lessons here in the hotel pool. We have an instructor."

"That's great," said Cora. "I can't swim—maybe I'll take lessons, too."

And so it went with much enthusiasm. I took time off to introduce them to people I thought they ought to know and then let them loose in Freeport. Before they went back to the States I took Debbie to dinner at the Xanadu Princess. I had engineered that tête-à-tête by sending Cora and Addy to Abaco with an introduction to Peggy.

As we got out of the car Debbie looked up at the hotel. "Does this belong to the Theta Corporation?"

I laughed. "No, I just like to keep tabs on what the opposition is up to."

Over cocktails I said, "I like Cora and Addy. Where did you find them?"

"Oh, I just asked around and hit the jackpot." She smiled. "Neither of them is married. From what I've observed in the last few days they could very well marry Bahamian boys. Your menfolk sure move in fast." The smile left her face and she said soberly, "How are you doing, Tom?"

"All right. The Theta Corporation is keeping me busy. So much so that I'm thinking of selling the house. I don't spend much time there now; usually I sleep at the hotel."

"Oh, you mustn't sell that beautiful house," she said impulsively.

"I rattle around in it. And there are too many memories."

She put her hand on mine. "I hope it's not too bad." We were quiet for a while, then she said, "Billy talked to me. He said you'd told him about Kayles. Any more news?"

"Nothing. Kayles seems to have vanished completely. If it weren't for all the inconsistencies I'd be inclined to believe he went down with *Lucayan Girl*—that it was a genuine accident."

I changed the subject deliberately and we talked of other and lighter matters, and it was pretty late when I took her back to the Royal Palm. As we walked toward the parking lot, something flashed out of the darkness and Debbie ducked, and gasped, "What was that!"

"Don't worry, it's harmless—it won't hurt you. It was just a bat. We call them money bats."

Debbie looked up doubtfully and I could see she did not altogether believe my claim that the bats were harmless. "That's an odd name? Why *money* bats?"

I chuckled. "Because the only time you see them is when they're flying away from you."

That night, lying sleepless in bed, I had a curious thought. Could the mind play tricks on one? Had I given Debbie Cunningham the idea of bringing American kids to the Bahamas just so I could see more of her? It had not been a conscious decision, of that I was sure. With Julie and Sue just dead a week I would not, could not, have made such a decision. But the mind is strange and complex, and perhaps it had put those words in my mouth, the idea into Debbie's mind, for reasons of its own.

All the same I felt happier than I had for a long time, knowing that I would be seeing Debbie Cunningham monthly for the foreseeable future.

Seven months after I became president of the Theta Corporation we had the grand opening of the Rainbow Bay Hotel on Eleuthera. I invited a crowd of notables: government ministers, a couple of film stars, a golf champion and so on. I also invited Deputy-Commissioner Howard Perigord and his wife, Amy. And the Cunninghams came: Billy and his father, Billy One; Jack Cunningham, who looked upon me with some mistrust, and, of course, daughter Debbie.

Before we flew to Eleuthera the Cunninghams and I had an informal board meeting. I handed out copies of the survey made by the American company, and added my report with its detailed recommendations. "You're not expected to read all this now, but I'll give you a brief summary."

I ticked off the points on my fingers. "We go into the Family Islands . . ." I paused, and said in parentheses, "They used to be known as the Out Islands but the Minister of Tourism thinks that the Family Islands sounds more cozy."

"He's right," said Billy. "And Shakespeare was wrong. There's a lot to names."

"Anyway, the future lies in the Family Islands. We go into real estate in a bit way on Crooked Island, Acklins Island, Mayaguana and Great Inagua. And we buy a couple of cays in the Ragged Island Range. All this is undeveloped and we get in there first, especially before the Swiss moneymen move in and send the prices up."

I tapped another finger. "We put together our own package deals and farm them out to travel agents in the States and in Europe. In order to do that we either make deals with a couple of airlines or charter planes ourselves to fly our customers into Grand Bahama or New Providence. From there we'll either have to do a deal with Bahamasair or set up our own islands airline."

Another finger went up. "Next I want one really top-class luxury hotel; not for the package tourist but for the people with money." I grinned. "Simple folks like yourselves. Ten percent of the visitors to the Islands come in their own aircraft and I want to capture that market."

"Sounds good," said Billy.

Billy One said, "Yeah, it seems to make sense."

Jack Cunningham had been flipping through the pages of my report. "What's this about you wanting to start a school?"

I said, "If we're building hotels we'll need staff to run them. I want to train them my way."

"The hell with that!" said Jack roundly. "We pay for training, then they leave and go to some other goddamn hotel like a Holiday Inn. No way are we doing that."

"The Ministry of Tourism is putting up half the cost," I said.

"Oh, well," said Jack grudgingly. "That may be different."

Billy said, "Jack, I'm chairman of this corporation and as far as I'm concerned you're the seventeenth Vice-President in Charge of Answering Stupid Questions. Don't stick your oar in here."

"Don't talk to your uncle like that," said Billy One. But his voice was mild.

"I've got my money in here," snapped Jack. "And I don't want this guy throwing it away. He's already filled Debbie's head with a lot of communistic nonsense."

Billy grinned. "Show me another commie with over ten million bucks."

"Two million of which we gave him," snapped Jack. He tossed the report aside. "Billy, you damn near swore a Bible oath that the government of the Bahamas was stable." He pointed at me. "You believed him. He gives us a report which makes nice reading, but I've been reading other words—in newspapers, for instance. There was a goddamn riot in Nassau three days ago. What's so stable about that?"

I knew about the riot and was at a loss to account for it. It had flashed into being from nowhere and the police had had a hard time in containing the disturbance. I said, "An American outfit pulled out and closed down a factory. They did it too damned fast and without consultation. People don't like being fired, especially when it's done without notice. I think that started the trouble. It's just a local difficulty, Jack."

He grunted. "It had better be. Some American tourists got hurt, and that's not doing the industry any good; an industry, I might point out, which we're into for fifty million dollars."

I could see that any relationship I had with Jack would be uneasy and I determined to steer clear of him as far as I could. As for the riot, I had given a glib enough explanation, but I was not sure it was the right one.

Billy One said, "Let's cool it, shall we?" He looked at me. "Would you happen to have any sour mash around?"

So it was smoothed over and next day we flew to Eleuthera. Eleuthera is one hundred and twenty miles long but at the place where I had built the hotel it was less than two miles wide, so that from the hotel one could see the sea on both sides. Billy One looked at this in wonder. "I'll be goddamned."

I said, "We get two beaches for the price of one. That's why I built here."

Even Jack was impressed.

During the course of the day I had a few words with Perigord and asked him about the riot in Nassau. "What caused it?" I asked.

He shrugged. "I don't really know. It's not in my jurisdiction. It's in Commissioner Deane's lap—and he's welcome to it."

"Any chance of a similar occurrence on Grand Bahama?"

He smiled grimly. "Not if I have anything to do with it?"

"Was it political?"

He went opaque on me and deliberately changed the subject. "I must congratulate you on this very fine hotel. I wish you every success."

That reaction worried me more than anything else.

But the grand opening was a tremendous success and I danced with Debbie all night.

The Theta Corporation was a success after its first year although more money was going out than coming in. After all, that was the point—we were still in the stage of expansion. Billy was satisfied with the way I was handling things and so, largely, was Billy One. How Jack felt I did not know; he kept his nose out of things and I did not care to ask. Everything was going fine in my business life, and my private life was perking up, too, to the point where I asked Debbie to marry me.

She sighed. "I thought you'd never ask."

So I took her to bed and we were married three weeks later over the protests of Jack, whose open objection concerned the disparity in our ages, but he did not like me, something I knew already. Billy and, I think, Billy One were for it, but Debbie's brother, Frank, followed Jack's line. Various members of the family took sides and the clan was split to some extent on this issue. But none of them could say that I was a fortune hunter marrying her for her money—I had enough of my own. As for my own feelings about it, I was marrying Debbie, not Jack.

We married in Houston in a somewhat tense atmosphere and then went back to the Bahamas to honeymoon briefly at the new Rainbow Bay Hotel. Then we went back to Grand Bahama via Abaco where we picked up Karen who seemed dubious about having a new mother. Debbie and Karen moved into the house at Lucaya and I went back to running the Corporation. Two months later she told me she was pregnant which made both of us very happy.

But then things began to go wrong again because people who were coming to the Bahamas on vacation were going home to die.

7

Legionella pneumophila.

I learned a lot about that elusive bug with the pseudo-Latin name in the next few months. Anyone connected with the hotel industry had to learn, and learn fast. At first it was not recognized for what it was because those afflicted were not dying in the Bahamas but back home in the States or in England or Switzerland or wherever else they came from. It was the World Health Organization that blew the first warning whistle.

Most people might know it as Legionnaires' disease because it was first discovered at the convention of the American Legion held at the Bellevue-Stratford Hotel in Philadelphia in 1976 where there was an almost explosive outbreak of pneumonia among those who had attended. Altogether 221 people became ill and 34 of them died. Naturally, Legionnaires' disease is bad news for any hotelier. No one is likely to spend a carefree vacation in a resort hotel from which he may be carried out feet first, and the problem is compounded by the fact that even those hotels which are well kept and disease-free feel a financial draught. Once the news gets around that a particular holiday resort is tainted then everybody gets hurt.

So it was that a lot of people, me among them, were highly perturbed to hear that Legionnaires' disease was loose in the Parkway Hotel in Nassau. I flew to New Providence to talk to Tony Bosworth, our corporation doctor. He had his base at the Sea Gardens Hotel because New Providence is fairly central and he could get to our other hotels reasonably quickly, using a corporation plane in an emergency. A company doctor was another of my extravagances of which Jack Cunningham did not approve, but he earned his salary on this, and other, occasions.

When I told him what was happening at the Parkway he gave a low whistle. "Legionellosis! That's a bad one. Are you sure?"

I shrugged. "That's what I hear."

"Do you know which form? It comes in two ways—Pontiac fever and Legionnaires' disease."

That was the first time I had heard of Pontiac fever, but not the last. I shook my head. "I wouldn't know. You're the doctor, not me."

"Pontiac fever isn't too bad," he said. "It hits fast and has a high attack rate, about ninety-five percent, but usually there are no fatalities. Legionnaires' disease is a killer. I'll get on to the Department of Public Health. Give me fifteen minutes, will you?"

I went away to look at the kitchens. I often make surprise raids on the kitchens and other departments just to keep the staff up to the mark. All departments are equally important but, to paraphrase George Orwell, the kitchen is more equal than others. Every hotelier's nightmare is an outbreak of salmonella. It was nearer half an hour before I got back to Tony and he was still on the phone, but he hung up a couple of minutes after my arrival.

"Confirmed," he said gloomily. "Legionnaires' disease. Suspected by a smart young doctor in Manchester, England, it was confirmed by the Communicable Disease Surveillance Center. The World Health Organization has identified a man dead in Paris and two more in Zurich; there's a couple of cases in Buenos Aires and a rash of them across the States."

"All these people stayed at the Parkway?"

"Yes. How many rooms there?"

I had all the statistics of my competition at my fingertips. "A hundred and fifty."

"What would you say the year-round occupation rate is?"

I considered. "It's a reasonably good hotel. I'd say between seventy-five and eighty percent."

Tony's lips moved silently as he made a calculation. "They'll have to contact about twelve thousand people, and they're spread all over the bloody world. That's going to be a job for someone."

I gaped at him. "Why so many?"

"There's been some work done on this one since 1976. Studies have shown that this deadly little chap can live in water for over a year, so that's how far back it's standard to check. One will get you ten that the bacteria are in the air-conditioning cooling tower at the Parkway, but we don't know how long they've been in there. Look, Tom, this is pretty serious. The attack rate among those exposed is between one and five percent. Let's split the different and call it two and a half. That means three hundred casualties. With a death rate among them of fifteen percent that gives us forty-five deaths."

In the event he was not far out. When the whole scare was over the final tally came to 324 casualties and 41 deaths.

"You seem to know a lot about it."

He gave me a lopsided grin. "I'm a hotel doctor; this is what I get my salary for. Those casualties who don't die won't be good for much for a few months, and there's a grave risk of permanent lung damage, to say nothing of the kidneys and the liver."

I took a deep breath. "All right, Tony; what do we do?"

"Nothing much. These outbreaks tend to be localized—usually restricted to a single building. They've turned off the air conditioning at the Parkway so there'll be nothing blown out."

"So you think our hotels are safe?"

He shrugged. "They should be."

"I'd like to make sure."

"Testing for *L. pneumophila* is a finicky business. You need a well-equipped laboratory with livestock—guinea pigs, fertilized eggs and so on. That's why the damned creature only turned up as late as 1976. And it takes a long time, too. I'll tell you what; I'll take samples of the water from the air conditioners in the four hotels and send them to Miami—but don't expect quick results." He turned and took a fat medical book from the shelf next to his desk and flipped through the pages. "We haven't developed an antibacterial agent for this one yet; nothing specific, anyway. Heavy chlorination would appear to be the answer."

"Tell me how it's done."

I did not wait for Bosworth to report on the samples he sent to Miami, but got working on the big air conditioners in each hotel, taking them out of service one at a time. An air conditioner in a moderately big hotel can handle up to one thousand gallons of water a minute and the cooling is effected by evaporation as the water pours over splash bars and has air blown through it.

A cooling tower will lose about ten gallons of water a minute as water vapor and there is another gallon a minute lost in what is known technically in the trade as "drift": very finely divided drops of water. Attempts are made to control the emission of drift by drift eliminators, but some always get out. Tony Bosworth told me that any infectious bacteria would probably be escaping in the drift. I chlorinated the hell out of that water.

I supervised it all myself to make sure it was done properly. I had to make sure it was done in the right way. There was a lot riding on this, apart from the fact that I did not want anyone to die just because he had patronized one of my hotels. *L. pneumophila* had a nasty habit of not only killing people, but hotels, too.

Tony Bosworth was also pretty busy flitting from island to island attending suspected cases of Legionnaires' disease which turned out to be the common cold. Our hotels were clean but the tourists were jittery and the whole of the Bahamas ran scared for a little while. It was not a good year for either the Bahamas or the Theta Corporation, and the Ministry of Tourism and I sat back to watch the people stay away. Tourism fell off by fifteen percent in the next three months. The Parkway Hotel was cleaned up and certified safe, but I doubt if the room occupancy even reached ten percent in the months that followed. The company that owned it later went broke.

Another thing it meant was that I was away from home

more often than I was there. Debbie grew annoyed and we had our first fights. I had never been that way with Julie but now, with hindsight, I remembered that when Julie was expecting Sue I had been always careful to stay close. That had been my first baby, too.

So, perhaps, in a sense our quarrels were equally my fault even if I did not recognize it at the time. As it was I took offense. I was working very hard, not only protecting against this damned disease which was worrying the hell out of me, but also taking the usual workload of the president of the Theta Corporation, and I did not see why I should have to be drained of my energies at home, too. So the quarreling became worse. It is not only jealousy that feeds on itself.

Debbie was still doing her thing with Cora, Addy and the Texan kids, but operating mainly from the Bahamian end. But then I noticed that she was spending more and more time back home in Texas. Her excuse was that Cora and Addy were hopeless at organization and she had to go back to iron out problems. I accepted that, but when her visits became more frequent and protracted I had the feeling I was losing a wife. It was not good for young Karen, either, who had lost one mother and looked like losing the surrogate. It was a mess and I could not see my way out of it.

My feelings were not improved when I saw the headlines in the *Freeport News* one morning. There had been a fire in Nassau and the Fun Palace had burned down. The Fun Palace was a pleasure complex built, I think, to rival Freeport's International Bazaar as a tourist trap. It contained movie theaters, restaurants and sports facilities and had been a shade too gaudy for my taste. As modern as the moment, it had a cheap feel to it of which I did not approve.

And now it was gone. Analyzing the newspaper report it would seem that the firemen never had a chance; the place had gone up in flames like a bonfire almost as though it had been deliberately built to burn easily, and it took eighty-two lives with it, most of them tourists and a lot of them children. That, coming of top of Legionnaires' disease, would certainly not help the image of the Bahamas. Come to the Islands and die! Take your pick of method!

Over the next few days I followed the newspaper reports and listened to people talking. There were muttered rumors of arson but that was to be expected; after any big fire there is always talk of arson. The Chief of the Fire Brigade in Nassau was eloquent in his damning of the construction of the Fun Palace and the materials used in its construction. In order to give it a light and airy appearance a lot of plastic had been used and most of the victims had died, not of burning, but of asphyxiation caused by poisonous fumes. He also condemned the use of polyurethane foam as furniture upholstery. "This is a real killer," he said. I made a note to check on what we were using in our hotels, and also to tighten up on fire precautions.

And it was at this point that Jack Kayles popped into sight.

8

STORM SIGNALS flew over the breakfast table one morning but I was too preoccupied to notice them until Debbie said, "I suppose you're going back to the office again today."

I poured myself a cup of tea. "I had thought of it."

"I never see you anymore."

I added sugar. "You do in bed."

She flared up. "I'm a wife—not a whore. When I married a man I expected all of him, not just his penis."

It was then I became aware that this was not a mere storm in a teacup. "I'm sorry," I said. "Things have been really tough lately." I reflected. "I suppose I don't really have to go in today, or even tomorrow. In fact, I can take the rest of the week off. Why don't we take one of Joe Cartwright's sailboats from the marina and cruise to one of the Family Islands? That would take us to the weekend and we could fly back."

She lit up like a Christmas tree. "Could we?" Then she frowned. "But we're going nowhere near any of your damned hotels," she warned. "This isn't a disguised business trip."

"Cross my heart and hope to die." I was drinking my tea as the telephone rang.

It was Jessie. "I think you'd better come in early this morning; we've got trouble."

"What kind of trouble?"

"Something to do with baggage at the airport. I don't really know what it is, but the lobby sounds like a hive of bees. Mr. Fletcher's at the dentist and the assistant manager isn't coping very well."

That was all I needed. "I'll be in." I hung up and said to Debbie, "Sorry, darling, but duty calls."

"You mean you're going in spite of what you just promised? You bastard!"

I left the house with recriminations clanging in my ears, and arrived at the Royal Palm to find that a minor bit of hell had broken loose.

I sat in Jack Fletcher's office listening to him moan. "Two hundred and eight of them, and without a damned toothbrush between them, not to mention other necessities. All they have is their hand baggage and what they stand up in."

I winced. "What happened? Did they arrive here and their baggage end up in Barcelona?"

He looked at me with mournful eyes. "Worse! You know that new baggage-handling carousel at the airport?" I nodded. It was an innovation for which we had been pressing for a long time. With increased flights of wide-bodied jets the airport had developed a baggage-handling bottleneck which the carousel was intended to alleviate.

Fletcher said, "It couldn't have done a better job if it had been designed for the purpose."

"A better job of what?"

"Opening the baggage without benefit of keys. The baggage was put on the conveyor, and somewhere in that underground tunnel something ripped open every suitcase. What spewed out on to the carousel were smashed suitcases and mixed-up contents."

"Didn't they try to turn it off when they saw what was happening?"

"They tried and couldn't. Apparently it wouldn't stop. And the telephone link between the carousel and the loading point outside hasn't been installed yet. By the time they'd fiddled around and sent someone outside to stop the loading it was too late. They'd pushed in the lot—the whole planeload of baggage."

I nodded toward the lobby. "Who is this crowd?"

"LTP Industries convention from Chicago. They're already raising hell. If you want a slice of gloom just go out into the lobby—you can cut it with a knife. One good thing; the Airport Authority carries the can for this—not us."

The Airport Authority might carry ultimate responsibility but the airport people did not have on their hands over two hundred unhappy and discontented Americans—and when Americans are discontented they let it be known, loud and clear. Their unhappiness would spread through the hotel like a plague.

Jack said, "That Boeing was full, every seat filled. We're not the only people with grief; Holiday Inn, Atlantik Beach, Xanadu—we've all got troubles."

That did not make me feel any better. "What's the Airport Authority doing about it?"

"Still trying to make up their minds."

"Oh, for God's sake!" I said. "You go out there and give them a pacifier—fifty dollars each for immediate necessities. I'll ring the airport to tell them I'll be sending them the bill. And make it a public relations service on the part of the hotel. Let them know clearly that we don't have to do it, but we're full of the milk of human kindness. We have to make some profit out of this mess."

He nodded and left, and I rang the airport. There followed a short but tempestuous conversation in which threats of legal action were issued. As I put down the telephone it rang under my hand. Jessie said, "Sam Ford wants to see you. By the way, he's acting as thought the matter is urgent."

"I'll be along." I went back to my office via the lobby, testing the atmosphere as I went. Fletcher had made an announcement and the tension had eased. A queue had already formed at the cashier's desk to receive their dole. I walked through Jessie's office, beckoning to Sam as I went, and sat behind my desk. "I thought you were down by Ragged Island."

The Ragged Island project was something I had developed by listening to Deputy-Commissioner Perigord. What he had said about the Ragged Island Range and the Jumento Cays had remained with me. My idea was to buy a couple of the cays and set up camps for those tourists who preferred to rough it for a few days on a genuine desert island. It was my intention to cater to all tastes and, being in the low tourist season, I had sent Sam Ford down in a boat to scout a few locations.

"I was," said Sam. "But something came up. You remember that fellow you wanted to know about?"

"Who?"

"Kayles. Jack Kayles."

I jerked. "What about him? Have you seen him?"

"No, but I've seen his boat."

"Where?"

"In the Jumentos—lying off Man-o'-War Cay. Now called *My Fair Lady* and her hull is blue."

I said, "Sam, how in hell can you be sure it's the same boat?"

"Easy." Sam laughed. "About a year and a half ago Kayles wanted a new masthead shackle for his forestay. Well, it's a British boat and I only had American fittings, so I had to make an adapter. It's still there."

"You got that close to her?"

" 'Bout a cable." That was two hundred yards. "And I put the glasses on her. I don't think Kayles was on board or he'd have come out on deck. They usually do in those waters because there are not that many boats about and folks get curious. He must have been ashore but I didn't see him." He looked at me seriously. "I thought of boarding her but I remembered what you said about not wanting him scared off, so I just passed by without changing course and came back here."

"You did right. When was this?"

"Yesterday. Say, thirty hours ago. I came back real fast."

He had indeed; it was over three hundred miles to the Jumentos. I pondered for a while. To get there quickly I could fly, but the only place to land was at Duncan Town and that was quite a long way from Man-o'-War Cay and

I would have to hire a boat, always supposing there was one to be hired with a skipper willing to make a one-hundred-mile round trip. For the first time I wished we had a seaplane or amphibian.

I said, "Are you willing to back now?"

"I'm pretty tired, Tom. I've been pushing it. I haven't had what you'd call a proper sleep for forty-eight hours. I had young Jim Glass with me but I didn't trust his navigation so all I got were catnaps."

"We'll go by air and see if he's still there, and you can sleep at Duncan Town. Okay?"

He nodded. "All right, Tom, but you'll get no words from me on the way. I'll be asleep."

I had completely forgotten about Debbie.

I took the first plane and the first pilot handy, and we flew southeast to the Jumentos, the pilot being Bill Pinder. I sat in the copilot's seat next to Bill, and Sam sat in the back. I think he was asleep before takeoff. I had binoculars handy and a camera with a telephoto lens. I wanted firm identification for Perigord, although how firm it would be was problematical because Kayle's boat changed color like a bloody chameleon.

Although I use aircraft quite a lot, flying being the quickest way for a busy man to get around the islands, I find that it bores me. As we droned over the blue and green sea, leaving the long chain of the Exumas to port, my eyes grew heavier and I must have fallen asleep because it took a heavy dig in the ribs from Bill to rouse me. "Man-o'-War Cay in ten minutes," he said.

I turned and woke Sam. "Which side of the cay was he?"

Sam peered from a window. "This side."

"We don't want to do anything unusual," I told Bill. "Come down to your lowest permitted altitude and fly straight just off the west coast of the cay. Don't jink about or circle—just carry on."

We began to descend and presently Bill said, "That little one just ahead is Flamingo Cay; the bigger one beyond is Man-o'-War."

I passed the binoculars back to Sam. "You know Kayles. Take a good look as we fly past and see if you can spot him. I'll use the camera."

"There's a boat," said Bill.

I cocked the camera and opened the side window, blinking as the air rushed in. The sloop was lying at anchor and I could see distinctly the catenary curve of the anchor cable under clear water. "That's her," said Sam and I clicked the shutter. I recocked quickly and took another snapshot. Sam said, "And that's Kayles in the cockpit."

By then the sloop was disappearing behind us. I twisted my neck to see it but it was gone. "Did he wave or anything?"

"No, just looked up."

"Okay," I said. "On to Duncan Town."

Bill did a low pass with his landing gear down over the scattered houses of Duncan Town, and by the time we had landed on the air strip and taxied to the ramp a battered car was already bumping towards us. We climbed out of the Navajo and Sam said, nodding towards the car, "I know that man."

"Then you can do the dickering," I said. "We want a boat to go out to Man-o'-War—the fastest you can find."

"That won't be too fast," he said. "But I'll do my best."

We drove into Duncan Town and I stood by while Sam bargained for a boat. I had never been to Duncan Town and I looked around with interest. It was a neat and well-maintained place of the size Perigord had said—less than two hundred population, most of them fishermen to judge by the boats. There were signs of agriculture but no cash crops, so they probably grew just enough food for themselves. But there were evaporation pans for the manufacture of salt.

Sam called me, and then led me to a boat. "That's it."

I winced at what I saw. It was an open boat about eighteen feet long and not very tidily kept. A tangled heap of nets was thrown over the engine casing and the thwarts were littered with fish scales. It smelled of rotting fish, too, and would have broken Pete Albury's heart. "Is this the best you can do?"

"Least it has an inboard engine," said Sam. "I don't think it'll break down. I'll come with you, Tom. I know Kayles by sight, and I can get six hours sleep on the way."

"Six hours!"

"It's forty miles, and I don't reckon this tub will do more than seven knots at top speed." He looked up at the sun. "It'll be about nightfall when we get there."

"All right," I said resignedly. "Let's get a seven-knot move on."

Five minutes later we were on our way with the owner and skipper, a black Bahamian called Bayliss, at the tiller. Sam made a smelly bed of fish nets and went to sleep, while I brooded. I was accustomed to zipping about the islands in a Navajo and this pace irked me. I judged the length of the boat and the bow wave and decided we were not even doing six knots. I was impatient to confront Kayles.

We came to Man-o'-War Cay just as the sun was setting and I woke Sam. "We're coming to the cay from the other side. How wide is it?"

" 'Bout half a mile."

"What's the going like?"

"Not bad." He peered at me. "What's all this about, Tom?"

"Personal business."

He shook his head. "A year back when I asked why you were interested in Kayles you damn near bit my head off. And then you brought the police in—Commissioner Perigord, no less. This is more than personal business. What are you getting me into?"

It was a fair enough question. If we were going to confront a man I believed to be a murderer then Sam had a right to know. I said, "How close were you to Pete Albury?"

"I knew him all my life. You know we both came from Abaco. I remember him and you together when I was a little nipper, not more than four years old. You'd be twelve or thirteen then, I reckon."

"Yes, he was my friend," I said quietly. "What about you?"

"Sure, he was my friend. We used to go turtling together. Biggest we ever caught was a two hundred-pounder. He taught me how to catch bush bugs with a crutch-stick."

That was Abaconian vernacular for catching land crabs with a forked stick. I said, "Kayles was on *Lucayan Girl* when she disappeared."

Sam went very still. "You mean . . ."

"I don't know what I mean, but I will when I get to the other side of that damn cay. Right now I'm working out the best way to go about it."

"Wait a minute." Sam called out to Bayliss, "Slow down," then turned back to me, the whites of his eyes reddened by the light of the setting sun. "If Kayles was on *Lucayan Girl,* if that's Kayles on that boat, then that means murder." Sam was as quick as any other Bahamian at adding up the facts of life—and death—at sea. "I read about the inquest in the *Freeport News*. It seemed to me then there was something left out."

"Perigord put the lid on it; he didn't want to frighten Kayles away. The picture of Kayles you saw was taken by my daughter, Sue, just before the *Girl* left for Miami. Perigord reckons Kayles is a cocaine smuggler. Anyway, that's not the point, Sam. I want to talk to Kayles."

"And you're thinking of walking across the island." He shook his head. "That's not the way. That boat is anchored nearly a cable offshore. You'd have to swim. It wouldn't look right. What we do is to go around and get next to him in a neighborly way like any other honest boat would." He pointed to the water keg in the bows. "Ask him for some water."

"Are you coming?"

"Sure I'm coming," said Sam promptly.

"He'll recognize you," I said doubtfully.

Sam was ironic. "What do you want me to do? Put on a white face? It doesn't matter if he knows me or not—he's not afraid of me. But he might know your face and that would be different. You'd better keep your head down."

So we went around Man-o'-War Cay with the engine gently thumping and made a few final plans. Although Sam had seen Kayles from the air through binoculars, it had been but a quick flash and firm identification would be made only when he talked to the man on the sloop. If Sam recognized Kayles he was to ask for water; if it wasn't Kayles he was to ask for fish. From then on we would have to play it by ear.

When we drifted alongside the sloop there was very little light. I took off the engine casing and stood with my back to *My Fair Lady* apparently tinkering with the engine. Bayliss took the way off and Sam bellowed, "Ahoy, the sloop!" He stood in the bows and held us off with a boathook.

A voice said, "What do you want?" The accent was American.

I think Sam went more by the voice than by what he could see. "We've run us a mite short of water. Can you spare us a few drops?"

A light stabbed from the cockpit and played on Sam. "Don't I know you?" said Kayles. There was a hint of suspicion in his voice.

"You could," said Sam easily. "I run a marina in New Providence. I know a lot of yachtsmen and they know me. Maybe you've been to my place—at the Sea Gardens Hotel, west of Nassau. I'm Sam Ford." He held his hand to shade his eyes, trying to see beyond the bright light.

"I remember you. You want water?"

"I'd appreciate it. We're damn thirsty."

"I'll get you some," said Kayles. "Got anything to put it in?"

Sam had taken the precaution of emptying the water keg. He passed it up to Kayles who went below. "He'll know if we go aboard," Sam whispered. "The sloop will rock. If we're going to take him it'll have to be when he comes up now. Get ready to jump him when I shout."

"You're sure it is Kayles?"

"Damn sure. Anyway, any ordinary yachtsman would have asked us aboard."

"All right, then."

The sound of a hand pump came from the sloop and after a few minutes it stopped. "Ready, now!" said Sam in a low voice.

The sloop rocked as Kayles came up into the cockpit. Sam said cheerfully, "This is kind of you, sir." He had shortened his grip on the boathook and when Kayles leaned over the side to hand down the keg, instead of taking it Sam gripped Kayles's wrist and pulled hard. With the other hand he thrust the end of the boathook into Kayles's stomach like a spear.

I heard the breath explode out of Kayles as I jumped for the sloop. Kayles stood no chance; he lay half in and half out of the cockpit fighting for breath and with Sam holding on to his wrist with grim tenacity. I got both knees in the small of his back, grinding his belly into the cockpit coaming. "Come aboard, Sam," I said breathily.

Bayliss shouted, "What's going on there?"

"Stick to your own business," said Sam, and came aboard. He switched on the compass light which shed a dim glow into the cockpit. "Can you hold him?"

Kayles's body writhed under mine. "I think so."

"I'll get some rope; plenty of that on a boat." Sam plucked the knife from Kayles's belt and vanished for a moment.

Kayles was recovering his breath. "You . . . you bastard!" he gasped, and heaved under me and nearly threw me off so I thumped him hard at the nape of the neck with my fist— the classic rabbit punch—and he went limp. I hoped I had not broken his neck.

Sam came with the rope and we tied Kayles's hands behind his back, and I knew Sam knew enough about seaman's knots to let him do it. When we had Kayles secure he said, "What do we do now?"

Bayliss had allowed his boat to drift off a little way in the gathering darkness. Now I heard his engine rev up and he came alongside again. "What you doin' to that man?" he asked. "I'm havin' nothin' to do with this."

I said to Sam, "Let's get him below, then you can talk to Bayliss. Cool him down because we might need him again."

We bundled Kayles below and stretched him on a bunk. He was breathing stertorously. Sam said, "What do I tell Bayliss?"

I shrugged. "Why not tell him the truth?"

Sam grinned. "Who ever believes the truth? But I'll fix him." He went into the cockpit and I looked around. Sam had been right about Kayles being a good seaman because it showed. Everything was neat and tidy and all the gear was stowed; a place for everything and everything in its place. Nothing betrays a bad seaman more than sloppiness, and if everything below was trim it would be the same on deck. That is the definition of shipshape. Given five minutes' notice Kayles could pull up the hook and sail for anywhere.

But a good seaman is not necessarily a good man; the history of piracy in the Bahamas shows that. I turned and looked at Kayles who was beginning to stir feebly, then switched on the cabin light to get a better look at him. I got a good sight of his face for the first time and was relieved to see that Sam had made no mistake—this definitely was the man whose picture had been taken by Sue.

I sat at the chart table, switched on the gooseneck lamp, and began going through drawers. A good seaman keeps a log, an honest seaman keeps a log—but would Kayles have kept a log? It would be useful to have a record of his movements in the past.

There was no log to be found so I started going through the charts. In recording a yacht's course on a chart it is usual to use a fairly soft pencil so that in case of error it can be easily erased and corrected, or when the voyage is over the course line can be erased and the chart used again. Most yachtsmen I know tend to leave the course on the chart until it is needed for another voyage. A certain amount of bragging goes on among boat people and they like to sit around in a marina comparing voyages and swapping lies.

Kayles had charts covering the eastern seaboard of the Americas from the Canadian border right down to and including Guyana, which is pretty close to the equator, and they covered the Bahamas and the whole of the Caribbean. On many of them were course lines and dates. It is normal to pencil in a date when you have established a position by a midday sun sight and you may add in the month, but no one I know puts in the year. So were these the records of old or recent voyages?

Sam came below and looked at Kayles. "Still sleeping?" He went into the galley, unclipped an aluminum pan, and filled it with water. He came back and dumped it in Kayles's face. Kayles moaned and moved his head from side to side, but his eyes did not open.

I said, "Sam, take a look at these charts and tell me if they mean anything." We changed places and I stood over Kayles. His eyes opened and he looked up at me, but there was no comprehension in them and I judged he was suffering from concussion. It would be some time before he would be able to talk so I went exploring.

What I was looking for I do not know but I looked anyway, opening lockers and boxes wherever I found them. Kayles's seamanship showed again in the way he had painted on the top of each food can a record of the contents. I found the cans stowed in lockers under the bunks and he had enough to last a long time. If water gets into the bilges labels are washed off cans, and Kayles had made sure that when he opened a can he thought was beef he was not going to find peaches.

I opened his first-aid box and found it well equipped with all the standard bandages and medications, including two throwaway syringes already loaded with morphine. Those were not so standard but some yachtsmen, especially single-handers, carry morphine by special permission. If so, the law requires that they should be carried in a locked box and these were not. There were also some unlabeled glass ampules containing a yellowish, oily liquid. Unlike the morphine syringes they carried no description or maker's name.

I picked up one of them and examined it closely. The ampule itself had an amateur look about it as though it was homemade, the ends being sealed as though held in a flame, and there was nothing etched in the glass to tell the nature of the contents. I thought that if Kayles was in the drug-running scene he could very well be an addict and this was his own supply of dope. The notion was reinforced by the finding of an ordinary reusable hypodermic syringe. I left everything where it was and closed the box.

I went back to Sam who was still poring over the charts. He had come to much the same conclusion that I had, but he said, "We might be able to tell when all this happened by relating it to weather reports."

"We'll leave that to Perigord," I said.

Sam frowned. "Maybe we should have left it all to the Commissioner. I think we should have told him about this man before we left. Are we doing right, Tom?"

"Hell, I didn't *know* it was Kayles before we left. It was just a chance, wasn't it?"

"Even so, I think you should have told Perigord."

I lost my temper a little. "All right, don't drive it home, Sam. So I should have told Perigord. I didn't. Maybe I wasn't thinking straight. Everthing has been going to hell in a handcart recently, from Legionnaires' disease at the Parkway to the fire at the Fund Palace. And we could do without those bloody street riots, too. Do you know what I was doing when you came to my office?"

"No—what?"

"Straightening out a mess caused by the Airport Authority. Their baggage-handling machinery ripped a plane-load of suitcases into confetti and I had over two hundred Americans in the lobby looking for blood. Any more of this and we'll all go out of business." I swung around as Kayles said something behind me.

"Who the hell are you?" Kayles's voice was stronger than I expected and I suspected he had been feigning unconsciousness for some time while working on his bonds. I did not worry about that—I had seen the knots.

"You know me, Mr. Kayles," said Sam, and Kayles's eyes widened as he heard his own name. "You're carrying no riding lights. That's bad—you could be run down." His voice was deceptively mild.

"Goddamn yacht-jackers!" said Kayles bitterly. "Look, you guys have got me wrong. I can help you."

"Do you know much about yacht-jacking?" I asked.

"I know it happens." Kayles stared at me. "Who are you?"

I did not answer him, but I held his eye. Sam said casually, "Ever meet a man called Albury? Pete Albury?"

Kayles moistened his lips, and said hoarsely. "For God's sake! Who are you?"

"You know Sam here," I said. "You've met him before. I'm Tom Mangan. You might have heard of me—I'm tolerably well known in the Bahamas."

Kayles flinched, but he mumbled, "Never heard of you."

"I think you have. In fact I think you met some of my family. My wife and daughter, for instance."

"And I think you're nuts."

"All right, Kayles," I said. "Let's get down to it. You were hired over a year ago by Pete Albury as crew on *Lucayan Girl* to help take her from Freeport to Miami. Also on board were my wife and daughter. The boat never got to Miami; it vanished without trace. But my daughter's body was found. How come you're still alive, Kayles?"

"I don't know what you're talking about. I don't know you, your wife or your daughter. And I don't know this guy, Albury." He nodded towards Sam. "I know him because I put my boat in his marina, that's all. You've got the wrong guy."

Sam said, "Maybe we have." He looked at me. "But it's easily provable, one way or the other." He regarded Kayles again. "Where's your logbook?"

Kayles hesitated, then said, "Stowed under this bunk mattress."

Sam picked up Kayles's knife which he had laid on the chart table. "No tricks or I'll cut you good." He advanced on Kayles and rolled him over. "Get it, Tom."

I lifted the mattress under Kayles, groped about and encountered the edge of a book. I pulled it out. "Okay, Sam." Sam released Kayles who rolled over on to his back again.

As I flipped through the pages of the logbook I said, "All you have to do is to prove where you were on a certain date." I tossed the book to Sam. "But we won't find it in there. Where's your last year's log?"

"Don't keep a log more'n one year," said Kayles sullenly. "Clutters up the place."

"You'll have to do better than that."

"That's funny," said Sam. "Most boat folk keep their old logbooks. As souvenirs, you know; and to impress other boat people." He chuckled. "And us marina people."

"I'm not sentimental," snarled Kayles. "And I don't need to impress anyone."

"You'll have to bloody well impress me if you expect me to turn you loose," I said. "And if I don't turn you loose you'll have to impress a judge."

"Oh, Christ, how did I get into this?" he wailed. "I swear to God you've got the wrong guy."

"Prove it."

"How can I? I don't know when your goddamn boat sailed, do I? I don't know anything about your boat."

"Where were you just before last Christmas but one?"

"How would I know? I'll have to think about it." Kayles's forehead creased. "I was over in the Florida keys."

"No, you weren't," said Sam. "I met you in the International Bazaar in Freeport, and you told me you were going to Miami. Remember that?"

"No. It's a hell of a long time ago, and how can I be expected to remember? But I did sail to Miami and then on down to Key West."

"You sailed for Miami, all right," I said. "In *Lucayan Girl.*"

"I sailed in my own boat," said Kayles stubbornly. "This boat." He jerked his head at me. "What kind of a boat was this *Lucayan Girl?*"

"A trawler—fifty-two feet—Hatteras type!"

"For God's sake!" he said disgustedly. "I'd never put foot on a booze palace like that. I'm a sailing man." He nodded towards Sam. "He knows that."

I looked towards Sam who said, "That's about it. Like I told you, he has this tidy little diesel about as big as a sewing machine which he hardly ever uses."

For a moment I was disconcerted and wondered if, indeed, we had the wrong man; but I rallied when Sam said, "Why do you keep changing the name of your boat?"

Kayles was nonplussed for a moment, then he said, "I don't."

"Come off it," I scoffed. "We know of four names already—and four colors. When this boat was in the marina of the Royal Palm in Freeport just over a year ago she was *Bahama Mama* and her hull was red."

"Must have been a different boat. Not mine."

"You're a liar," said Sam bluntly. "Do you think I don't know my own work? I put up the masthead fitting."

I thought back to the talk I had had with Sam and Joe Cartwright in my office a year previously. Sam had seen Kayles in the International Bazaar but, as it turned out, neither Sam nor Joe had seen the boat. But he was not telling Kayles that; he was taking a chance.

Kayles merely shrugged, and I said, "We know you're a cocaine smuggler. If you come across and tell the truth it might help you in court. Not much, but it might help a bit."

Kayles looked startled. "Cocaine! You're crazy—right out of your mind. I've never smuggled an ounce in my life."

Either he was a very good actor or he was telling the truth, but of course he would deny it so I put him down as a good actor. "Why did you go to Cat Island?"

"I'm not saying another goddamn word," he said sullenly. "What's the use? I'm not believed no matter what I say."

"Then that's it." I stood up and said to Sam, "Where do we go from here?"

"Sail this boat back to Duncan Town and hand him over to the local government commissioner. He'll contact the police and they'll take it from there. But not until daylight."

"Scared of sailing in the dark?" jeered Kayles.

Sam ignored him, and said to me, "I'd like a word with you on deck."

I followed him into the cockpit. "What did you tell Bayliss?"

"Enough of the truth to shut him up. He'd heard of the disappearance of *Lucayan Girl* so he'll stick around and cooperate." He picked up the flashlamp Kayles had used and swept a beam of light into the darkness in a wide arc. There came an answering flicker from a darker patch of blackness about two hundred yards to seaward. "He's there."

"Sam, why don't we sail back now? I know it's not true what Kayles said."

"Because we can't," said Sam, and there was a touch of wryness in his voice. "I was a mite too careful. I was figuring on what might happen if Kayles got loose and I wanted to hamstring him, so I got some of Bayliss's fish net and tangled it around the propeller. That engine will never turn over now. Then I cut all the halyards so Kayles couldn't raise sail. Trouble is neither can we. I'm sorry, Tom."

"How long will it take to fix?"

"Splicing the halyards and re-reeving will take more than an hour—in daylight. Same with the engine."

"We could take Kayles back in Bayliss's boat, starting right now."

"I don't think he'd do it," said Sam. "Fishermen aren't the same as yachtsmen who sail for fun. They don't like sailing around at night because there's no call to do it, so they don't have the experience and they know it." He pointed south. "There are a lot of reefs between here and Duncan Town, and Bayliss would be scared of running on to one. You don't know these folk; they don't work by charts and compasses like pleasure boat people. They navigate by sea color and bird flight—things they can see."

"You'd be all right on the tiller," I said.

"But Bayliss wouldn't know that. It's his boat and he wouldn't want to lose her."

"Let's ask him anyway," I said. "Call him in."

Sam picked up the lamp and flashed it out to sea. There were a couple of answering winks and I heard the putt-putt of the engine as Bayliss drew near. He came alongside, fending off with the boathook, and then passed his painter up to Sam who secured it around a stanchion. Sam leaned over the edge of the cockpit still holding the light. "Mr. Mangan wants to know if you'll take us back to Duncan Town now."

Bayliss's face crinkled and he looked up at the sky. "Oh, no," he said. "Might if there was a full moon, but tonight no moon at all."

I said, "Sam here is willing to navigate and take the tiller, too. He's a good man at sea."

It was just as Sam had predicted. Bayliss became mulish. "How do I know that? This is the only boat I got—I don't want to lose her. No, Mr. Mangan, better wait for sunrise."

I argued a bit but it was useless; the more I argued the more Bayliss dug in his heels. "All right," I said in the end. "We wait for sunrise."

"Jesus!" said Sam suddenly. "The knife—I left it on the chart table." He turned and looked below. "Watch it!" he yelled. "He's coming through the forehatch."

I looked forward and saw a dark shape moving in the bows, then there was a flash and a flat report and a *spaaaang* as a bullet ricocheted off metal. Sam straightened and cannoned into me. "Over the side!"

There was no time to think but it made immediate sense. You could not fight a man with a gun on a deck he knew like the back of his own hand. I stepped on to the cockpit seat and jumped, tripping on something as I did so and because of that I made a hell of a splash. There was another splash as Sam followed, and then I ducked under water because a light flashed from the sloop and the beam searched the surface of the water and there was another muzzle flash as Kayles shot again.

It was then I thanked Pete Albury for his swimming lessons on the reefs around Abaco. Scuba gear had just been introduced in those days and its use was not general; anyway, Pete had a hearty contempt for it. He had taught me deep diving and the breath control necessary so that I could go down among the coral. Now I made good use of his training.

I dribbled air from my mouth, zealously conserving it, while conscious of the hunting light flickering over the surface above. I managed to kick off my shoes, being thankful that I was not wearing lace-ups, and the swimming became easier. I was swimming in circles and, just before I came up for more air, I heard the unmistakable vibrations of something heavy entering the water and I wondered what it was.

I came to the surface on my back so that just my nose and mouth were above water. Filling my lungs I paddled myself under again, trying not to splash. I reckoned I could stay underwater for two minutes on every lungful of air, and I came up three times—about six minutes. The last time I came up I put my head right out and shook the water from my ears.

Then I heard the regular throb of the engine of Bayliss's boat apparently running at top speed. Ready to duck again if it came my way I listened intently, but the noise died away in the distance and presently there were nothing to be heard. The sound of a voice floated softly over the water. "Tom!"

"That you, Sam?"

"I think he's gone."

I swam in what I thought was Sam's direction. "Gone where?"

"I don't know. He took Bayliss's boat."

"Where's Bayliss?" I saw the ripples Sam was making and came up next to him.

"I don't know," said Sam. "I think he went overboard, too. He may still be in the boat, though."

"Let's not jump to conclusions," I said. "That might have been Bayliss running away, and Kayles might still be around."

Sam said, "I was bobbing under the bows and Kayles was swearing fit to bust a gut. First, he tried to start the engine and it seized up. Then he tried to hoist sail and found he couldn't. I think it's fairly certain he took Bayliss's boat."

"Well, if we're going to find out, let's do it carefully," I said.

We made a plan, simple enough, which was to come up simultaneously on both sides of the sloop, hoping to catch Kayles in a pincer if he was still there. On execution we found the sloop deserted. Sam said, "Where's Bayliss?"

We shouted for a long time and flashed the light over the water but saw and heard nothing. Sam said, "It's my fault, Tom. I botched it. I forgot the knife."

"Forget it," I said. "Which way do you think Kayles went?"

"I don't know, but in his place I'd head north. He has fifty miles of fuel and maybe more, and there are plenty of cays up there to get lost in. He might even have enough fuel to get to Exuma." He took a deep breath. "What do we do now?"

I had been thinking about that. "We wait until sunrise, do the repairs, find Bayliss if we can, go back to Duncan Town and report to the government commissioner, and have Bill Pindler make an air search for that son of a bitch."

It was an uneasy night and a worse morning because, while Sam was repairing the halyards, I went under the stern to cut the fish net from around the propeller and found Bayliss jammed in there entangled in the net. He had been shot through the head and was very dead.

That broke up Sam Ford more than anything else and it did not do me much good.

9

DEPUTY-COMMISSIONER Perigord was thunderous and he gave the definite impression that invisible lightning was flashing around his head. "You had Kayles and you let him go!" he said unbelievingly.

"Not deliberately," I said. "There wasn't much we could do about it—he had the gun."

"But you did go off half-cocked. I warned you about that. Why in God's name didn't you tell me you knew where Kayles was?"

"I didn't know where he was. I thought I knew where his boat was. And I wasn't even sure of that. I know that Sam Ford knows his boats but I couldn't be entirely sure. I went down to the Jumentos to make the identification."

"Instead of which you made a stinking mess," said Perigord cuttingly. "Mr. Mangan, I told you this is a professional matter and you were not to butt in. You are responsible for the death of a man; an innocent bystander whom you casually took along on a hunt for a murderer. Fred Bayliss was a married man with a wife and four children. What of them?"

I felt like hell. "I'll look after the family," I muttered.

"Oh, you will? Big deal. You know what it's like to lose your family. How do you suppose Mrs. Bayliss is feeling now? Do you think you can cure her grief with a few dollars?"

Perigord was a man who knew how to go for the jugular. "Christ, what can I say beyond that I'm sorry?"

"Neither your sorrow nor your money is of much help. And now I have an armed man loose in the Bahamas who knows he is being hunted, and it is my men who will have to do the hunting. How much sorrow will you feel if one of them is killed in the process?"

"Jesus, Perigord, enough is enough!"

He nodded. "I think so, too. Go back to running your hotels, Mr. Mangan. Go back to making money—but stay out of this business." He paused. "I may want to question you and Sam Ford further—I'll let you know. That's all."

I left Perigord's office feeling so low I could walk under a snake's belly wearing a top hat. He was a man who knew how to use words as weapons, and the hell of it was that I knew I had it coming. I had been irresponsible. When Sam had come with the news of Kayles's boat I should have taken him to Perigord immediately and let the police handle it.

My disposition did not improve when I returned to my office and telephoned home. Luke Bailey answered. "Is Mrs. Mangan at home?"

"No, Mr. Mangan."

"Have you any idea where she is?"

"She left for Houston this morning."

"Thanks, Luke." I put down the telephone feeling more depressed than ever.

A few days later Perigord asked to see me and Sam Ford and we met him, not in his office, but in the Customs Department at the harbor. He had had Kayles's sloop brought up from Duncan Town and, as I thought he might, he had enlisted the aid of Customs officers to give it a real going-over.

The boat had been taken out of the water and put into a warehouse where she looked enormous. It is surprising how much larger a sailing boat looks out of the water than in; one tends to forget that most of a boat is under water. The Customs officers had taken most of the gear out of her and it was stacked on the floor of the warehouse and on tables in small heaps, each heap labeled as to where it was found. Again, it is surprising how much you can cram into a twenty-seven-footer.

Perigord took us into a small glassed-in office in a corner of the warehouse and put us through the hoops again, this time with a tape recorder on the desk. It was a grueling interrogation and it hit Sam hard because he blamed himself for everything, knowing that if he had not left the knife on the chart table then Bayliss might still be alive.

It was a two-hour grilling, occasionally interrupted by a Customs officer who would come in to show Perigord something or other. At last he switched off the recorder and took us out into the warehouse where he had Sam show him the masthead fitting by which he was able to identify the boat, even with its name and color changed.

I said, "Have you found anything useful?"

"Nothing of interest." There was that in Perigord's voice which told me that even if he had found something he was not going to inform me.

"Not the drugs?" I asked in surprise.

His interest sharpened. "What drugs?"

"The stuff in the first-aid box."

He beckoned to a Customs man and the box was produced. It was empty. The Customs man said, "We've laid out the contents over there." We walked over to the trestle table and I scanned through the articles. The morphine syringes were there but there were no glass ampules.

I described them, and said, "I thought if Kayles was a drug-runner he might be a user, too, and that this was his personal stock."

"Yes," said Perigord thoughtfully. "If he was a user he would certainly take it along, no matter in how much of a hurry he was. It was a liquid, you say?"

"That's right; a faintly yellowish liquid." I described the ampules and told of the homemade look they had.

The Customs officer picked up the reusable hypodermic syringe. "It's funny he didn't take this." He shook his head. "A yellow liquid. That's new to me."

"They're always coming up with something new to blow their minds," said Perigord. "So now we've got a hopped-up gunman. It gets worse, doesn't it, Mr. Mangan? Once his supplies run out he might start raiding pharmacies to resupply. Another headache."

"Have you any idea where he might be?" I asked.

Bayliss's boat had not been found and, according to Perigord's gloomy prediction, it never would be. He thought it had been sunk. A small sailing yacht had been stolen from George Town in the Exumas. "And it could be anywhere now, with a change of name and color," said Perigord. "If Kayles has any sense he'll be getting clear of the Bahamas."

I was about to turn away, but thought of something. "There are rumors floating around that the fire at the Fun Palace was due to arson. Is there anything in that?"

"Not to my knowledge," he said. "Squash those rumors, if you can."

"I do," I said. "It's in my interest to do so."

So I went home and found that Debbie had returned.

She was sitting in an armchair, her long legs crossed. She did not get up. "Where were you? You're never here when I want you."

"I could say the same for you," I returned acidly. "In point of fact I was being shot at down in the Jumentos."

"Shot at!" Her blue eyes darkened in disbelief. "Who by?"

"A man called Kayles—remember him? He killed a man down there, and damn near killed me and Sam Ford."

"Who is Sam Ford?"

"If you took more interest in me and my doings you'd know damn well who Sam Ford is. He's boss of the marinas division."

"So you found Kayles."

"Sam did, and you're looking at a damn fool. I tried to take him myself and got a poor bloody fisherman killed. I'm beginning to make myself sick." I poured myself a stiff drink and sat down. "Commissioner Perigord doesn't think a great deal of me these days. Just about as much as you seem to do."

"And whose fault is that?" she flared. "What interest are you taking in me? You're never around anymore."

"My God, you know the problems I've had recently, what with one thing and another. And a new one has just come up—the Fun Palace fire. There's a meeting of the Hoteliers'

Association and the Ministry of Tourism in Nassau tomorrow. I'll have to leave early."

"That was bad," she said. "I read about it in the Houston papers."

"You would. If you were in Timbuktu you'd have read about it. That's the problem."

"But what has it got to do with you? Why should you fly to Nassau?"

I looked at Debbie thoughtfully and decided to cool it. She was in a worse temper than I had ever seen, but even though she was being unreasonable she deserved an explanation. "Because I'm in the business," I said patiently. "It affects the Theta Corporation. The Bahamas seems to have become a disaster area lately and we're trying to figure out ways of minimizing the damage. My guess is that the Ministry of Tourism will propose a levy on the industry to fund a new advertising campaign."

"Oh, I see."

I adopted a more conciliatory tone. "Debbie, I know I haven't been around much lately, and I'm sorry—truly I am. I'll tell you what. Let me get straightened out here and we'll take a holiday. Maybe go to Europe—London and Paris. We've never had a holiday together, not a real one."

"A second honeymoon so soon after the first?" she said ruefully. "But will you get straightened out? Won't there be something else come along to need your personal attention? And then something else? And something else? Won't it be like that?"

"No, it won't be like that. No man is indispensable in a decently run organization, not even the boss. And this run of bad luck can't go on forever."

She shook her head slowly. "No, Tom. I'm going away to think this out."

"Think what out, for God's sake?"

"Us."

"There's nothing wrong with us, Debbie. And can't you do your thinking here?"

"I'd rather go home—be among my own family."

I took a deep breath. "I wish you wouldn't, Debbie, I really do, but if you must I don't suppose I can stop you."

"No, you can't," she said, and left the room.

I poured myself another drink, again a stiff one. As I sat down I reflected that although I had told Debbie I had been shot at, never once had she asked if I had been hurt. We had gone so far down the line. The Mangan marriage appeared to be another part of the Bahamian disaster area.

Bobby Bowen flew me to Nassau early next morning and I spent the day arguing with Ministry of Tourism officials and a crowd of apprehensive and tight-wadded hoteliers. Everyone agreed that something must be done; the argument was about who was going to pay for it. The argument went on all day and ended as I had predicted; there would be a levy on the industry and the Government would put up dollar for dollar.

I got home at about seven in the evening to find that Debbie had gone, but had left a note.

Dear Tom,

I meant what I said yesterday. I have gone back to Houston and will stay until the baby has come. I don't want to see you until then, but I suppose you will want to come just before the birth. That's all right with me, but I don't want to see you until then.

I have not taken Karen with me because I think it would be unfair to take her from her school and her friends and into what is a foreign country. Besides, she is your daughter.

I can't see clearly what has gone wrong between us, but I will be thinking hard about it, and I hope you do the same. It's funny but I still love you, and so I can end this note with

Love,
Debbie

I read that letter five times before putting it into my wallet, and then sat down to write my own letter asking her to come back. I had no great hopes that she would.

10

THE WEEK after Debbie left we lost Bill Pinder.

He was taking four American fishermen to Stella Maris on Long Island which they were going to use as a base for hunting marlin and sailfish off Columbus Point and on the Tartar Bank in Exuma Sound. I was going with them, not because I am particularly charmed by American fishermen, but because Bill was flying me on to Crooked Island, one hundred miles farther south, where I was to look at some property on behalf of the Theta Corporation.

As it happened I did not go because the previous evening I slipped in the bathroom and broke a toe which proved to be rather painful. To look at property and to walk a few miles on Crooked Island in that condition was not a viable proposition, so I canceled.

Bill Pinder took off in a Navajo early next morning with the Americans. He was flying over Exuma Sound and was filing his intentions with Nassau radio when suddenly he went off the air in midsentence, so we know exactly when it happened. What happened I know now but did not know then. The Bahamas may be the Shallow Sea but there are bits like the Tongue of the Ocean and Exuma Sound which are very deep; the Tartar Bank rises to within seven fathoms of the surface in Exuma Sound but the rest is deep water.

The Navajo was never found, nor any wreckage, and Bill Pinder disappeared. So did the four Americans, and two of them were so influential on Wall Street that the event caused quite a stir, more than I and the Bahamas needed. After a couple of weeks some bits and pieces of clothing were washed up on one of the Exuma cays and identified as belonging to one of the Americans.

The death of Bill Pinder hit me hard. He was a good man, and the only better light pilot I know is Bobby Bowen. It is hard for blacks like Bill and Bobby to get a commercial pilot's license, or at least it was when they pulled it off. I suppose it is easier now.

There was a memorial service to which I and many of the Corporation employees came, as many as could be spared without actually closing down the hotels. A lot of BASRA pilots were there, too. After the service I went over to Bobby Bowen. "What happened, Bobby?"

He shrugged. "Who knows? There'll be no evidence coming out of Exuma Sound." He thought for a moment. "He was filing with Nassau at the time so he'd be flying pretty high, about ten thousand feet, to get radio range. But why he fell out of the sky . . . ?" He spread his hands. "That was a good plane, Tom. It had just had its one hundred-hour check, and I flew it myself three days earlier." He grimaced a little. "You'll hear talk of the Bermuda Triangle; pay no heed—it's just the chatter of a lot of screwy nuts who don't know one end of an airplane from the other."

I said, "We'll need another plane and another pilot."

"You won't get one like Bill," said Bobby. "He knew these Islands right well. About another plane—something bigger?" he said hopefully.

"Perhaps. I'll have to talk it over with the board. I'll let you know."

We watched the Pinder family walking away from the church. Bobby said, "It's bad for Meg Pinder. Bill was a good husband to her."

"She'll be looked after," I said. "The pension fund isn't broke yet."

"Money won't cure what's wrong with her," said Bobby, echoing what Perigord had said about Bayliss's wife, and I felt a stab of shame.

But how could I have known that someone was trying to kill me?"

Billy Cunningham paid a flying visit. He came without warning at a weekend and found me at the house where I was packing a few things to take to my suite at the Royal

Palm. We talked about Bill Pinder and he said the usual conventional things about what a tragedy it was, and we talked about getting another aircraft. He appeared to be a little nervous so I said, "Stop pussy-footing, Billy. Sit down, have a drink, and get it off your chest. Are you an emissary?"

He laughed self-consciously. "I guess so. I've had obligations laid on me."

"Cunningham obligations?"

"Score one for you—I never did think you were stupid. You had that subtle look in your eye when you were inspecting us back home when you married Debbie. I suppose you didn't miss much."

"A tight-knit bunch," I observed.

"Yeah. The advantages are many—one for all and all for one—that stuff. A guy always has someone guarding his back. But there are disadvantages, like now. Old Jack's not been feeling too well lately so he couldn't come himself."

"I'm sorry to hear that," I said sincerely.

Billy waved his hand. "Nothing serious. Frank had a business meeting in California—important. So I was elected."

I said, "Tell me one thing. Does Debbie know about this? Does she know you're here?"

He shook his head. "No. It's just that Jack wants to know what the hell is going on. Personally, I think it's none of our business, but. . . ."

"But the Cunninghams look after their own."

"That's about it. Hell, Tom, I told Jack that interfering between man and wife is pure poison, but you think he'd listen? You know the old man."

"Not too well," I said coolly. "What do you want to know?"

"It's not what I want to know—it's what Jack wants to know. Jack and Frank both. They're both mad at you." Billy paused, then said meditatively, "If Frank had come on this mission he might have taken a poke at you. Very protective is Frank."

"Why should he do that?" I demanded. "I don't beat up his little sister every Friday night as a regular routine."

He grinned crookedly. "It might have been better if you had. The Cunningham women—" He stopped short. "Anyway, Jack wants to know why his little girl has come running home looking as blue as a cold flounder."

"Didn't he ask her?"

"She clammed up on him—and on Frank. Me—I didn't bother to ask. What is it, Tom?"

"I don't know," I said. "It appears that she wants me to stay home and hold her hand. Says I'm neglecting her. But, God, you know what's been happening here. If it hasn't been one bloody thing it's been another. Did she tell you about Kayles?"

"No. What about him?"

I told Billy in some detail, and said, "I know I made a damn fool of myself and I'm sorry a man was killed—but Debbie didn't even ask if I'd been hurt."

"Self-centered," observed Billy. "She always was, and I've told her so to her face, many times. So where do you go from here?"

I took out my wallet and showed Billy the note Debbie had left and he made a sour face. "If she wasn't family I'd call her a bitch," he said. "What are you doing about Karen?"

"She's staying with me at the hotel for the moment. I doubt if it's good for her but it's the best I can do right now."

"Do you want me to talk with Debbie?"

"No," I said. "Keep out of it. She must work this thing through herself. And tell Jack and Frank to keep out of it, too."

He shrugged. "I've already told them, but I'll pass on the message from you."

"Do that."

And so we left it there and began to discuss our problems in the Bahamas. Billy said, "The way things are going you'd better start another division—staffed by morticians. It should show a profit."

"Not if the bodies aren't found," I said. "Anyway, the Theta Corporation was only directly involved in one of these incidents, the air crash."

"We don't want another like that," warned Billy. "The waves are still rocking the New York Stock Exchange. Those guys who were killed weren't ready to die; their financial affairs weren't exactly in order. I hear the Securities and Exchange Commission might start an investigation and that'll cause grief all around. Tom, the name of the Bahamas is coming up too often in headlines and it's beginning to stink. And don't give me that crap about any publicity being good publicity as long as they get the name right."

"It's just a streak of bad luck. It'll come right." I told him of the deal made between the Hoteliers' Association and the Ministry of Tourism, ending with, "So we're doing something about it."

"You'd better do something about it. Jack's getting worried; he's talking about pulling out."

"We've had a run of three bad incidents and Jack runs scared?"

"Three incidents and one hundred twenty-eight dead," said Billy. "Jack's been counting; he's keeping score." He sighed. "Trouble is he never really wanted to come into the Bahamas anyway. It was my idea and Billy One backed me. Jack went along but his heart was never really in it."

"On top of which he's never cottoned to me," I said a little bitterly.

"He thinks you run a loose ship," said Billy frankly. "That you give too much away. According to Jack at best you're a do-gooder; at worst, when his bile really starts to rise, you're an agent of the Kremlin."

I gave Billy a level look. "What do you think?"

"I think Jack is a fossilized dinosaur. Times are changing but he isn't. As for me I'm willing to play along with your plans of operation as long as they show a profit—a reasonable return on a fifty-million-buck investment, a return comparable to what we'd get anywhere else. I know you're a Bahamian and you want to help your own people; all I ask is that you don't do it *too* much at corporate expense."

"Fair enough. But, Billy, all those things which Jack thinks are giveaways—the pension fund, the hotel doctor, the hotels' school, and so on—all those are investments for the Corporation. They'll pay off in staff service and corporate loyalty, and that's hard to buy."

"You're probably right," acknowledged Billy. "But Jack's an old-time Texan. He even accused Nixon of being a commie when he pulled out of Vietnam. Sometimes I think he's a nut. But look at you from his side of the fence. You're a foreigner who first subverted his daughter into mixing with black kids, then took her away, and now she's back home looking goddamn unhappy. Add all that together and you'll see he's just looking for an excuse to pull out of here. It won't take much."

"How much of the Theta Corporation does he control?"

"As an individual, nothing; our eighty percent of Theta is owned by the Cunningham Corporation. But he has some clout in there. With some fast talking he could line up enough proxies to vote for a pull-out from the Bahamas."

"That would be a personal disaster for me," I said slowly. "I'm too deeply committed now."

"I know. That's why you'd better pray there isn't an earthquake here next week, or an outbreak of infectious dandruff. No more headlines, Tom."

As though I did not have enough to worry about I now had Jack Cunningham gunning for me. And, as Billy had said, all I could do was pray.

11

THAT WAS on Saturday. Billy stayed to lunch and then departed, saying that he was going to Miami on business for the Cunningham Corporation, and from there to New York. He gave me telephone numbers where I could find him. On Sunday I caught up with paperwork.

Monday was—well, Monday was Monday—one of those days when nothing goes really wrong but nothing goes really right; a day of niggling futilities and a rapidly shortening temper. I suppose we all have days like that.

I dined in the restaurant and went to my room early, after seeing Karen to bed, intending to go to bed myself and to scan some managerial reports before sleeping. I have never known why one is supposed to be vertical while working, and I can read perfectly well while flat on my back. I had just got settled when the telephone rang and a voice said in my ear, as clear as a bell, "Mangan? Is that you?"

"Yes. Who's speaking?"

"Jack Cunningham here. Is Debbie there?"

"No, I thought she was with you. Where are you?"

"Houston." His voice suddenly receded although he was still speaking. I caught a few scattered words and concluded he was consulting with someone else. ". . . not there . . . must be right . . . Billy . . ." He came back full strength. "Is young Billy there?"

"No," I said. "He was here on Saturday. He'll be in Miami if he hasn't gone on to New York."

Again he withdrew and I heard incomprehensible bits of a conversation nearly one thousand miles away. ". . . Miami . . . airplane . . . both . . ." then Jack said loudly, "Tom, you pack a bag and be ready to get your ass over here."

I resented that rasping tone of command. "Why? What's happening?"

"I'm not going to talk about it now. There's a satellite up there spraying this conversation all over the goddamn planet."

"I don't see—"

"Damn it! Do as I say and don't argue. There'll be a jet at Freeport International in about two hours. Don't keep it waiting, and be prepared to stay over awhile." The connection broke and silence bored into my ear.

I checked the time. It was 9:30 in the evening.

Much against my will I got out of bed and dressed, impelled by the fizzing urgency in Jack Cunningham's voice. Then I thought of Karen, asleep in the next room. Damn Jack Cunningham! Damn the whole blasted family! I rang the desk and asked the clerk to find Kitty Symonette and send her up to my suite, then I started to pack a bag.

I was just finishing a letter when Kitty Symonette tapped at the door and I let her in. "Sit down, Kitty. I have problems and I want you to help me."

She looked slightly surprised. "I'll do what I can."

Kitty was the hotel nurse and I liked her very much, and so did Karen. She was totally unflappable and equally reliable. "I'm not interrupting anything, am I?"

"No. I was going to have an early night."

"Good. I have to go away and I don't know for how long. Tomorrow I want you to take Karen to stay with my sister on Abaco. I've just spoken to Peggy and Karen is expected." I scribbled my signature. "These are instructions for Bobby Bowen to take you."

"No problem there," said Kitty.

"Karen is asleep in that room there. I don't want her to wake alone so you'd better sleep in my room tonight."

"You're going right away?"

"This minute. I don't want to wake Karen now, but you tell her I'll be back as soon as I can make it."

Kitty stood up. "I'll collect some things from my room."

I gave her the key to the suite, picked up my bag, and went to my office where I collected my passport from the office safe. As an afterthought I took the packet of two thousand American dollars which I kept there for an emergency and put them in my wallet.

The wait at the airport was long and boring. I drank coffee until it sickened me, then had a couple of Scotches. It was after midnight when the public address speakers said, "Will Mr. Mangan please go to the inquiry desk?"

I was met by a pretty girl dressed in a yellow uniform trimmed with black and with a badge on her lapel, two letters "C" intertwined in a monogram. The outfit made her look waspish, about as waspish as I was feeling. "Mr. Mangan?"

"Yes," I said shortly.

"This way, sir." She led the way from the concourse and through a side door. Standing on the apron not very far away was a Lockheed JetStar in gold with black trim; on the tailfin was the Cunningham monogram. Around it was a collection of airport vehicles like workers around a queen bee. I followed her up the gangway and paused as she stopped inside the door to take my bag. "Glad to have you with us, Mr. Mangan."

I could not reciprocate her feelings, but I murmured, "Thank you," and passed on into the main cabin.

Billy Cunningham said explosively, "Now, will you, for Christ's sweet sake, tell me what's going on?"

From Freeport to Houston is about one thousand miles across the Gulf of Mexico. We droned across the Gulf at five hundred miles an hour and Billy was morose—sore because he had been yanked out of Miami as unceremoniously as I had from Freeport—and he was irritated when he found I could tell him nothing. "What bugs me," he said, "is that for the first time in my life I'm going somewhere in an airplane and I don't know why. What the hell's got into Jack?"

"I don't know," I said slowly. "I think it's something to do with Debbie."

"Debbie! How come?"

"The first thing Jack asked was if she was with me—in Freeport."

"He knew she wasn't," said Billy. "She was in Houston."

I shrugged. "Air travel is wonderful. A girl can get around fast."

"You think she's taken off again?" He snorted. "That girl wants her ass spanked—and if you won't do it, then I will. It's time she settled down and learned how to behave."

There was nothing more to say so we did not say it.

There was a car waiting at Houston airport and an hour later I was at the start of a Cunningham conference. At least it was the start for me; the others had evidently been arguing the toss for a long time—and it showed. Jack Cunningham was at the head of the table, his silver hair making him look senatorially handsome as usual, and Billy One sat next to him, his bald head shiny under the fluorescent lighting. Debbie's brother, Frank, eyed me with arrogant and ill-concealed hostility, the resulting sneer marring his good looks. As background there were half a dozen other collateral Cunninghams, most of whom I did not know, ready to take their cue from the powerful tribal bosses. But I did recognize Joe Cunningham whom I remembered from the wedding; he favored me with a flat, hard stare. This was the Cunningham clan in full deliberation and, predictably, there wasn't a woman in sight.

Our arrival brought instant silence which did not last long. Billy flipped a hand at his father, surveyed the gathering, and drawled, "Morning, y'all." Uproar broke out, everybody talking at once, and I could not distinguish a word until Jack hammered the long table with a whiskey bottle and yelled, "Quiet!"

It could have been the traditional smoke-filled room but for the air conditioning and, indeed, they did look like a crowd of old-time political bosses carving up next year's taxes. Most had their jackets off and had loosened their neckties and the room smelled of good cigars. Only Jack had kept on his coat, and his tie was securely knotted at his neck. Even so he looked decidedly frayed around the edges, and there was a persistent twitch in his left cheek.

He said, "Tom, do you know what's happened to Debbie?"

The question could have had two meanings—he really wanted to know if I knew, or it was rhetorical—and there was no way of knowing from the inflection of his voice. I said, "How would I know? She left me."

"He admits it," said Frank.

"Admit! I admit nothing—I'm *telling* you, if she hasn't told you already. She's her own woman and she ran away."

Billy casually walked up to the table and picked up a whiskey bottle. "Any clean glasses around?" Then he swung on Frank. "Shut up."

"You can't . . ."

"Shut it," said Billy quietly, but there was a cutting edge to his voice. "Your sister's a brat. Everything she ever wanted she got, but she wouldn't know a man if she saw one, not a real man. When she found she couldn't handle him she picked up her marbles and wouldn't play anymore." He looked at Jack. "Nobody's going to hold a kangaroo court on Tom. Hear?"

Billy One stirred. "Quiet, boy."

"Sure," said Billy easily. "I've said it, y'all know that." He dropped into a chair. "Come sit here, Tom; you look as though you need a drink."

I suppose I did; we both did. And it was half past three in the morning. I took the chair he offered and accepted the drink, then I said, "If you want to know what happened to Debbie why don't you ask her?"

I was now facing Billy One across the table. He laid his hands flat. "That's just it, son. She's not around to be asked."

"Jesus!" said Billy, and stared at Jack. "Your little girl runs away again, and you jerk me from making the sweetest deal you ever saw?"

The tic convulsed Jack's cheek; he looked defeated. "Tell him, Billy One," he said in an old man's voice.

Billy One stared at the back of his hands. He said slowly,

"We weren't sure at first, not really, not even this afternoon when. . ." He looked up at me. "Now you're here we're pretty sure Debbie's been kidnapped."

Suddenly it all did not seem real. My head swam for a moment as a host of questions crowded in. I picked the first at random. "Who by?"

"Who the hell knows?" said Frank disgustedly. "Kidnappers don't hand out business cards."

He was right; it was a stupid question. Billy said, "When?"

"Saturday, we think; maybe Sunday early." And today was late Monday or, rather, very early Tuesday. Billy One nodded down the table. "Last one of us to see her was Joe's wife."

"Yeah," said Joe. "Linda and Debbie went shopping Saturday morning—Sakowitz and Nieman-Marcus. They lunched together."

"Then what?" asked Billy.

Joe shrugged. "Then nothing. Linda came home."

"Did she say what Debbie was going to do Saturday afternoon?"

"Debbie didn't tell her."

This did not seem to be getting anywhere. I cleared my throat, and said, "How do you know she's been kidnapped? Billy, here, jumped to the conclusion that she'd taken off again. So did I. So how do you *know?*"

"Because the goddamn kidnappers told us," said Frank.

Billy One said, "We got a letter yesterday—least, Jack did. Tell the truth, I don't think we believed it at first, neither of us. Thought it was some kind of hoax until we discovered she really wasn't around."

"Where was Debbie staying?"

"At my place," said Jack. He looked at me reproachfully. "My girl was very unhappy."

"She was last seen by the family at midday on Saturday and it took you until Monday to find out she'd disappeared?" I looked at Jack. "Wasn't her bed slept in?"

"Take it easy, Tom," said Billy One. "We thought she'd gone back to you."

"She'd have left word," I said. "She may be irresponsible, but she's not that irresponsible. When she left me she at least had the decency to leave a note telling me where she'd gone, if not why. What about her clothes? Didn't you check to see if any were missing? Or, more to the point, not missing?"

"Oh, Christ!" said Frank. "She'd been living away. Who knew what clothes she had?" He waved an impatient hand. "We're wasting time."

"I agree," I said emphatically. "Have you notified the police?"

There was silence around the table and Jack evaded my eye. Finally Billy One said quietly, "Kidnapping is a federal offense."

He tented his fingers. "If it was just a matter for the state police we'd be able to keep control—we draw a lot of water here in Texas. But once the Federal government gets into the act—and that means the FBI—then anything could happen. Since Watergate every government department has been as leaky as a goddamn sieve!" In his voice was the contempt of the old-line Republican for a Democratic administration. "The FBI is no exception, and if the newspapers get hold of this I wouldn't give a bent nickel for our chances of getting Debbie back safely."

"We can control our press down here, but those newspapers back east would really screw things up," said Frank.

"To say nothing of the professional bleeding hearts on TV," Joe commented.

"So you haven't told the police," I said bleakly.

"Not yet," said Billy One.

"Hell, we can pay," said Billy. He grinned sardonically. "And stop it out of Debbie's allowance when we get her back."

"If we get her back," said Jack. There was agony in his voice.

"Right," said Billy. "But if you don't call the cops you

don't get her back unless you pay—so let's start opening the coffers."

"It's not as easy as that," said Billy One. "Not by a long shot. There are . . . difficulties."

"What difficulties? These guys want dough, we want Debbie. We give them however many dollars they want and we get Debbie." Billy's voice turned savage. "Then we go hunting and we get the money back and maybe some scalps. But I don't see any difficulty."

"You brought one with you," said Frank.

"What the hell do you mean by that?"

Frank jerked his thumb at me. "I mean that this son of a bitch is the problem."

"Shut up!" snapped Billy One. "He could be the answer, too." He sighed. "These guys don't want money, Billy. They want him." He was pointing at me. "He's the ransom."

12

DAWN WAS breaking as I got to bed that morning but I did not sleep much. I just lay there in bed, staring into the darkness of the curtained room, and thinking. The trouble was that I could not think very well; fugitive thoughts chittered about in my skull like bats in an attic. Nothing seemed to connect.

I moved restlessly in bed and again saw the face of Billy One and the finger pointing directly at me. That finger had been a little unsteady; it trembled with age or fatigue—or possibly both. "Don't ask me why," said Billy One. "But they want Tom for Debbie—an even deal."

"Bullshit!" said Billy. He did not believe it, and neither did I. It made no sense.

"Show him the ransom note," said Frank.

Jack took a folded letter and tossed it onto the table. I grabbed it and read it with Billy peering over my shoulder. It was in typescript, addressed to Mr. John D. Cunningham, and written with a stilted formality which contrasted oddly with the rawness of the contents.

Dear Mr. Cunningham,

You will have difficulty in believing this but we have in our possession the person of your daughter, Deborah Mangan. In short, we have kidnapped her. In the belief that you will want her back unharmed we now give you our terms. They are not subject to negotiation.

You will cause your son-in-law, Thomas Mangan, to travel to Houston. How you do this is your concern. We will know when he has arrived. Our price for your daughter's safety and, possibly, her life is the person of Thomas Mangan delivered to us intact and unhurt. Your daughter will then be returned in fair exchange. You will be notified as to the manner of this transaction upon the arrival of Mr. Mangan in Texas.

It goes without saying that the police should not be informed of these arrangements nor should any of those steps be taken which might seem obvious in such a dramatic situation as this.

You will understand my motives in not signing this communication.

"For Christ's sake!" said Billy. He looked at me with a baffled expression. "Who'd . . ." He stopped and shook his head in wonder.

"I don't know." What I did know was the reason for Jack Cunningham's peremptory summons to Houston.

"You must be quite a guy," said Frank, his tone belying his words. He looked around the table. "Any hoodlum knows a Cunningham woman is worth hard cash money. How much? Quarter of a million dollars? Half a million? A million? Christ, we'd pay five million if we had to. Course, any hoodlum with sense would know he wouldn't live long enough to spend it. But this guy would rather have Mangan than the dough." He eyed me challengingly. "So what the hell makes you so valuable?"

"Cut it out," said Billy.

Billy One said pointedly, "We want to make friends and influence people."

"Yeah," said Billy. "Tom hasn't said much yet. He hasn't said he wants any part of this."

"He's not a man if he runs out," said Frank hotly.

"Oh, I don't know," said Billy in a detached voice. "How much would you do for a wife who's run out on you?"

For some reason that seemed to hit Frank where it hurt. He flushed and was about to say something, but thought better of it and sat back in his chair, drumming his fingers on the table.

There was a long silence. Jack Cunningham sat at the head of the table, looking along its length with dead eyes; Billy pulled the letter closer and read it again; Frank fidgeted while Billy One studied him with watchful eyes. The rest, the family underlings, said nothing.

Billy One, apparently satisfied that Frank had shot his bolt, at least temporarily, said, "Okay, Tom." His voice was neutral but not unfriendly. "Frank has a point, you know. What makes you so valuable that someone would kidnap a Cunningham to get you?"

That was a good question and I did not have an answer. "I don't know," I said flatly. "You know who I am and what I do. Jack had me thoroughly investigated, didn't he? Twice. Once before the merger and again before the wedding. You don't think I can't recognize private detectives when they're floating around my hotels?"

Billy One smiled slightly. "You checked out fine," he said. "Both times."

"It wasn't necessary," I said. "All you had to do was to come to me and ask. My life is a pretty open book. But I thought that if that's the way you operate, then that's the way you operate, and there was nothing I could do about it. Which isn't to say I liked it."

"We didn't give a damn if you liked it or not," said Frank.

Jack said, "That will be enough, Frank."

"Jack was dead set against the marriage," said Billy One. "He had his reasons. Frank was, too; but Billy was for it—he thought you were a right guy. Me, I had no druthers either way. As it turned out, what we all thought didn't matter a damn because Debbie got her own way, as always."

He reached out and poured a measure of whiskey into a glass. "Now, we've got two things here, both separate—I think. Debbie left you, and she's been kidnapped. Can you think of any connection?"

"No," I said. "As you know, I've had my hands full lately—you've read the reports—and perhaps I couldn't, or didn't, give Debbie enough of my time. That's what she thought, anyway, so she quit. But I don't know why she should be kidnapped with me as ransom. That fits nowhere."

"Has anything out of the ordinary happened lately?"

"Yes," said Billy. "Tell him about Kayles."

So I told the story of me and Kayles. When I had finished Frank said, "And this guy is still loose?"

"Yes—so far."

"That's it, then," he said. "There's your answer."

"What would Kayles want with me?" I demanded, and prodded at the ransom demand on the table. "I've met and talked with Kayles—he wouldn't and couldn't write a thing like this. It's way above his head—he's not that educated."

Billy One said, "And where does that leave us? What makes you so goddamn valuable, Tom?"

"I have no idea," I said tiredly. "And does it matter? The point at issue here is what to do about Debbie."

"Mangan, I'd say you lose wives awful easy," said Frank nastily.

"That does it," said Billy, and hit Frank before I could get my own hands on him. It was a backhander across the jaw which caught Frank by surprise. He went over backwards and his chair went with him, and he sprawled on the floor with Billy standing over him. He looked up, rubbing his jaw, and Billy said, "Cousin Frank, I've always been able to whip your ass, and if you don't stay off Tom's back I'm ready to do it again right now."

Billy One glanced at Jack who was silent. He said, "That was uncalled for, Frank. Now, you'll stand up and apologize to Tom or you leave this room right now, and maybe you won't be back—ever. Understand? Help him up, Billy."

Billy hoisted Frank to his feet. Frank rubbed his mouth and looked at the blood on the back of his hand. "I guess I'm sorry," he mumbled, then looked at me directly. "But what are you going to do about my sister?"

"I'm going to make the exchange." I looked at the expression on his face, and then at Billy One. "Did you have any doubt I would?"

A suppressed chuckle came from Billy. "You're damn right they had doubts."

Billy One exhaled a long sigh. "Maybe I misjudged you, Tom," he said quietly.

"Well, now we can plan," said Billy. He sat down and picked up the letter. "Frank was talking about hoodlums, but Tom's right; this wasn't written by any illiterate jerk. He used a typewriter—they can be traced."

"Typewriters are cheap," said Frank as he picked up his chair. "That one is probably at the bottom of Galveston Bay by now." He sat down. "And what's to plan? This guy is doing the planning. We can't do a goddamn thing until we get instructions on how we do the deal."

"You're wrong," said Billy. "What's the use of having a security section in the Corporation if we don't use it? Those guys know all about bugs."

Billy One lifted a shaggy eyebrow. "So?"

"So we bug Tom. A transmitter in the heel of a shoe, maybe. In a ballpoint pen or sewn into his pants. We bug him until he's crawling."

"And then?"

"Then we . . ."

Billy One had a sudden thought. He held up his hand and looked about the table. "Hold it! There are too many damn people in here. Let's do some pruning. Tom stays, of course—and Billy. Jack stays, too, if he wants." He peered at the far end of the table. "Jim, you stay. The rest of you clear out." Jim Cunningham was a quiet young man who had remained silent throughout the wrangling.

There was a general murmur of disapproval but no one objected overtly except Frank. "What the hell!" he said tightly. "We're talking about my sister. I'm staying."

Billy One scowled at him. "Okay. But quit riding Tom; we're talking about his wife and that's a closer relationship." He turned to Jack. "It's after four in the morning and you look beat. You sure you want to stay? You've been grinding at this all night."

"So has Frank. So have you."

"Yeah, but Frank is young—and I'm not as close to it as you. I'm more objective. Why don't you catch some sleep and come up tomorrow full of the old moxie?"

"Maybe you're right," said Jack. His face was gray with fatigue as he stood up slowly. "Frank, fill me in tomorrow morning. Hear?"

"I'll do that." A frown creased Frank's forehead as he watched his father walk to the door.

I had a sudden insight into the workings of the Cunningham Corporation. It operated remarkably like the Kremlin—collective leadership. Everybody had a vote but some votes were heavier than others. Every so often the old bulls at the top would do battle over some issue and the weaker would be tossed out. I had the idea that this was happening now; that Billy One was in the process of tossing out Jack, just as Brezhnev had got rid of Podgorny.

Billy and Frank were fighting for second place. Where Jim Cunningham came into this I did not know; probably Billy One was sealing an alliance with a faction of the clan. Jim was lucky—he had been promoted to top table.

This was confirmed when, as the door closed, Billy One called, "Jim, come sit up here." He glowered at us from under white eyebrows. "From now on we operate on "need to know," and what they don't know won't hurt us, or Debbie. Hell, it only needs Joe to drop a loose word at home and Linda would spread it over half Houston."

Frank said, "If she shoots her mouth off about what's happened to Debbie she'll wish she never married a Cunningham. I'll see to it if Joe doesn't."

Billy One nodded. "Jim, you know more about the security angle than any of us. Got any ideas on this?"

Jim was a young chap of about twenty-five, dressed casually in jeans. He had a sleepy look about him which proved to be deceptive because he was sharp as a tack. He said, "Billy is right." He turned to me. "I'll need your clothes—coat, pants, everything you wear down to socks and underwear. The outfit you'll use when you go to make this lousy deal. We'll have you radiating right through the electromagnetic spectrum." To Billy One he said, "We'll need cars, light airplanes and maybe choppers. Better lay on a couple of fast boats, too; Tom might be taken out to sea."

"We'll use my boat," said Frank. "Nothing faster in Texas."

"No!" said Jim quickly. "We use nothing Cunningham. We rent everything."

"My job," said Billy.

I said, "But no one makes a move until Debbie's safe."

"That's understood," said Billy One. "What about a gun?"

I shook my head. "No gun. I don't want to kill anybody."

He looked disappointed; my way was not the Texan way. "You might need a gun to stop someone killing *you.*"

"A gun wouldn't stop them—not the way I use one," I said dryly. "Anyway, they'll search me. The joker who wrote this ransom note doesn't sound like a damn fool."

Jim agreed. "Finding a gun might make him nervous; and nervous is dangerous."

A telephone beeped discreetly in a corner of the room. Billy One jerked his head and Jim got up to answer it. Even though he had got to the inner cabinet he knew his place in the pecking order; he was still a messenger boy. Presently he said, "It's the Security Officer speaking from the lobby. He says an envelope has been handed in addressed to Jack."

Billy One grunted. "Have him bring it up."

"Our security force might need beefing up," said Billy. "The way this is turning out we might be spread thin. What about a detective agency?"

"I don't know about that," said Billy One doubtfully. "I'm trying to keep things tight."

Frank said, "We might not have time for all that. I have a gut feeling trouble is coming up in the elevator right now."

Billy One looked at his watch. "If you're right, it's bad news." He picked up the ransom letter. "I know this guy said he'd know when Tom arrives, but Tom's been here not much over an hour."

"Good intelligence service," said Billy.

"Too goddamn good." Frank frowned. "Inside information? From this building, maybe?"

"Who knows?" Billy One irritably threw down the sheet of paper. "We'll wait and see."

If the information of my arrival had come from the inside of the building then it was bad news indeed, because we were sitting in the penthouse of the slab-sided glass tower that was the Cunningham Building, the latest addition to the Houston skyline. It would mean the Cunningham Corporation itself had been penetrated.

The long moments dragged by. Billy One must have paralleled my train of thought because he ceased his finger-tapping and said, "Jim, have security check this room for bugs first thing in the morning."

"Will do."

There was a discreet tap at the door and Jim got up. After a brief colloquy he came back carrying a large envelope which he laid on the table. Billy One bent forward to read the superscription, then pulled the ransom letter to him and compared. "Could be the same typewriter. Probably is."

"The guy has confidence," said Billy with a sideways glance at Frank.

"Lot of stuff in here," said Billy One, hefting the envelope. "Who delivered it?"

"A guy who said he'd been given five bucks in a bar." As Billy One picked up a letter opener Jim said sharply. "Let's do this right. Let's not get our fingers all over what's in there."

"You do it."

Jim slit open the envelope and shook its contents on to the table. Most of it appeared to be eight-by-ten glossy black-and-white photographs, but there were also a couple of sheets of paper covered with typescript, single-spaced. Jim took a ballpoint pen and separated it all out, being careful not to touch anything with his fingers. He said, "I'll have these put in glassine envelopes later. You can look at them now, but don't touch."

The two pages of typescript were complicated instructions of what to do and when to do it. The photographs were of places where certain actions had to be done, and had been annotated with a red felt-tip pen. On one, for instance, were the instructions, "Wait here exactly four minutes. Flash headlamps twice at end of each minute." There were eleven photographs, each numbered, and the eleventh showed the edge of a road with open country beyond and trees in the distance. A red-dashed line traced a path from the road to the trees, and an inscription read, "Mangan goes this way alone. Deborah Mangan comes out same way ten minutes later. No tricks, please."

It was all very complicated.

Billy was studying the first typed page. "What a nerve! This one begins: 'Mr. Thomas Mangan, welcome to Houston, the fastest growing city in America.'"

Frank said, "Well, he gives us until Thursday—three days. Enough time to get ready for the son of a bitch."

Billy One grunted, but said nothing.

Jim looked down at the photographs. "I don't think this guy is American. Look here, Billy." His finger hovered an inch over the table. "An American wouldn't refer to head-lamps—he'd say headlights."

"Yeah, could be. European usage, maybe."

"Why not come right out and say British?" Frank looked at me unsmilingly. "What do you say in the Bahamas, Mangan? Headlamps or headlights?" He could not resist needling me.

I shrugged. "I use them interchangeably. Both usages are valid. We're being penetrated by the American language because most of our tourists are American."

Billy One yawned. "Since we have time to spare I'm going home to bed. I want y'all in my office downstairs at ten A.M. Jim, don't forget to have this room debugged. Where are you sleeping tonight, Tom? I don't believe Jack made arrangements."

"Come home with me," said Billy. He rubbed his eyes wearily. "Jesus, but I'm tired."

13

TUESDAY MORNING, early but not very bright. I had had
about three hours' sleep and my body felt as heavy as my
spirits, and even the forceful shower in the guest bathroom
did not help. I dressed lightly; Houston was like a permanent
sauna and it was already fairly steamy.

Breakfast was on the patio outside the house, a low ram-
bling structure of stone, timber and glass. I do not know if
Billy's wife, Barbara, knew anything about the kidnapping
of Debbie; she made no reference to it as she served breakfast
so I concluded that probably Billy had not told her. It is a
characteristic of Texans, and Cunninghams in particular,
not to involve their womenfolk.

Over breakfast we talked of the weather, of baseball, and
other mundane matters. A couple of times I caught Barbara
giving me a sidelong glance and I knew what she was thinking—why was I there and not at Jack's place with Debbie?
The gossiping close-knit Cunningham women would know,
of course, that the marriage was in trouble, but Barbara was
too disciplined to refer to it and hid her curiosity well if not
entirely.

After breakfast I went with Billy to his study where he
picked up a red telephone and depressed a button. "Hi, Jo-
Ann; anything I ought to know?" I realized he had a direct
line to his office in the Cunningham Building. He listened
for a while then said abruptly. "Cancel all that." Standing
ten feet away I was able to hear the cry of protest which
came from the earphone.

"No, I can't tell you," he said. "But it'll be a week. Damn
it, don't argue with me, Jo-Ann. Here's what you do. I want
to see Harry Pearson of Texas Aviation and Charlie Alvarez
of the Gulf Fishing Corporation—both this morning—*not* at

the Cunningham Building, someplace else. Sure, the Petroleum Club will do fine. You can tell me when you see me—half an hour."

He put down the telephone and grinned. "I have a strong-minded secretary—but efficient." He became serious. "If we want helicopters and fast boats to be used in the way we want them used I'll have to tell Harry and Charlie the reason. No chopper jockey or boat skipper will do what we want without their bosses' say-so—we may have to skirt the law. So Harry and Charlie have to know. They'll keep their mouths shut, I promise."

"I don't mind," I said. "It's my skin you're protecting. Just so you don't take action before you have Debbie safe."

"Right," he said. "Have you got the clothing Jim wants?"

"All packed."

"Then let's go downtown."

Houston.

Not so much a city as a frame of mind—a tribute to the dynamism of American technology. Too far from the sea? Bring the sea fifty miles to the city and make Houston the third biggest port in the United States. Want to produce gasoline? Build seven refineries and produce a flood of fifteen billion gallons a year. Want to go to the moon? Spend ten years, forty billion dollars, and make Houston the nerve center of the operation. Want to play baseball when it is too hot and steamy to move? Put a roof over a stadium which holds fifty-two thousand people and cool it to a constant 74° F.—cool for Houston—using seven thousand tons of air-conditioning machinery. The grass in the stadium won't grow? For Christ's sake, man; design a special plastic grass.

The latest proposal was to roof over the entire business district of the city—much simpler than to air-condition individual buildings.

Houston—Baghdad-on-the-Bayou. I hated the place.

We went downtown in Billy's air-conditioned car without once taking a breath of the nasty, polluted, natural stuff outside. Billy's secretary, I was interested to note, was a middle-aged lady with a face like a prune. As we passed through the outer office she said quickly, "Mr. Pearson and Mr. Alvarez—eleven o'clock—Petroleum Club."

Without breaking stride Billy said, "Right. Find Cousin Jim—might be in security." We went into his office and he picked up a telephone and stabbed a button. "Pop, we're in and ready to go." He listened for a moment and his expression changed. "Oh, God, no!" Pause. "Yeah, I guess so. Okay."

He put down the telephone. "Jack had a heart attack an hour ago. He's being taken to the Texas Medical Center. Frank is with him and Pop is going there now. Of all the times...."

"Because of the times," I said. "It probably wouldn't have happened if Debbie hadn't been kidnapped. He wasn't looking too good last night."

He nodded. "That leaves you, me and Jim to plan and execute this operation. Not enough—I'll draft a couple more."

Jim came in and Billy told him about Jack. "Tough," said Jim. "Poor old guy."

"Well, let's get to it," said Billy. "Tom's outfit is in that case there."

"Fine." Jim frowned. "I've been worrying about something. What happens if they strip Tom? His bugged clothes might be going one way and Tom in another direction."

"That's a chance we have to take," said Billy.

Jim smiled. "Not so. I've got something, if Tom will go for it." He produced a capsule of plastic, about an inch long, three-eighths of an inch in diameter, and with rounded ends. "You have to swallow it."

"What!"

"It's a transponder—it returns a signal when interrogated by a pulsed transmitter; not a powerful signal but good enough to get a direction finder on it. It goes into action when the gastric juices work on it, so you swallow it at the last minute."

Jim laughed. "How about it, Tom?"

I looked at it distastefully. "All right—if I have to. Where did you get it?"

"I have a pipeline into the CIA. I borrowed it."

"Borrowed!" said Billy, grimacing. "Anyone going to use it afterwards?"

Jim said, "It's good for thirty-six to forty-eight hours before peristalsis gets rid of it."

"Just don't crap too much, that's all," said Billy. "Anything else?"

"I had the contents of the second envelope checked for fingerprints. Result negative. No dice, Billy."

"Okay," said Billy. "I have things to do. Tom, why don't you go along with Jim and watch him ruin your coat and pants? I'm going out to round up some transportation."

So I went with Jim to the security section in the Cunningham Building which meant having my photograph taken in color by a Polaroid camera and wearing a plastic lapel badge with my name, signature and aforesaid photograph. Jim wore one too, as did everybody else.

I was introduced to an electronics genius named Ramon Rodriguez who displayed and discussed his wares, all miracles of micro-miniaturization. "Do you wear dentures, Mr. Mangan?" he asked.

"No."

"A pity." He opened a box and displayed a fine set of false teeth. "These are good; they'll transmit anything you say— range over a mile. If you keep your mouth a little open they'll also catch what the guy you're talking to is saying— those two front top incisors are microphones." He put them away.

"We'll put a bug in the car you'll be driving," said Jim.

"Two," said Rodriguez. "Know anything about bugs, Mr. Mangan?"

"Not a thing."

"There are many kinds. Most fall into one of two categories—active and passive. The active bugs are working all the time, sending out a signal saying, 'Here I am! Here I am!'

The passive bugs only transmit when asked by a coded impulse, like the gadget Mr. Cunningham showed me this morning."

Jim chuckled. "The pill."

"That's to economize on power where space is limited. Those bugs send out an unmodulated signal, either steady or pulsed. When it comes to modulation, a voice transmission, it becomes a little harder. You'll be wired up with every kind of bug we have."

Rodriguez put a familiar-looking box on the bench. "Pack of cigarettes; genuine except for those two in the back right corner. Don't try to light those or the sparks will fly." Something metallic went next to the cigarette pack. "Stickpin for your necktie—will pick up a conversation and transmit it a quarter-mile. Belt to hold up your pants—bug in buckle, but will transmit a mile because we have more room to play with. Try to face the man you're talking with, Mr. Mangan."

"I'll remember that."

Two identical objects joined the growing heaps. "These go in the heels of your shoes. This one sends a steady signal so we can get a direction finder on it. But this one has a pressure transducer—every time you take a step it sends out a beep. If you're being hustled along on foot we'll know it— we might even be able to calculate how fast. And if it stops we know you've stopped moving—if you're not in an automobile, that is. Now, this is important. You know the rhythm of shave-and-a-haircut?"

I smiled and knocked it out with my knuckles on the bench.

"Good. If you're being taken for a ride tap it out once for a car, twice for a boat, three times for an airplane. Repeat at five-minute intervals. Got that?"

I repeated his instructions. "Just tap it out with my heel? Which one?"

"The right heel." Rodriguez picked up my jacket and trousers. "I'm giving you two antennae—one in your coat sewn into the back seam, the other in your pants. Don't worry; they won't show. And there'll be a few other things— I'll give you a new billfold and there'll be the coins in your pockets—anything I can cook up between now and Thursday. You don't have to know about them, just be glad they're there."

The Cunninghams were going to a great deal of trouble and it occurred to me that if they had all this stuff handy then they were probably up to their necks in industrial espionage. I wondered if they had used it on me in the course of their investigations.

Rodriguez looked at his watch. "I have to make a phone call. I won't be long, Mr. Cunningham." He walked away into his office.

Jim said, "That man once said he could make a working microphone out of three carpenter's nails, a foot of copper wire, and a power cell. I bet he couldn't. I lost." He laughed. "He even made his own power cell from a stack of pennies and nickels, a piece of blotting paper and some vinegar."

"He seems a good man."

"The best," said Jim, and added casually, "Ex-CIA."

I looked longingly at the pack of cigarettes on the bench. I had run out and I knew Jim did not smoke. "I'll be back in a minute," I said. I remembered there was a newsstand in the lobby of the Cunningham Building so I went down in the elevator to street level.

There was a short line but I bought two packs of cigarettes within minutes. As I turned, opening one of them, I bumped heavily into a man. "Watch it, buster!" he said nastily, and walked past me.

I shrugged and headed toward the elevator. In a climate like that of Houston anyone was entitled to be short-tempered. I stood waiting for the elevator and looked at the half-opened pack in my hand while absently rubbing my thigh. The health warning on the side of the pack shimmered strangely.

"You okay, mister?" The elevator starter was looking at me oddly.

I said distinctly, "I'm per-fect-ly all right."

"Hey!" He grabbed my arm as I swayed. Everything was swimming and my legs felt like putty. Slowly and majestically I toppled forward like a falling tree, and yelled "Timber!" at the top of my voice. Oddly enough, not a sound passed my lips.

The next thing I knew was that I was being turned over. I looked at the ceiling and heard someone say, "Just fell down right there." Someone else said, "Drunk, I guess." And again: "At this time of day!"

I tried to speak. My brain worked all right in a somewhat crazy manner—but there seemed to be interference with the connection to my voice box. I experimented with "Mary had a little lamb," but nothing came through. It was weird.

From a distance a man said, "I'm a doctor—let me through." He bent over me and I stared up at him, past a big nose and into his eyes, yellow flecks in green irises. He felt my pulse then put his hand over my heart. "This man is having a heart attack," he said. "He must be taken to the hospital immediately." He looked up. "Someone help me— my car is outside."

I was lifted bodily and carried to the entrance, shouting loudly that this was no bloody heart attack and this was no bloody doctor, either. My brain told me I was shouting loudly but not a sound did I hear from my lips, and neither could I move a muscle. They put me on the back seat of a limousine and off we went. The man in the front passenger seat twisted around and took my limp arm. I saw the flash of glass and felt the prick of a needle, and soon the bright world began to go gray.

Just before I passed out I reflected that all the Cunninghams' organization and the painstaking work of Ramon Rodriguez was going for nothing. The kidnappers had jumped the gun.

14

IT WAS dark when I woke up. I was lying on my back and staring into blackness and feeling no pain, at least not much. When I stirred I found that I was naked—lying on a bed and covered by a thin sheet—and my left thigh ached a little. I turned my head and saw a rectangular patch of dim light which, when I propped myself up on one elbow, appeared to be a window.

I tossed aside the sheet, swung my legs out of bed, and tentatively stood up. I seemed to be in no immediate danger of falling so I took a step towards the window, and then another. The window was covered with a coarse-fibered cloth which I drew aside. There was nothing much to see outside, just the darker patches of trees silhouetted against a dark sky. From the west came the faint loom of the setting moon. There were noises, though; the chirping of cicadas and the distant, deeper croaking of bullfrogs.

There were bars on the window and no glass.

The breeze which blew through the window was warm and smelled of damp and rotting vegetation. Even so, I shivered as I made my way back to the bed, and I was glad to lie down again. That brief journey had taken the strength out of me; maybe I could have lasted two seconds with Muhammad Ali, but I doubted it. I pulled up the sheet and went back to sleep.

When next I woke I felt better. Perhaps it was because of the sunlight slanting through the room, making a yellow patch at the bottom of the bed. The window was now uncurtained and next to the bed was a tray which contained a pitcher of orange juice, an empty glass, a pile of thick-cut bread slices, a pot of butter and a crude wooden spatula with which to spread it.

The orange juice went down well and my spirits rose when

I saw the pot of honey which had been hidden behind the pitcher. I breakfasted stickily, sitting on the edge of the bed with the sheet draped around me, and doing an inventory of the room. Against one wall was another table holding a basin and a water jug together with a piece of kitchen soap. And there was a chair with clothing draped over it—not mine. And that, apart from the bed and the bedside table, was all.

After breakfast I washed, but first looked through the un-curtained window. There was nothing much to see—just trees baking under a hot sun. The air was humid and dank.

After washing I turned to the clothing—a pair of jeans, a T-shirt with the words HOUSTON COUGARS embla-zoned across the chest, and a pair of dirty white sneakers. As I was putting on the jeans I examined the bruise on the out-side of my thigh; it was livid and there seemed to be a small pinhole in the middle of it. It did not hurt much as I put on the jeans, then the shirt, and sat on the bed to put on my shoes. And there I was—dressed and almost in my right mind.

I might have hammered on the door then, demanding to be released, and what the hell is going on. I refrained. My captors would see me in their own time and I needed to think. There is a maneuver in rugby football known as "sell-ing the dummy," a feint in which the ball goes in an unex-pected direction. The Cunningham family had been sold the dummy and I would bet that Billy Cunningham would be spitting bullets.

I mentally reviewed the contents of the first and second ransom letters. The object of the first was to get me to Hous-ton. The second was so detailed and elaborate that no one thought it would be the dummy we were being sold. It was a fake all the way through.

One thing was certain: the Cunninghams would be wild. To kidnap a Cunningham was bad enough, but to add a double cross was to add insult to injury. Right at that mo-ment the Cunningham Building would be like a nest of disturbed rattlesnakes; all hell would be breaking loose and, perhaps, this time they would bring in the police. Not that it would help me, I thought glumly, or Debbie.

Which brought me to Debbie. Was she here or not? And where the hell was here? I went to the window again and looked out through the bars and again saw nothing but trees. I tested the bars; steel set firmly in concrete, and immovable.

I turned at a metallic noise at the door. The first man to enter held a shotgun pointing at my belly. He was dressed in jeans and a checkered shirt open almost to the waist, and had a lined grim face. He took one pace inside the room and then stepped sideways, keeping the gun on me. "On the bed." The barrel of the gun jerked fractionally.

I backed away and sidled sideways like a crab to the bed. The muzzle of that gun looked like an army cannon.

Another man came into the room and closed the door behind him. He was dressed in a lightweight business suit and could have been anybody. He had hair, two eyes and a mouth, with a nose in the middle—a face-shaped face. He was nobody I had seen before or, if I had, I had not noticed him. He was my most forgettable character.

"Good morning, Mr. Mangan. I hope you had a quiet night and slept well."

English—not American, I thought. I said, "Where's my wife?"

"First things first." He gestured sideways. "This man is armed with an automatic shotgun loaded with buckshot. Anything that will kill a deer will kill a man—men die more easily. At ten feet he couldn't miss; he could put five rounds into you in five seconds. I think you'd be chopped in half."

"Two seconds," said the shotgunner flatly and objectively.

I was wrong about his being English; at the back of those perfectly modulated tones was the flavor of something I could not pin down. I repeated, "Where's my wife?"

"She's quite safe," he said reassuringly.

"Where? Here?"

He shrugged. "No harm in your knowing. Yes, she's here."

"Prove it. I want to see her."

He laughed. "My dear Mr. Mangan, you are in no position to make demands. Although . . ." He was pensive for a moment. "Yes, my dear chap, that might be a good idea. You shall see her as soon as we have finished our initial conversation. I trust you are fit and well. No ill effects from the curious treatment we were forced to administer?"

"I'm all right," I said shortly.

He produced a small cylinder from his pocket and held it up; it looked like a shotgun cartridge. "It was one of these that did the trick. Issued to NATO soldiers for use against nerve-gas attacks. You put one end against the arm or leg—so—and push. A spring-loaded plunger forces a hypodermic needle right through the clothing and into the flesh, then injects atropine. I admit that the needle going through clothing is not hygienic; there's a small risk of tetanus—but that is preferable to heart failure from nerve gas, so the risk is acceptable. I don't think you even felt the prick of the needle."

"I didn't."

"Of course we used something other than atropine," he said. "A muscle relaxant derived from curare, I believe; used when giving electric shock therapy. You're lucky I wasn't a Middle Eastern guerrilla; they use something totally lethal. Very useful for street assassinations."

"Very interesting," I said. "But I can do without the technical lecture."

"It has a point," he said, and laughed. "Just like the needle. It's to tell you we're most efficient. Remember that efficiency, Mr. Mangan, should you be thinking of trying anything foolish."

"Who are you?"

"Does it matter?" He waved his hand. "Very well, if you must call me something call me . . . Robinson."

"Okay, Robinson. Tell me why."

"Why you're here? Rest assured I shall do so, but in my own time." He looked at a point over my head. "I was about to begin your interrogation immediately, but I have changed my mind. Don't you think it is a mark of efficiency to be flexible?"

He had a formal, almost pedantic, way of speech which fitted well with the tone of the ransom letters, and could very well have typed "headlamps" instead of "headlights." I said, "I couldn't give a damn. I want to see my wife."

His gaze returned to me. "And so you shall, my dear chap. What is more, you shall have the privilege of seeing her alone so that you may talk freely. I am sure she will be able to tell you many things of which you are, as yet, unaware. And vice versa. It will make my later interrogation so much easier—for both of us."

"Robinson, quit waffling and get her."

He studied me and smiled. "Quite a one for making demands, aren't you? And in the vernacular, too. But I shall accede to . . . er . . . shall we call it your request?"

He put his hand behind him, opened the door, and backed out. The man with the shotgun went out, gun last, and the door closed. I heard it lock.

I thought about it. The man with the shotgun was local, a Texan. He had spoken only a total of five words but the accent was unmistakable. Robinson was something else. Those cultured tones, those rolling cadences, were the product of a fairly long residence in England, and at a fairly high social level.

And yet . . . and yet . . . there was something else. As a Bahamian, class differences, as betrayed by accent, had been a matter of indifference to me, but my time in England had taught me that the English take it seriously, so I had learned the nuances. It is something hard to explain to our American cousins. But Robinson did not ring true—there was a flaw in him.

I looked with greater interest at my prison. The walls were of concrete blocks set in hard mortar and whitewashed. There was no ceiling so I could look up into the roof which was pitched steeply and built of rough timbers—logs with the bark still on—and covered with corrugated iron. The only door was in the gable end of the building.

From the point of view of escape the wall was impossible. I had no metal to scrape the mortar from between the blocks, not even a belt buckle; and they had carefully not put a knife on the tray with which to spread the butter, just a flat piece of wood. As Robinson had said—efficiency. A careful examination of the furniture told me that I was probably in a rural area. The whole lot had not a single nail in them, but were held together by wooden pegs.

Not that I was intending to escape—not then. But I was looking at the roof speculatively when I heard someone at the door. I sat on the bed and waited, and the door opened and Debbie was pushed in, then it slammed behind her quickly.

She staggered, regained her balance, then looked at me unbelievingly. *"Tom!* Oh, Tom!" The next moment she was in my arms, dampening the front of my Houston Cougars' T-shirt.

It took some time to get her settled down. She was incoherent with a mixture of relief, remorse, passion and, when she understood that I, too, was a prisoner, amazement, consternation and confusion. "But how did you get here?" she demanded. "To Texas, I mean. And why?"

"I was drawn into it by bait," I said. "You were the bait. We were all fooled."

"The family," she said. "How are they?"

"Bearing up under the strain." There were a few things I was not going to tell Debbie. One was that her father had just suffered a heart attack. Others would doubtless occur to me. "How were you snatched?"

"I don't know. One minute I was looking in the window of a store on Main Street, then I was here."

Probably Robinson had used his NATO gadget; but it did not matter. "And where is here? You're the local expert."

She shook her head. "I don't know. Somewhere on the coast, I think."

I disentangled myself, stood up, and turned to look at her. The dress she was wearing certainly had not come from a plushy Main Street store—it was more reminiscent of Al Capp's Dogpatch and went along with my jeans and T-shirt. From where I stood it seemed to be the only thing she was wearing. "All right, Daisy Mae, has anyone told you why you were kidnapped?"

She caught on and looked down at herself, then involuntarily put a hand to her breast. "They took my clothes away."

"Mine, too."

"I must look terrible."

"A sight for sore eyes." She looked up at me and flushed, and we were both silent for a moment. Then we both started to talk at the same time, and both stopped simultaneously.

"I've been a damned fool, Tom," she said.

"This is not the time—or place—to discuss our marital problems," I said. "There are better things to do. Do you know why you were kidnapped?"

"Not really. He's been asking all sorts of questions about you."

"What sort of questions?"

"About what you were doing. Where you'd been. Things like that. I told him I didn't know—that I'd left you. He didn't believe me. He kept going on and on about you." She shivered suddenly. "Who is this man? What's happening to us, Tom?"

Good questions; unfortunately I had no answers. Debbie looked scared and I did not blame her. That character with the automatic shotgun had nearly scared the jeans off me and I had just arrived. Debbie had been here at least three days.

I said gently, "Have they treated you badly?"

She shook her head miserably. "Not physically. But it's the way some of them look at me." She shivered again. "I'm scared, Tom. I'm scared half to death."

I sat down and put my arm around her. "Not to worry. How many are there?"

"I've seen four."

"Including a man whose name isn't Robinson? An English smoothie with a plummy voice?"

"He's the one who asks the questions. The others don't say much—not to me. They just look."

"Let's get back to the questions. Was there anything specific he wanted to know?"

Debbie frowned. "No. He asked general questions in a roundabout way. It's as though he wants to find out something without letting me know what it is. Just endless questions about you. He wanted to know what you'd told the police. He said you seemed to spend a lot of time in the company of Commissioner Perigord. I said I didn't know about anything you might have told Perigord, and that I'd only met Perigord once, before we were married." She paused. "There was one thing. He asked when I'd left you, and I told him. He then commented that it would be the day after you'd found Kayles."

I sat upright. *"Kayles!* He mentioned him by name?"

"Yes. I thought he'd ask me about Kayles, but he didn't. He went off on another track, asking when we were married. He asked if I'd known Julie."

"Did he, by God! What did you say?"

"I told him the truth; that I'd met her briefly but hadn't known her well."

"What was his reaction to that?"

"He seemed to lose interest. You call him Robinson—is that his name?"

"I doubt it; and I don't think he's English, either." I was thinking of the connection between Robinson and Kayles and sorting out possible relationships. Was Robinson the boss of a drug-running syndicate? If so then why should he kidnap Debbie and me? It did not make much sense.

Debbie said, "I don't like him, and I don't like the way he talks. The others frighten me, but he frightens me in a different way."

"What way?"

"The others are ignorant white trash but they look at me as a woman. Robinson looks at me as an object, as though I'm not a human being at all." She broke down into sobs. "For God's sake, Tom; who are these people? What have you been doing to get mixed up in this?"

"Take it easy, my love," I said. "Hush, now."

She quieted again and after a while said in a small voice, "It's a long time since you've called me that."

"What?"

"Your love."

I was silent for a moment, then said heavily, "A pity. I ought to have remembered to do it more often." I was thinking of a divorce lawyer who had told me that in a breaking marriage there were invariably faults on both sides. I would say he was right.

Presently Debbie sat up and dried her eyes on the hem of her dress. "I must look a mess."

"You look as beautiful as ever. Cheer up, there's still hope. Your folks will be turning Texas inside out to find us. I wouldn't like to be anyone who gets on the wrong side of Billy One."

"It's a big state," she said somberly.

The biggest—barring Alaska—and I could not see the Cunninghams finding us in a hurry. The thought that chilled me was that Robinson had made no attempt at disguise. True, his face was not memorable in the normal way, but I would certainly remember it from now on, and so would Debbie. The rationale behind that sent a shudder up my spine—the only way he could prevent future identification was by killing us. We were never intended to be released.

It was cold comfort to know that the Cunninghams were roused and that sooner or later, with the backing of the Cunningham Corporation, Robinson would eventually be run down and due vengeance taken. Debbie and I would know nothing of that.

Debbie said, "I'm sorry about the way I behaved."

"Skip it," I said. "It doesn't matter now."

"But you could be a son of a bitch at times—a real cold bastard. Sometimes you'd act as though I wasn't there at all. I began to think I was the invisible woman."

"There was no one else," I said. "There never was."

"No one human."

"Nor a ghost, Debbie," I said. "I accepted Julie's death a long time ago."

"I didn't mean that—I meant your goddamn job." She looked up. "But I ought to have known because I'm a Cunningham." She smiled slightly. " 'For men must work and women must weep.' And the Cunningham men do work. I thought it might be different with you."

"And the sooner it's over, the sooner to sleep." I completed the quotation, but only in my mind; it was too damned apposite to say aloud. "Why should it have been different? The Cunningham men haven't take out a patent on hard work. But maybe I did go at it too hard."

"No," she said thoughtfully. "You did what you had to, as all men do. The pity is that I didn't see it. Looking back, I know there's a lot I didn't see. Myself, for one thing. My God, you married an empty-headed ninny."

That was a statement it would be politic not to answer. I said, "You had your problems."

"And piled them on your back. I swear to God, Tom, that things will be different. I'll make an effort to change if you will. We've both, in our own ways, been damned fools."

I managed a smile. The likelihood that we would have a future together was minimal, "It's a deal," I said.

She held out her hand and drew me down to her. "So seal it." I put my hands on her and discovered that, indeed, she wore nothing beneath the shift. She said softly, "It won't hurt him."

So we made love, and it was not just having sex. There is quite a difference.

15

ROBINSON GAVE us about three hours together. It was difficult to judge time because neither of us had a watch and all I
could do was to estimate the hour by the angle of the sun. I
think we had three hours before there was a rattle at the
door and the Texan came in, gun first.

He stepped sideways, as before, and Robinson came in
with another man who could have been the Texan's brother
and possibly was. He was armed with a pistol. Robinson surveyed us and said benignly, "So nice to see young people
getting together again. I hope you have acquainted your
husband with the issue at hand, Mrs. Mangan."

"She doesn't know what the hell you want," I said. "And
neither do I. This is bloody ridiculous."

"Well, we'll talk about that later," he said. "I'm afraid I
must part you lovebirds. Come along, Mrs. Mangan."

Debbie looked appealingly at me, but I shook my head
gently. "You'd better go." I could see the man's finger tightening on the trigger of the shotgun.

And so she was taken from me and escorted from the room
by the man with the pistol. "We won't starve you," said
Robinson. "That should be an earnest of my good intentions—should you doubt them."

He stood aside and a woman came in with a tray which
she exchanged for the breakfast tray. She was a worn woman
with sagging breasts and hands gnarled and twisted with
arthritis. I pointed to the pitcher and basin on the other side
of the room. "What about some fresh water?"

"I see no reason why not. What about it, Leroy?"

The Texan said, "Belle, git th' water."

She took the pitcher and basin outside, and I had a couple
more names, for what they were worth. Robinson looked at

the tray from which steam rose gently. "Not the best of cuisine, I'm afraid, but edible . . . edible. And it's very much a case of fingers being made before forks. I think you'll need the water."

I said, "What about coming to the point?"

He wagged a finger at me. "Later . . . I said later. There is something which I must think over rather carefully. There's really plenty of time, my dear chap."

Belle came back, put the basin on the table and stood the pitcher in it. When she left Robinson said, *"Bon appetit,"* and backed out, followed by Leroy.

The meal was fish or, rather, wet cotton wadding mixed with spiky bones. I ate with my fingers and the flesh tasted of mud. When I had eaten rather less than my fill, but could stomach no more, I walked over to the water pitcher and was about to pour water into the basin to wash my slimy hands when I stopped and looked at it thoughtfully. I did not pour the water but dabbled my hands in the pitcher, then wiped them dry on my jeans.

The pitcher held more than two gallons. That, plus the weight of the pitcher itself, would be about twenty-five pounds. I went back to bed, spread butter on a thick slice of bread, and munched while looking at the pitcher, hoping it would tell me what to do. The first faint tendrils of an idea began to burgeon.

Robinson came back about two hours later with his usual bodyguard, and Leroy took his position just to the left of the door. Robinson closed the door and leaned on it. "I'm sorry to learn of your marital troubles, Mr. Mangan," he said suavely. "But from what I heard I gather you are on your way to solving them." He smiled at my startled expression. "Oh, yes, I listened to your conversation with your wife with great interest."

I cursed silently. Ramon Rodriguez had shown me what could be done with bugs, and I might have known that Robinson would have the place wired. "So you're a voyeur, too," I said acidly.

He sniggered. "I even recorded your love play. Though not my main interest, it was very entertaining. If set to music it could hit the top twenty."

"You bastard!"

"Now, now," he said chidingly. "That's not the way to speak when you're at the wrong end of a gun. Let us come to more serious matters—the case of Jack Kayles. I noted when listening to the tape that you showed interest when your wife mentioned his name. My interest is in how you tracked him down. I would dearly like to know the answer to that."

I said nothing but just looked at him, and he clicked his tongue. "I advise you to be cooperative," he said. "In your own interest—and that of your wife."

"I'll answer that if you tell me why he killed my family."

Robinson regarded me thoughtfully. "No harm in that, I suppose. He killed your family because he is a stupid man; how stupid I am only now beginning to find out. In fact, it is essential that I now find the degree of his stupidity, and that is why you are here."

He took a pace forward and stood with his hands in his pockets. "Kayles was supposed to sail from the Bahamas to Miami in his own boat. There was a deadline, but Kayes was having problems—something technical to do with boats." Robinson waved the technicality aside. "At any rate he found he could not meet the deadline. When he heard that a skipper needed a crewman to help take a boat to Miami the next day he jumped at the chance. Do you follow me?"

"So far."

"Now, Kayles was carrying something with him, something important." Robinson waved his hand airily. "There is no necessity for you to know what it was. As I say, he is stupid and he let your skipper find it, so Kayles killed him with the knife he invariably carries. His intention was to conveniently lose that poor black man overboard but, unfortunately, the killing was seen by your little girl and then . . ." He sighed and shrugged. ". . . then one thing led to another. Now, Mr. Mangan, I don't mind telling you that I was very angry about this—very angry, indeed. It was a grievous set-back to my plans. Disposing of your boat was a great problem, to begin with."

"You son of a bitch," I said bitterly. "You're talking about my wife, my daughter and my friend." I stuck my finger out at him. "And you've no need to be coy about what Kayles was carrying. It was a consignment of cocaine."

Robinson stared at me. "Dear me! You do jump to conclusions. Now, I wonder. . . ." He broke off and looked up at the roof, deep in thought. After a while his gaze returned to me. "Well, we can take that up later, can't we? I've answered your question, Mangan. Now answer mine. How did you trace the idiot?"

I saw no reason not to answer, but I was becoming increasingly chilled. If Robinson saw no reason not to gossip about three murders then it meant that he thought he was talking to a dead man, or a man as good as dead. I said, "I had a photograph of him," and explained how it had come about.

"Ah!" said Robinson. "So it *was* the little girl's camera. That really worried Kayles. He was pretty sure she had taken his photograph, but he couldn't find the camera on our boat. Of course, it was a big boat and he couldn't search every nook and cranny, but it still worried him. So he solved his problem—as he thought—by sinking your boat, camera and all. But it wasn't there, was it? You had it. I suppose you gave the photograph to the police."

"There'll be a copy of it in every police office in the Bahamas," I said grimly.

"Oh, dear!" said Robinson. "That's bad, very bad, isn't it, Leroy?"

Leroy grunted, but said nothing. The shotgun aimed at me had not quivered by as much as a millimeter.

Robinson took his hands from his pockets and clasped them in front of him. "Well, to return to the main thrust of our conversation. You tracked Kayles to the Jumentos. How did you do that? I must know."

"By his boat."

"But it was disguised."

"Not well enough."

"I see. I told you the man is an idiot. Well, the idiot escaped and reported back to me. He told me a strange story which I found hard to credit. He told me that you knew all my plans. Now, isn't that odd?"

"Remarkable, considering that I don't know who the hell you are."

"I thought so, too, but Kayles was most circumstantial. Out it all came, information which even he was not supposed to know about—and all quite accurate."

"And I told him all this?" I said blankly.

"Not quite. He eavesdropped while you were talking to the man, Ford. I must say I was quite perturbed; so much so that I acted hastily, which is uncharacteristic of me. I ordered your death, Mr. Mangan, but you fortuitously escaped." Robinson shrugged. "However, the four Americans were quite a bonus—I believe the Securities and Exchange Commission is causing quite a stir on Wall Street."

"The four Am—" I broke off. "You caused that crash? You killed Bill Pinder?"

Robinson raised an eyebrow. "Pinder?" he inquired.

"The pilot, damn you!"

"Oh, the pilot," he said uninterestedly. "Well, by then I had time to think more clearly. I needed to interrogate you in a place of my own choosing—and so here you are. It would have been difficult getting near to you on Grand Bahama; for one thing, you were tending to live in Commissioner Perigord's pocket. But that worried me for other reasons; I want to know how much information you have passed on to him. I must know, because that will influence my future actions."

"I don't know what you're talking about," I said, wishing I did.

"I will give you time to think about it; to think and remember. But first I will do you a favor." He turned and opened the door, saying to Leroy, "Watch him."

A couple of minutes later the pistol carrier came in. He jerked his head at Leroy. "He wants you." Leroy went out and I was left facing the muzzle of a pistol instead of a shotgun. Not a great improvement.

Presently Robinson came back. He looked at me sitting on the bed, and said, "Come to the window and see what I have for you."

"The only favor I want from you is to release my wife."

"I'm afraid not," he said. "Not for the moment. But come here, Mangan, and watch."

I joined him at the window and the man with the pistol moved directly behind me, standing about six feet away. There was nothing to be seen outside that was new, just the trees and hot sunlight. Then Leroy came into view with another man. They were both laughing.

"Kayles!" I said hoarsely.

"Yes, Kayles," said Robinson.

Leroy was still carrying the shotgun. He stopped to tie the lace of his shoe, gesturing for Kayles to carry on. He let Kayles get ten feet ahead and then shot him in the back from his kneeling position. He shot again, the two reports coming so closely together that they sounded as one, and Kayles pitched forward violently to lie in a crumpled heap.

"There," said Robinson. "The murderer of your family has been executed."

I looked at Kayles and saw that Robinson was right—buckshot does terrible things to a man's body. Kayles had been ripped open and his spine blown out. A pool of blood was soaking into the sandy earth.

It had happened so suddenly and unexpectedly that I was numbed. Leroy walked to Kayles's body and stirred it with his foot, then he reloaded the shotgun and walked back the way he had come and so out of sight.

"It was not done entirely for your benefit," said Robinson. "From being an asset Kayles had become a liability. Anyone connected with me who has his photograph on the walls of police stations is dangerous." He paused. "Of course, in a sense the demonstration *was* for your benefit. An example—it could happen to you."

I looked out at the body of Kayles and said, "I think you're quite mad."

"Not mad—just careful. Now you are going to tell me what I want to know. How did you get wind of what I am up to, and how much have you told Perigord?"

"I've told the police nothing, except about Kayles," I said. "I know nothing at all about what other crazy ideas you might have. I know nothing about you, and I wish I knew less."

"So do I believe you?" he mused. "I think not. I can't trust you to be honest with me. So what to do about it? I could operate on you with a blunt knife, but you could be stubborn. You could even know nothing, as you say, so the exercise would be futile. Even if your wife saw the operation with the blunt knife there would be no profit in it. You see, I believe she knows nothing and so torturing you could not induce her to speak the truth. In fact, anything she might say I would discount as a lie to save you."

I said nothing. My mouth was dry and parched because I knew what was coming and dreaded it.

Robinson spoke in tones of remote objectivity, building up his ramshackle structure of crazy logic. "No," he said. "We can discard that, so what is left? Mrs. Mangan is left, of course. Judging from the touching scene of reconciliation this morning it is quite possible that you still have an attachment for her. So, we operate on Mrs. Mangan with a blunt knife—or its equivalent. Women have soft bodies, Mr. Mangan. I think you will speak truly of what you know."

I nearly went for him then and there, but the gunman said sharply, "Don't!" and I recoiled from the gun.

"You son of a bitch!" I said, raging. "You bloody bastard!"

Robinson waved his hand. "No compliments, I beg of you. You will have time to think of this—to sleep on it. I regret we can waste no more good food on you. But that is all for the best—the digestion of food draws blood from the brain and impedes the thought processes. I want you in a condition in which you think hard and straight, Mr. Mangan. I will ask you more questions tomorrow."

He went out, followed by the gunman, and the door closed and clicked locked, leaving me in such despair as I had never known in my life.

16

THE FIRST thing I did when I had recovered the power of purposive thought was to find and rip out that damned microphone. A futile gesture, of course, because it had already fulfilled Robinson's purpose. It was not even very well hidden, not nearly as subtle as any of Rodriguez's gadgets. It was an ordinary microphone such as comes with any standard tape recorder and was up in the rafters taped to a tie-beam, and the wire led through a small hole in the roof. Not much sense in it, but it gave me savage satisfaction in the smashing of it.

As I hung from the tie-beam, my feet dangling above the floor preparatory to dropping, I looked at the door at the end of the room and then at the roof above it. My first thought was that if I was up in the roof when Leroy came in I might drop something on to his head. That idea was discarded quickly because I had seen that every time he entered he had swung the door wide so that it lay against the wall. That way he made sure that, if I was not in sight, then I would not be hiding behind the door. If he did not see me in that bare room he would know that the only place I could be was up in the roof, and he would take the appropriate nasty action.

If there was anyone watching what I did next he would have thought I had lost my marbles. I stood with my back to the door, imitating the action of a tiger—the tiger being Leroy. I had no illusions about him; he was as deadly as any tiger—possibly more dangerous than Robinson. I do not think that Robinson was the quintessential man of action; he was more the cerebral type and thought too much about his actions. Leroy, however vacant in the head, would act automatically on the necessity for action.

So I imitated Leroy coming in. He booted the door wide

open; I had to imagine that bit. The door swung and slammed against the wall. Leroy looked inside and made sure I was on the bed. Satisfied he stepped inside, fixing me with the shotgun. I stood, cradling an imaginary shotgun, looking at an imaginary me on the bed.

Immediately behind came Robinson. In order that he could enter I had to cease blocking the doorway, so I took a step sideways, still holding the gun on the bed. That was what Leroy had done every time—the perfect bodyguard. I looked above my head towards the roof and was perfectly satisfied with what I saw.

Then I studied the water pitcher and basin. I had seen a piece of a similar basin before. As part of my education I had studied the English legal system and, on one Long Vacation, I had taken the opportunity of attending a Crown Court to see what went on. There had been a case of a brawl in a seamen's hostel, the charge being attempted murder. I could still visualize the notes I took. A doctor was giving evidence.

Prosecutor: Now, Doctor, tell me; how many pints of blood did you transfuse into this young man?

Doctor: Nine pints in the course of thirty hours.

Prosecutor: Is that not a great quantity of blood?

Doctor: Indeed it is.

Judge (breaking in): How many pints of blood are there in a man?

Doctor: I would say that this man, taking into account his weight and build, would have eight pints of blood in him.

Judge: And you say you transfused nine pints. Surely, the blood must have been coming out of him faster than you were putting it in?

Doctor (laconically): It was.

The weapon used had been a pie-shaped fragment of such a basin as this, broken in the course of the brawl, picked up at random, and used viciously. It had been as sharp as a razor.

I next turned my attention to the window curtain; a mere flap of sackcloth. I felt the coarse weave and decided it would serve well. It was held in place by thumb tacks which would also be useful, so I ripped it away and spent the rest of the daylight hours separating the fibers rather like a nineteenth-century convict picking oakum.

While I worked I thought of what Robinson wanted. Whatever Kayles had told him was a mystery to me. I went back over the time I had spent with Kayles, trying to remember every word and analyzing every nuance. I got nowhere at all and began to worry very much about Debbie.

I slept a little that night, but not much, and what sleep I had was shot with violent dreams which brought me up wide awake and sweating. I was frightened of oversleeping into the daylight hours because my preparations were not yet complete and I needed at least an hour of light, but I need not have worried—I was open-eyed and alert as the sun rose.

An hour later I was ready—as much as I could be. Balanced on a tie-beam in the roof was the pitcher full of water, held only in place by the spatula with which I had spread my butter. I had greased it liberally so that it would slide away easily at the tug of the string I had made from the sackcloth. The string ran across the roof space, hanging loosely on the beams to a point in the corner above my bed where it dropped close to hand. Lacking a pulley wheel to take care of the right-angle bend I had used two thumb tacks and I hoped they would hold under the strain when I pulled on the string.

The pitcher was just above the place where Leroy usually stood, and I reckoned that a weight of twenty-five pounds dropping six feet vertically on to his head would not do him much good. With Leroy out of action I was fairly confident I could take care of Robinson, especially if I could get hold of the shotgun.

Making my hand weapon had been tricky but fortunately I was aided by an existing crack in the thick pottery of the basin. Afraid of making a noise, and thankful that I had destroyed the microphone, I wrapped the basin in the bed sheet and whacked it hard with a leg I had taken from the table. It had not been difficult to dismantle the table; the wooden pegs were loose with age.

It took six blows to break that damned basin and after each one I paused to listen because I was making a considerable row. On the sixth blow I felt it go and unwrapped the bed sheet to find I had done exactly what I wanted. I had broken a wedge-shaped segment from the basin, exactly like the fortuitous weapon I had seen in that distant courtroom in England. The rim fitted snugly into the palm of my hand and the pointed end projected forward when my arm was by my side. The natural form of use would be an upward and thrusting slash.

Then, after gently pulling on the string to take up the slack I sat on the bed to wait. And wait. And wait.

The psychologists say that time is subjective, which is why watched pots never boil. I never believe them. I do not know whether it would have been better to have had a watch; all I know is that I counted time by the pace of shadows creeping across the floor infinitesimally slowly and by the measured beat of my heart.

Debbie had said there were four of them. That would be Leroy, Robinson, Kayles and the man with the pistol—I did not think Debbie had counted Belle. Kayles was now dead and I reckoned that if the pitcher took care of Leroy and I tackled Robinson I would have a chance. I would have the shotgun by then and only one man to fight—I did not expect trouble from Belle. The only thing which worried me was Leroy's trigger finger; if he was hit on the head very hard there might be a sudden muscular contraction, and I wanted to be out of the way when that shotgun fired.

Time went by. I looked up at the pitcher poised on the beam and worked equations in my head. Accelerating under the force of gravity it would take nearly two-thirds of a second to fall six feet, by which time it would be moving at twenty-two feet a second—say, fifteen miles an hour. It might seem silly but that is what I did—I worked out the damned equations. There was nothing else to do.

The door opened with a bang and the man who came in was not Leroy but the other man. He had the shotgun, though. He stood in the doorway and just looked at me, the gun at the ready. Robinson was behind him but did not come into the room. "All right," he said. "What did you tell Perigord?"

"I still don't know what you're talking about."

"I'm not going to argue," he said. "I'm done with that. Watch him, Earl. If you have to shoot, make sure it's at his legs."

He went away. Earl closed the door and leaned his back against it, covering me with the shotgun. It was all going wrong—he was in the wrong place. A break in the pattern was ruining the plan.

I said, "What did he say your name was?" My mouth was dry.

"Earl." The barrel of the shotgun lowered a fraction.

I slid sideways on the bed about a foot, going towards him. "How much is he paying you?"

"None of your damn business."

Another foot. "I think it is. Maybe I could pay better."

"You reckon?"

"I know." I moved up again, nearly to the end of the bed. "Let's talk about it."

I was getting too close. He stepped sideways. "Get back or I'll blow yo' haid off."

"Sure." I retreated up the bed to my original position. "I'm certain I could pay better." I was cheering silently because friend Earl had been maneuvered into the right place. I leaned back casually against the wall and felt behind me for the string. "Like to talk about it?"

"Nope."

I groped and could not find the bloody string. The pottery knife was hidden by my body ready to be grasped by my right hand, but the string had to be tugged with my left hand, and not too obviously, either. I had to be casual and in an apparently easy posture, an appearance hard to maintain as I groped behind me.

As my fingertips touched the string there came a scream from outside, full-throated and ending in a bubbling wail. All my nerves jumped convulsively and Earl jerked the gun warningly. "Steady, mister!" He grinned, showing brown teeth. "Just Leroy havin' his fun. My turn next."

Debbie screamed again, a cry full of agony. "Christ damn you!" I whispered and got my index finger hooked around the string.

"Let's have your hands in sight," said Earl. "Both of 'em."

"Sure." I put my left hand forward, showing it to him empty—but I had tugged that string.

I dived forward just as the shotgun blasted. I think Earl had expected me to move up the bed as I had before, but I went at right-angles to that expectation. My shoulder hit the ground with a hell of a thump and I rolled over, struggling to get up before he could get in a second shot. There was no second shot. As I scooped up the fallen shotgun I saw that nearly six hundred foot-pounds of kinetic energy had cracked his skull as you would crack an egg with a spoon. A fleeting backward glimpse showed the mattress of the bed ripped to pieces by the buckshot.

I had no time for sightseeing. From outside Debbie screamed again in a way that raised the hair on my neck, and there was a shout. I opened the door and nearly ran into a man I had not seen before. He looked at me in astonishment and began to raise the pistol in his right hand. I lashed out at him with my home-made knife and ripped upwards. A peculiar sound came from him as the breath was forcibly ejected from his lungs. He gagged for air and looked down at himself, then dropped the pistol and clapped both hands to his belly to stop his entrails falling out.

As he staggered to one side I ran past him, dropping the pottery blade, and tossed the shotgun from my left hand to my right. It was then I realized I had made a dreadful mistake; this was no small crowd of four people—I could see a dozen, mostly men. I had a hazy impression of clapboard houses with iron roofs arranged round a dusty square, and a mongrel cur was running towards me, snapping and barking. The men were running, too, and there were angry shouts.

Someone fired a gun. I did not know where the bullet went, but I lifted the shotgun and fired back, but nothing happened because I had forgotten to pump a round into the breech. There was another shot so I ducked sideways and ran like hell for the trees I saw in the middle distance. There was no time to stop and argue—I had probably killed two men and their buddies would not be too impressed by exhortations from Robinson to shoot at my legs.

And, as I ran for my life, I thought despairingly of Debbie.

17

THEY CHASED me; by God, how they chased me! The trouble was that I did not know the country and they did. And damned funny country it was, too; nothing like anything I had heard of in Texas. Here were no rolling plains and barren lands but fetid, steaming swamp country, lush with overripe growth, bogs and streams. I had no trail knowledge, not for that kind of country, and my pursuers had probably grown up in the place. I think that had it been the Texas we all know from Hollywood movies where a man could see for miles, I would not have stood a chance, but here was no open ground and that saved me.

At first I concentrated on sheer speed. There would be confusion back there for a while. They would find Earl and the other man and there would be a lot of shouting and waste of time if I knew human nature. Those first few minutes were precious in putting distance between me and my nemesis. As I ran I tried not to think of Debbie. Giving myself up would not help her, and I doubted if I *could* give myself up. Leroy would just as soon kill me as step on a beetle—there had been a close resemblance between him and Earl.

So I pressed on through this strange wilderness, running when I could and glad to slow down when I could not run. I considered myself to be a reasonably fit man, but this was the equivalent of going through an army battle course and I soon found I was not as fit as I thought.

My clothing was not really up to the job as I found when I inadvertently plunged into a brier patch. Sharp spines raked my arms and ripped the T-shirt, and I cursed when I had to go back again, moving slowly. My shoes, too, were not adequate; the rubber soles slipped on mud and one of the sneakers was loose on my foot. To lose even one shoe would be fatal; my feet were not hardened enough for me to run barefoot.

And so I plunged blindly on. I could just as well be running away from help as toward it. What I wanted to find was a house, preferably with a telephone attached to it. Then I could find out where I was and phone Billy Cunningham so that he could send one of his lovely helicopters for me—to call the police and then go and beat the bejesus out of Robinson. There were no houses. There were no roads which would lead to houses. There were no telephone lines or power lines I could follow. Nothing but tall stands of trees interspersed with boggy meadows.

After half an hour I stopped to get my breath back. I had traveled about three miles over the ground, I reckoned, and was probably within two miles of the place where I had been held captive. I fiddled with the shotgun and opened the magazine to find out what I had—four full rounds and one fired. I reloaded, pushed one up the spout, and set the safety catch.

Then I heard them, a distant shout followed by another. I went on, splashing up a shallow stream in the hope of leaving no trail. Presently I had to leave the stream because it was curving back in just the direction I did not want to go. I jumped onto the bank and ran south, as near as I could estimate by the sun.

I went through a patch of woodland, tall trees dappling the ground with sun and shadow, then I came to a river. This was no brook or stream; it was wide and fast-flowing, too deep to wade and too dangerous to swim. If I was spotted halfway across I would be an easy target. I ran parallel with it for some way and then came to a wide meadow.

There was no other way so I ran on and halfway across heard a shout behind me and the flat report of a shot. I turned in the waist-high grass and saw two men coming from different angles. Raising the shotgun I aimed carefully, banged off two shots, and had the satisfaction of seeing them drop, both of them. I did not think I had hit them because the shouts were not those of pain, but nobody in his right mind would stand up against buckshot. I turned and ran on, feeling an intolerable itch between my shoulder blades. I was not in my right mind.

I got to the cover of the trees and looked back. There was movement; the two men were coming on and others were emerging on to the meadow. I ejected a spent cartridge and aimed and fired one shot. Again both men dropped into cover but the rest came on so I turned and ran.

I ran until my lungs were bursting, tripping over rocks and fallen trees, slipping into boggy patches, and cannoning off tree trunks. My feet hurt. In this last mad dash I had lost both shoes and knew I was leaving a bloody trail. I was climbing a rise and the pace was too much. I threw myself to the ground beneath a tree, sobbing with the rasping agony of sucking air into my lungs.

This was it. One last shot and they would be upon me. I put my hand out to where the shotgun had fallen and then stopped because a foot pinned down my wrist. I twisted around and looked up and saw a tall man dressed in faded denims. He had a shotgun under his arm.

"All right," I said, defeated. "Get it over with."

"Get what over with?" He turned his head and looked down the hill at the sound of a shout. "You in trouble?"

Someone else moved into sight—a busty brunette in skin-tight jeans and a shirt knotted about her middle. I suddenly realized these were not Leroy's people. "They're going to kill me," I said, still gasping for breath. "Chased me—"

He showed polite interest. "Who are?"

"Don't know all the names. Someone called Leroy. Torturing my wife."

He frowned. "Whichaway was this?"

I pointed with my free arm. "That way."

He turned to the girl. "Could be the Ainslees."

"It is." She was looking down the hill. "I see Trace."

The man released my wrist, then picked up my shotgun. "Any load in this?"

"One round of buckshot."

"Enough. Can you climb a tree?" He was looking at my feet.

"I can try."

"If you admire yo' skin you better climb this tree," he advised. He tossed my shotgun to the girl. "Over there, behind that rock. Watch my signal."

"Okay, Pop."

The man gave me a boost into the tree. For a skinny old man he was surprisingly strong. "Stay on the upslope side an' keep yo' haid down." I managed the rest by myself and got lost in the leafy branches. I could not see down the hill but I had a good view to one side, and I saw him walk out and look towards my pursuers. I heard heavy breathing as someone came up the hill fast, and the old man said sharply, "Just hold it there, son."

"Hell, Dade—"

"I mean it, Trace. You stop right there." The shotgun Dade carried was held steady.

Trace raised his voice in a shout. "Hey, Leroy; here's old Dade."

There was the sound of more movement and presently Leroy said breathily, "Hi, there, Dade."

"What you huntin', Leroy?" asked Dade. "T'ain't razorback hog 'cause you ain't gotten dogs. An' yo' makin' too much damn noise for deer."

"Ah'm huntin' one son of a bitch," said Leroy. He came into sight.

"I don't care what yo' huntin'," said Dade. "I told you before. If you came huntin' on my land agin I'd kick yo' ass. I don't care if yo' huntin' a man or Hoover hog—you git offen my land."

"You don't understand," said Leroy. "This guy kilt Earl—smashed his haid in like a watermelon. An' Tukey—he's like to die; he ain't hardly got no belly left. Belle's tendin' to him, but ah don't know. . . ."

"If Belle's tendin' him he's sure to die," said Dade flatly. "Now git the hell outta here."

Leroy looked around. "You reckon you can make us?"

"Think I'm crazy?" said Dade. "I've got six of my boys within spittin' distance."

Leroy eyed him speculatively. Dade took an apple from his pocket. "I was goin' to enjoy this, an' that's somethin' else I have agin you, Leroy." He suddenly tossed the apple into the air, and shouted, "Hit it!"

There was a shotgun blast from the rock behind me and the apple disintegrated in midair. Wetness splattered against my cheek.

"Could have been yo' haid, Leroy," said Dade. "It's bigger. Mighty fine target is a swelled head." His voice sharpened. "Now, you heard me tellin' you, an' you know I tells no one twice. Move yo' ass." His hand pointed down the hill. "That's the shortest way offen my land."

Leroy looked uncertainly at the shotgun pointing at his belly, then he laughed shortly. "Okay, Dade. But, listen, old man, you ain't heard the last."

"An' yo' not the last to tell me that. Better men, too." Dade spat at Leroy's feet.

Leroy turned on his heel and went out of sight and I heard the sound of many men going down the hill. Dade watched them go, his sparse gray hair moving in the slight breeze. He stood there for a long time before he moved.

From somewhere behind me the girl said, "They're gone, Pop."

"Yeah." Dade came up to the tree. He said, "I'm Dade Perkins an' this is my girl, Sherry-Lou. Now, suppose you come down outta that tree an' tell me just who the hell you are."

18

IT NEARLY went sour even then.

I climbed down from the tree, wincing as the rough bark scraped my bruised and bloody feet. As I reached the ground I said, "Where's the nearest telephone? I need help."

Sherry-Lou laughed. She looked me up and down, taking in my bleeding arms, the tattered T-shirt with its incongruous inscription, the ripped jeans and my bare feet. "You sure do," she said. "You look like you tangled with a cougar." She saw the expression on my face and the laughter vanished. "Got a telephone back at the house," she offered.

"How far?"

"Two—three miles."

"You won't make that in under an hour," said Dade. "Yo' feet won't. Can Sherry-Lou go ahead an' talk for you?"

I was not feeling too well. I leaned against the tree, and said, "Good idea."

"Who do I talk with?" she asked. "What number?"

I had forgotten the number and had no secretary handy to ask. "I don't know—but it's easy to find. Houston—the Cunningham Corporation; ask for Billy Cunningham.

There was an odd pause. Sherry-Lou seemed about to speak, then hesitated and looked at her father. He glanced at her, then looked back at me. "You a Cunningham?" he asked, and spat at the ground. That ought to have warned me.

"Do I sound like a Cunningham?" I said tiredly.

"No," he admitted. "You talk funny. I reckoned you was from Californy—someplace like that."

"I'm a Bahamian," I said. "My name's Mangan—Tom Mangan."

"What's the Cunninghams to you?"

"I married one," I said. "And Leroy's got her." Perkins said nothing to that. I looked at his expressionless face and said desperately, "For Christ's sake, do something! She was screaming her head off when I busted out this morning. I couldn't get near her." I found I was crying and felt the wetness of tears on my cheek.

Sherry-Lou said, "Those Ainslees. . . ."

"Cunningham or Ainslee—dunno which is worst," said Dade. "Ainslee by a short haid, I reckon." He nodded abruptly. "Sherry-Lou, you run to the house an' talk to Billy Cunningham." He turned to me. "The young sprout or Billy One?"

"Young Billy would be best." I thought he would be better able to make quick decisions.

Dade said, "Tell young Billy he'll need guns, as many as he can get. An' tell him he'd better be fast."

"How far are we from Houston?" I did not even know where I was.

"Mebbe hundred miles."

That far! I said, "Tell him to use helicopters—he'll have them."

"An' tell him to come to my place," said Dade. "He sure knows where it is. Then come back an' bring a pair of Chuck's sneakers so as Tom here can walk comfortable."

"Sure," said Sherry-Lou, and turned away.

I watched her run up the hill until she was lost to sight among the trees, then I turned to look about. "Where is this place?"

"You don't know?" said Dade, surprised. "Close to Big Thicket country." He pointed down the hill to the right. "Neches River down there." His arm swung in an arc. "Big Thicket that way, an' Kountze." His thumb jerked over his shoulder. "Beaumont back there."

I had never heard of any of it, but it seemed I had just come out of Big Thicket.

Dade said, "Seems I remember Debbie Cunningham marryin' a Britisher a few months back. That you?"

"Yes."

"Then it's Debbie Leroy's got," he said ruminatively. "I think you'd better talk."

"So had you," I said. "What have you got against the Cunninghams?"

"The sons of bitches have been tryin' to run me offen my own land ever since I can remember. Tried to run my Paw off, too. Been tryin' a long time. They fenced off our land an' big city sportsmen came in an' shot our hogs. They reckoned they was wild; we said they belonged to people—us people. We tore down their fences an' built our own, an' defended 'em with guns. They ran a lot of folks offen their land, but not us Perkinses."

"The Cunninghams don't want your land just to hunt pigs, do they?"

"Naw. They want to bring in bulldozers an' strip the land. A lot of prime hardwood around here. Then they replant with softwoods right tidy, like a regiment of soldiers marchin' down Pennsylvania Avenue in Washington like I seen on TV once. Ruinin' this country."

Dade waved his arm. "Big Thicket was three million acres once. Not much left now an' we want to keep it the way it is. Sure, I cut my timber, but I do it right an' try not to make too many big changes."

I said, "I can promise you won't have trouble with the Cunninghams ever again."

He shook his head. "You'll never get that past Jack Cunningham—he's as stubborn as a mule. He'll never let go while there's a dollar to be made outta Big Thicket."

"Jack will be no trouble; he had a heart attack a couple of days ago."

"That so?" said Dade uninterestedly. "Then it's Billy One—that old bastard's just as bad."

"I promised," I said stubbornly. "It'll hold, Dade."

I could see he was skeptical. He merely grunted and changed the subject. "How come you tangled with Leroy Ainslee?"

"Debbie was kidnapped from Houston," I said. "So was I.

Next thing I knew I was at the Ainslee place locked up in a hut with Leroy on guard with a shotgun. That one," I added, pointing to the shotgun leaning against the tree where Sherry-Lou had left it.

"Kidnappin'!" said Dade blankly. He shook his head. "Ainslees have mighty bad habits, but that ain't one of 'em."

"They didn't organize it. There was an Englishman; called himself Robinson, but I doubt if that's his real name. I think all the Ainslees provided was muscle and a place to hide. Who are they, anyway?"

"A no account family of white trash," said Dade. "No one around here likes 'em. An' they breed too damn fast. Those Ainslee women pop out brats like shelling peas." He scratched his jaw. "How much did they ask for ransom?"

"They didn't tell me." I was not about to go into details with Dade; he would never believe me.

"Did you really kill Earl? An' gut Tukey?"

"Yes." I told him how I had done it and he whistled softly. I said, "And Debbie was screaming all the time and I couldn't get near her." I found myself shaking.

Dade put his hand on my arm. "Take it easy, son, we'll get her out of there." He looked down at my feet. "Think you can walk a piece?"

"I can try."

He looked down the hill. "Them Ainslees might take it into their haids to come back. We'll go over the rise an' find us a better place to be." He picked up Leroy's shotgun and examined it. "Nice gun," he said appreciatively.

"You can have it," I said. "I doubt if Leroy will come calling for it."

Dade chuckled. "Ain't that so."

Just over an hour later Dade nudged me. "Here's Sherry-Lou. Got my boy Chuck with her, too." He put two fingers in his mouth and muttered a peculiar warbling whistle, and the two distant figures changed course and came toward the tumble of rocks where Dade and I were sitting.

Sherry-Lou had brought more than footwear. She produced a paper bag full of chunky pork sandwiches and I suddenly realized I had not eaten for about twenty-four hours. As I ate them she rubbed my feet with a medicine and then bandaged them.

More important than this was the news she brought. When Billy had heard her story he exploded into action and promised all aid short of the US Navy as fast as humanly possible. "He's flyin' here direct," she said. "I told him to bring a doctor." She avoided my eyes and I knew *my* hurts were not in her mind when she said that.

"What's all this about?" asked Chuck.

I let Dade tell the story—I was too busy eating. When he had finished Chuck said, "I always knew the Ainslees were bad." He shook his head. "But this . . ." He stared at me. "An' you kilt Earl?"

"He's dead, unless he can walk around with his brains leaking out," I said sourly.

"Jeez! Leroy will be madder than a cornered boar. What's to do, Pop?"

Dade said, "Did Billy Cunningham say how long he'd be?"

" 'Bout three o'clock," said Sherry-Lou.

Dade hauled out an old-fashioned turnip watch and nodded. "Chuck, you get back to the house. When Billy drops by in his whirlybird you show him the big meadow near Turkey Creek. We'll be there. No reason for Tom to walk more'n he has to."

"Jeez!" said Chuck with enthusiasm. "Never flown in one of them things." He loped away. I thought that Dade Perkins's kids would stand a chance in the Olympics marathon; they did everything on the dead run.

Sherry-Lou snorted. "He's never been in the air in his life—in anythin'." She finished knotting a bandage over the deepest gash on my arm. "You all right, Tom?"

"I'll be better when I know Debbie's all right."

She veiled her eyes. "Sure."

Dade stood up. "Take us fifteen minutes to get down to the creek. Might as well start."

• • •

When the helicopter came down in the meadow Billy had the door open before the shock absorbers had taken up the weight, and came running across the grass toward us, stooping as people always do when they know rotors are turning overhead. He took in my condition in one swift glance. "Christ! How are you? How's Debbie?"

Dade and Sherry-Lou moved tactfully to one side, out of earshot, and were joined by Chuck who was talking nineteen to the dozen and windmilling his arms wildly. I gave Billy the gist of it, leaving out everything unimportant; just outlining the "whats" and ignoring the "hows" and "whys." He winced. "Torturing her!" he said incredulously.

"She was screaming," I said flatly. "I was being shot at—I had to move fast." I paused. "I should have stayed."

"No," said Billy, "you did the best you could." He looked back at the helicopter. "The State Police and some of our own security men are coming up behind. We'd better get back to the Perkins place."

"One more thing," I said. "Seems Dade Perkins doesn't like Cunninghams, and from what little he told me I know why. Now, he just saved my life, so from now on you haul off your dogs."

"It's not up to me," said Billy. "Jack won't . . ."

"Jack doesn't matter any more and you know it."

"Yeah, but Dad won't be buffaloed either." He frowned. "Let me think about it. Come on."

A few minutes later we dropped next to the Perkins's family residence and to two more helicopters with police markings. More were in the air coming in. When all six were on the ground we had a conference—a council of war.

Dade Perkins outlined on a table what the Ainslee place was like, using matchbooks and tobacco tins. Then there was a brief argument when Sherry-Lou announced that she was coming along.

The senior police officer was Captain Booth who was inclined to want to know the whys and wherefores until he was cut down by Billy. "For Christ's sake, Captain, quit yammering! We can hold the inquest after we've gotten my cousin out of there." It was a measure of Cunningham influence that Booth stopped right then and there.

Now he said decidedly, "No place for a woman. There might be shooting."

"Miz Mangan will need a woman if she's. . . ." Sherry-Lou swallowed the words "still alive," and continued, "I know Leroy Ainslee."

Dade turned red in the face. "Has he interfered with you?"

"No, he hasn't!" she retorted. "Not since I laid a rock against his head an' then got me a gun an' told him I'd perforate him."

Dade glowered, and Booth said thoughtfully, "There'll be one chopper in the air all the time. They might scatter and we'll want to see where they go. I reckon Miss Perkins could be in that one."

We left in the helicopters and descended like a cloud of locusts on the Ainslee place less than five minutes later with the precision of a military operation. I was in the chopper which dropped right in the middle. No one shot at us because there was no one there to shoot. All the Ainslee menfolk were absent and only the women and a few kids were left. The children were excited by the sudden invasion but the slatternly women merely looked at us with apathetic eyes.

Billy had a gun in his hand when he jumped out, and Dade carried Leroy's shotgun. I looked about and saw cops closing in from all sides. Billy holstered his pistol. "They're not here."

"Still out lookin' for Tom, I reckon," said Dade. He squinted up at the helicopter hovering overhead. "They'll know somethin's wrong. Been nothin' like this since I seen the Vietnam war on TV. They won't be back in a hurry."

I said, "For God's sake, let's find Debbie." I picked out the biggest house, a ruinous shack, and began to run.

It was Billy who found her. He came out of a smaller

shack bellowing, "A doctor! Where is that goddamn doctor?" He caught me by the shoulders as I tried to go in. "No, Tom. Let the doctor see her first. Will you quit struggling?"

A man ran past us carrying a bag and the door of the shack slammed shut. Billy yelled at me, "She's alive, damn it! Let the doctor tend to her."

I sagged in his arms and he had to hold me up for a moment, then I said, "Okay, Billy, I'm all right now."

"Sure," he said. "I know you are." He turned and saw Booth. "Hey, Captain, better get the Perkins girl down here."

"Right, Mr. Cunningham." Booth spoke to one of the pilots standing by, then came over to us. "Mr. Mangan, I'd like you to come with me." I nodded and was about to follow him, but he was looking at Billy. "You okay, Mr. Cunningham?"

Billy had developed a curious greenish pallor and beads of sweat stood out on his forehead. He sat down on the stoop of the shack. "I'll be all right. You go with the Captain, Tom."

I followed Booth to the shack in which I had been held prisoner. Earl's body had been laid out parallel to the wall and beneath the window. The big pitcher was lying on its side, still intact, and a pool of water lay on the floor, as yet unevaporated. Tukey lay on the bed; he was dead and stank of feces.

Booth said, "Know anything about this?"

"Yes. I killed them."

"You admit it," he said in surprise. I nodded, and he said, "You'd better tell me more."

I thought about that, then shook my head. "No, I'll say what I have to say in a courtroom."

"I don't think I can accept that," he said stiffly. "Not in a case of murder."

"Who said anything about murder?" I asked. "When you lift Tukey you'll find the bed has been ripped up by buckshot. I happened to be sitting there when Earl pulled the trigger. I stabbed Tukey when he was going to shoot me.

Don't prejudge the case, Captain; it's for a court to decide if it was murder." He made a hesitant movement, and I said, "Are you going to arrest me?"

He rubbed his chin and I heard a faint rasping sound. "You're not an American, Mr. Mangan. That's the problem. How do I know you'll stay in our jurisdiction?"

"You can have my passport, if you can find it," I offered. "I had it on me when I was snatched. It may be around here somewhere. Anyway, Billy Cunningham will guarantee I'll stay, if you ask him."

"Yeah, that'll be best." Booth seemed relieved.

"There *was* a murder." I nodded towards the window. "It happened out there. Leroy Ainslee shot a man in the back. I saw it."

"There's no body."

"Then have your men look for a new-dug grave." I turned on my heel and walked out of that stinking room into the clean sunlight. The hovering helicopter had come down, and I saw Sherry-Lou hurrying into the shack the doctor had gone into. I felt curiously empty of all feeling, except for a deep thankfulness that Debbie was still alive. My rage was muted, dampened down, but it still smoldered deep in my being, and I knew it would not take much for it to erupt.

I went over and stood in the shade of a helicopter. Presently I was found by Chuck Perkins. "Jeez, you sure kilt Earl," he said. His face sobered. "Tukey died bad."

"They deserved it."

"Pop's been looking for you." He jerked his thumb. "He's over there."

I walked around the helicopter and saw Dade talking to Sherry-Lou. His face was serious. As I approached I heard Sherry-Lou say, ". . . tore up real bad."

He put his hand on her arm in a warning gesture as he saw me. He swallowed. "Sherry-Lou's got something to tell you," he said. "I'm sorry, Tom, real sorry."

I said, "Yes, Sherry-Lou?"

"Did you know Miz Mangan was pregnant?"

"Yes." I knew what was coming.

"She lost the baby. I'm sorry."

I stared blindly into the sky. "Rape?"

"An' worse."

"God damn their souls to hell!" I said violently.

She put out her hand to me. "Some women are hurt more in birthin' a baby," she said. "She'll be all right."

"In her body, maybe."

"She'll need a lot of love . . . lot of attention. She'll need cherishin'."

"She will be. Thanks, Sherry-Lou."

They brought her out on a stretcher, the doctor walking alongside, and a nurse holding up a bottle for an intravenous drip. All that could be seen of her was her face, pale and smudgy about the eyes. I wanted to go with her in the helicopter back to Houston, but the doctor said, "There's no use in it, Mr. Mangan. She'll be unconscious for the next twenty-four hours—I guarantee it. Then we'll wake her up slowly. We'll want you there then."

So the helicopter lifted without me aboard and I turned to find Captain Booth standing close by talking to Dade. I said bitterly, "If I find Leroy Ainslee before you, Captain, I can guarantee you'll have a murder case."

"We'll get him," Booth said soberly, but from the way Dade spat on the ground I judged he was skeptical.

Billy came up. He had recovered something of his color. "Dade Perkins, I want to talk with you. You too, Tom."

Dade said, "What do you want?"

Billy glanced at Booth, then jerked his head. "Over here." He led us out of earshot of Booth. "I know we've been putting pressure on you, Dade."

Dade's face cracked in a slow smile. "An' not gettin' far."

"All I want to say is that it stops right now," said Billy.

Dade glanced at me, then looked at Billy speculatively. "Reckon you big enough to make yo' Paw eat crow?"

"This crow he'll eat with relish," said Billy grimly. "But there's something I want from you."

"Never did know the Cunninghams to give anything away free," observed Dade. "What is it?"

"I want the Ainslees out of here," said Billy. "I don't want to feel there's folks like that dirtying up the place."

"The cops'll do that for you," said Dade. "Why pick me?"

"Because I saw your face when Sherry-Lou said what she did about Leroy back at your place. Where do you suppose Leroy is now?"

"Easy. Hidin' out in Big Thicket."

"Think the cops will find him there?"

"Them!" Dade spat derisively. "They couldn't find their own asses in Big Thicket."

"See what I mean." Billy stuck his forefinger under Dade's nose. "I don't want that son of a bitch getting away. I'd be right thankful if he didn't."

Dade nodded. "There's a whole passel of folks round here that don't like the Ainslees. Never have—but never gotten stirred up enough to do anythin'. This might do it. As for Leroy—well, if the devil looks after his own, so does the Lord. So let's leave it to the Lord." Dade spat again, and said thoughtfully, "But mebbe he could do with a little help."

Billy nodded, satisfied. "That make you happy?" he said to me.

"It'll do—for now." I was thinking of Robinson.

"Then let's go home."

I said goodbye to the Perkinses, and Dade said, "Come back some time, you hear? Big Thicket ain't all blood. There's some real pretty places I'd like to show you."

"I'll do that," I said and climbed up into the helicopter. I slid the door closed and we rose into the sky and I saw Big Thicket laid out below. Then the chopper tilted and there was nothing but sky as we slid west towards Houston.

Ten days after we came out of Big Thicket Leroy Ainslee's body was found by the track of the Southern Pacific railroad. Apparently he had been run over by a train.

"Where exactly did it happen?" I asked Billy.

"Just north of Kountze. Little town which might be described as the capital of Big Thicket."

" 'Leave him to the Lord,' " I quoted ironically.

"I got the pathologist's report," said Billy. "Most of the injuries were consistent with tangling with a freight train."

"Most?"

Billy shrugged. "Maybe the Lord had help. Anyway the cops have written it down as accidental death. He's being buried in Kountze."

"I see." I saw that Texas could be a pretty rough place.

"It's best this way," said Billy. "Oh, by the way, Dade Perkins sends his regards."

But Robinson had disappeared and it was to be a long time before I caught up with that murderous bastard.

19

MEDICAL SCIENCE made Debbie's wakening mercifully easy, and when she opened her eyes mine was the first face she saw. She was not fully conscious, lapped in a drug-induced peace, but enough so to recognize me and to smile. I held her hand and she closed her eyes, the smile still on her lips, and slipped away into unconsciousness again. But her fingers were still tight on mine.

I stayed there the whole afternoon. Her periods of semi-consciousness became more frequent and longer-lasting, monitored by a nurse who adjusted the intravenous drip. "We're bringing her out slowly and smoothly," the nurse said in a low voice. "No sudden shocks."

But Debbie did have the sudden shock of remembrance. In one of her periods of wakefulness her eyes widened and she gave a small cry. "Oh! They ... they...."

"Hush, my love," I said. "I'm here, and I won't leave. It's finished, Debbie, it's all over."

Her eyes had a look of hazy horror in them. "They...."

"Hush. Go back to sleep."

Thankfully she closed her eyes.

Much later, when she was more coherent, she tried to talk about it. I would not let her. "Later, Debbie, when you're stronger. Later—not now. Nothing matters now but you."

Her head turned weakly on the pillow. "Not me," she said. "Us."

I smiled then because I knew that she—we—would be all right.

I talked with her doctor and asked bluntly if Debbie would be able to have another baby. His answer was almost the same as Sherry-Lou's. "Women are stronger than most men think, Mr. Mangan. Yes, she'll be able to have children.

What your wife has suffered, in terms of physical damage, is no more than some women suffer in childbirth. Cesarean section, for instance."

"Cesarean section is usually done more hygienically," I said grimly. "And with anesthetics."

He had the grace to look abashed. "Yes, of course," he said hurriedly. "She may need a great deal of care of the kind that is out of my field. If I could recommend a psychiatrist . . . ?"

Sherry-Lou had said Debbie would need cherishing, and I reckoned that was my department; the cherishing that comes from a psychiatrist is of an arid kind. I said, "I'll be taking her home."

"Yes," said the doctor. "That might be best."

I was hedged about by the law. The Cunninghams retained a good lawyer, the best trial lawyer in Texas I was assured. His name was Peter Heller and his only command was that I keep my mouth shut. "Don't talk to anyone about the case," he said. "Not to the police and especially not to newsmen."

One thing troubled him. "The reef we're going to run onto is that of intent," he said. "You see, Mr. Mangan, you made certain preparations, way ahead of the event, to kill one of the Ainslees—and you did kill Earl Ainslee and, subsequently, Tukey. Now, we might just get away with Tukey because you could have had no knowledge he'd be there when you opened the door, but Earl is a different matter— that was deliberately planned. The pitcher did not walk up into the roof by itself. The jury might not like that."

The case did not come to trial or, at least, not to the kind of trial we have in the Bahamas where the law is patterned after the British style. It went to the grand jury which was supposed to establish if there was a case to be answered at all. I never did get to the bottom of the intricacies of the American legal system, but I suspect that a considerable amount of string-pulling was done by the Cunninghams behind the scenes.

Because it involved kidnapping, a federal offense, the argument before the grand jury was not conducted by a local district attorney but by a state attorney from Austin. As far as I could judge, Heller and the state attorney—a man called Riker—had no adversary relationship at all. The whole hearing was conducted in such a way as to get a cool assessment of the facts.

There was a tricky moment when I was on the stand and Riker was interrogating me. He said, "Now, Mr. Mangan; you have stated that you made certain preparations—and quite elaborate preparations—involving a pitcher of water to kill Earl Ainslee."

"No," I said. "I thought it would be Leroy Ainslee."

"I see," he said thoughtfully. "Did you have anything against Leroy Ainslee?"

I smiled slightly. "Apart from the fact that he was keeping me prisoner at gunpoint, and that he was keeping my wife from me—nothing at all." There was a rumble of amusement from the jury. "I'd never met the man before."

"Yes," said Riker. "Now, to return to the man you actually killed—Earl Ainslee. He actually had you at gunpoint at that time?"

"Yes. It was a twelve-bore shotgun."

Riker looked puzzled. "Twelve what?"

"I'm sorry," I said. "It would be called twelve-gauge here."

"I see. Did you know the gun was loaded?"

"I had been so informed. Robinson said buckshot."

"The mysterious Mr. Robinson said that?"

"Yes. I found his information to be accurate when Earl pulled the trigger."

"Earl fired a shot at you?"

"That's right. The buckshot ripped up the bed I was sitting on."

"Now, I want you to answer this question very carefully, Mr. Mangan. Did Earl Ainslee pull that trigger involuntarily as a result of being struck on the head with the heavy pitcher, or did he shoot first?"

"I don't know," I said. "I was too busy getting out of the way." Again there came a murmur from the jury.

"But, at all events, you did pull the string which released the pitcher?"

"Yes."

"Why?"

Into the sudden silence I said, "My wife was screaming." I moistened my lips. "Earl said Leroy was having fun, and that it was his turn next."

Riker waited until the stir had died away. "Mr. Mangan, had your wife not screamed would you have pulled that string?"

Again there was silence.

"I don't know. I honestly don't know."

Heller put up his hand. "Objection. The witness can testify only as to matters of fact. That is a hypothetical question."

"I withdraw the question," said Riker.

And that was the worst of it as far as I was concerned. There were more questions concerning the death of Tukey and the chase through Big Thicket, but Heller steered me past all the pitfalls. Then I retired because I was not allowed to hear other witnesses giving evidence.

Debbie told me afterwards that they handled her gently and considerately, and her time on the stand was brief. I believe the evidence of the doctor who had attended Debbie at the Ainslee place, and that of Sherry-Lou, damned Leroy thoroughly.

Anyway the whole thing was tossed out as being no case of murder or culpable homicide to answer at trial. There appeared to be a slight incredulity mixed with gratification that a Britisher, as I was popularly supposed to be, could be as red-blooded as any American and, I suppose, the unwritten law had a lot to do with it. Anyway, it was over and I was a free man.

• • •

Before I went home to Grand Bahama Billy One convened another conference. Again it was confined to his kitchen cabinet; present were Billy, Frank and young Jim. Jack was absent; although out of the hospital he was still confined to his home. I was there, too, and waiting to find out why.

Billy One started by saying to Frank, "Your Pa is a sick man and I don't reckon he'll be attending to business for some time. But decisions have to be made and someone has to make them, and I think it's up to me. Of course, it'll be put to a full meeting of the board as soon as we get around to it, but we don't have time to wait on that." He looked around the table. "Any objections?"

Billy smiled and Jim merely shrugged—he was not going to argue with the man who had promoted him to top table—but Frank said, "I think it should be put to the board."

"No time," said Billy One. "Joe's in Scotland wrapping up that North Sea oil deal and I don't want to pull him from that. Besides, I'd want to have Jack at the meeting and he's not up to it yet."

Frank nodded and accepted defeat. "Okay—but what's he doing here?" His finger stabbed at me.

"He's here because he's a Cunningham," said Billy One flatly. "And because I want him here." He ignored Frank's perplexed look and turned to me. "How's Debbie today?"

"Not too bad," I said. "She's mended in body but. . . ." I shrugged. "She has nightmares."

"Tom, I know you want to get back to her, but this won't take long." Billy One leaned back and surveyed us. "I want to remind you young fellows of some history—family history. We Cunninghams originally came from Scotland. Two brothers, Malcolm and Donald, settled here in tidewater Texas when it was still Mexico. They were piss-poor but it was a goddamn sight better than crofting back home."

He clasped his hands. "Over the years the family prospered. We helped Sam Houston take Texas from the Mexicans, and the family were among the leaders who pressured

Tyler into admitting Texas to the Union. We grew rich and strong and now we're not only powerful in Texas but over the whole goddamn world. And the way we did it was this." He raised his clasped hands before him, the knuckles white under firm pressure. "The family stays together and works as a team."

Frank said in a bored voice. "We know all that."

"Sure," said Billy One mildly. "But I want Tom to know the score. It was Billy's idea to bring him into the Bahamas deal. Me, I was neutral but willing to go along. I didn't think all that much of Tom but I had nothing against him. Same when he married Debbie."

"He cut himself a fair slice in that Bahamas deal," said Frank.

"Sure he did," agreed Billy One. "And my respect for him went up a notch." He looked at me. "Why did you set it up that way?"

"I like my independence."

"That can be good—but solidarity can be better. How would you like to join the Cunningham Corporation?"

"As what?"

"You'll be on the board making policy."

"The hell he will!" said Frank outraged.

Billy One swung on him. "You've still got a sister and Jack's still got a daughter on account of this guy, and he killed two men making it that way. He's shed blood and lost some of his own. In my book that makes him family—a Cunningham." He stared Frank down and then sighed. "Okay, Tom, what do you think?"

It was a handsome offer but there had to be a catch. As Dade Perkins had remarked, the Cunninghams were not notorious for offering free handouts. There had to be a catch in spite of Billy One's rhetoric, and he confirmed it by saying, "Before being appointed to the board there's something you'll have to do."

"And that is?"

"Well, there's something I want. Another thing about us

Cunninghams is that we take insults from nobody. Now, my brother nearly died in that damn hospital, and my niece—your wife—was raped, and that's the biggest insult you can offer a woman." His voice trembled. "I want this guy, Robinson, and I want him real bad."

Jim said, "The State Police haven't gotten far on it."

"They don't have our reasons," snapped Billy One. He stared at me. "You'll have the whole family right behind you, and that means the Cunningham Corporation. You can have any resources we have and, believe me, that's plenty."

I said, "Wow!" but not aloud. I did not know how many billions of dollars the Cunningham Corporation controlled, but it was a respectable chunk of the GNP. It was not the biggest corporation in the United States, but it was not the smallest, either, not by a long shot.

"It might not be a question of money," I said. "In any case, I have plenty of that." I held Billy One's eye. "And I don't need any reasons from you why I should find Robinson; I have plenty of my own." I leaned back. "The problem is that we have a total lack of information."

Jim said, "We have a pretty fair intelligence unit; you can put that to work." I nodded, thinking of the ready way Rodriguez had hustled up bugging devices.

"Anything you want you get through Billy or Jim," said Billy One. "You'll contact them."

"What about me?" said Frank.

"You and me have the Corporation to run. Have you any immediate ideas, Tom?"

"I think the answer lies in the Bahamas," I said. "That's the reason why your State Police have come up with nothing. I don't think Robinson is in Texas, or even in the United States. I think he's in the Bahamas. That's where I'm going to look for him, anyway. I'm leaving tomorrow with Debbie."

"With Debbie?" said Frank. "Wouldn't it be better if she stays here?"

I said deliberately, "We've had enough of separate lives—both of us." I turned to Jim. "But I'd like a twenty-four-hour bodyguard on her until this thing is settled. Can you arrange that?"

"Sure, no problem. We have some dandy bodyguards—Treasury-trained."

I did not see the point of that remark. "What's that got to do with anything?"

Billy said, "The Department of the Treasury guards the President of the United States. Those guys are very good." He smiled. "We get to hire them because we pay better than the Treasury. But I've had an idea, Tom. I know you did a composite of Robinson for the cops, but they've gotten no place with it. I have a kissing cousin who is a pretty fair portrait painter. Maybe she can produce something better."

So it was that I was introduced to Cassie Cunningham, aged about twenty-five, who came armed with a sketching block, pencils and water colors. She was quite a good portraitist and, after a few false starts, I began to feel hopeful of success. When we had done Robinson, for good measure I asked Cassie to do another of the fake doctor who had whipped me from the lobby of the Cunningham Building.

The next day we flew to Freeport in the Cunningham Corporation JetStar. Apart from Debbie and myself there were six large men with bulges under their arms. "Six!" I said to Jim Cunningham. "I'm not going to start a bloody war."

"Billy thought you ought to have a bodyguard, too. Anyway, allocate them as you choose."

After thinking that one over I thought that Billy could very well be right. "One thing," I said. "They're not employed by me. The Bahamian Government is very strict about firearms, and if these men are caught they're on their own."

So we went home and I installed Debbie back in the house, with Kitty Symonette as attendant and companion.

After making arrangements to bring Karen back from Abaco I went to see how the Theta Corporation had fared in my enforced absence. But it was just going to be a quick look because I was not going to leave Debbie for long. I had learned that lesson well.

20

STEVE WALKER, the boss of the bodyguard team, went with me to the office. I introduced him to Jessie in the outer office, then we went into my own. Walker looked around. "Two doors," he commented. "Where does that one lead?"

"To the corridor."

The key was in the lock so he turned it, locking the door. "I'd rather you use just the one door," he said. "Can I have a desk in the corner of your secretary's office?"

"Sure. I'll have Jessie set it up." So I did, much to her mystification, and when Walker had settled in I sat behind my own desk to do some heavy thinking.

I went over everything Robinson had said and latched on to something. He had said that Kayles had reported that I knew all about his plans, whatever they were, and that I had not told Kayles directly, but that Kayles had overheard a conversation between me and Sam Ford.

I thought back to the conversation on *My Fair Lady*. Kayles could have listened when Sam and I were talking in the cockpit, but we had not talked about any mysterious plans, only about how to get Kayles back to Duncan Town. Anyway, Kayles would have been too busy cutting himself free and grabbing his gun to listen to us.

The only other time he could have listened to Sam and me was when he was tied up on the bunk. I vaguely remembered that I had a notion he had been feigning unconsciousness at the time, so what had I said to Sam about anyone's plans? I remember I had been a bit irritable and had blown my top about something, but what it was I could not remember—a lot had happened since then. But perhaps Sam would know.

I snapped on the intercom. "Jessie, get Sam Ford on the telephone. I don't know where he'll be; you'll have to track him down."

"But didn't you know?" she said.

"Know what?"

"He's in a hospital in Nassau. A boat fell on him."

"Come in here and tell me more."

It appeared that Sam had been supervising the removal of a yacht from the water. Halfway up the slip it had fallen sideways from the cradle, and Sam happened to be in the way. It was a ten-ton ketch. "He's in the intensive care unit of the Princess Margaret Hospital," said Jessie. "He was still in a coma the last I heard."

"When did this happen?"

"About a week ago."

I was filled with a cold rage. If Robinson had tried to kill me because of what Kayles overheard he would certainly not leave Sam out. This was as much of an ordinary accident as the disappearance of Bill Pinder. I said, "Ask Mr. Walker to come in."

Jessie stood up, then hesitated. "Who is he?" she asked. "He's just sitting there reading magazines. And he asked me to give him a signal if a stranger comes in."

"Don't worry about him, but do as he says. And I'd appreciate it if you didn't talk about him—to anyone."

All the same she looked a bit worried as she left. When Walker came in I said, "We have another bodyguard job," and filled in the details. "I don't want anyone getting to Sam."

Walker tugged his ear. "That might be tricky. Do we get the cooperation of the hospital?"

"I'll see what I can do about that. In the meantime have a couple of your men on alert, ready to fly to Nassau."

He nodded and left, and I was about to ask Jessie to put me through to the hospital in Nassau when she buzzed me. "Commissioner Perigord to see you."

I had been expecting Perigord but not as soon as this. He was quick. "Send him in."

Perigord came in, as trim and elegant as ever in his well-cut uniform. "What can I do for you?" I asked. "Please sit down."

He took off his cap and laid it on the desk, together with the swagger stick he always carried, and sat in the chair opposite. He regarded me with dark brown eyes set in a dark brown face, and said quietly, "Don't be bland with me, Mr. Mangan. You have much to tell me. When a Bahamian of some eminence is kidnapped in Texas and kills two men in the act of escaping it tends to make headlines in the newspapers. You are a man of some notoriety."

I should have expected that but it had not occurred to me. True, Jessie had looked at me wide-eyed when I had walked into the office, but I had kept her on the run and we had not had time to be chatty. "I must get the clippings for my scrapbook," I said ironically.

"Captain Booth of the Texas State Police telephoned me. He wanted to know about you, naturally enough. Your status in the community, had you a criminal record, and so forth. I gave you a clean bill of health."

"Thanks for the testimonial."

"We also talked about our common problems—drug-running, for instance. Texas has a long border with Mexico."

"Do you still think this case has to do with drugs? I'm beginning to wonder about that."

Perigord shrugged. "I'm keeping an open mind. I read the transcript of the grand jury hearing with great interest."

I was surprised. "You did? That hearing was held in private."

Perigord's lips quirked into a smile. "Like you, I have friends in Texas. It made . . . how shall I put it? . . . empty reading. For example, there was the mysterious Mr. Robinson, your kidnapper, floating about the case with no visible means of support—never found. And there was the body of Kayles which, again, has never been found."

"It wouldn't be too hard to make a body vanish in Big Thicket," I said. "You could toss it into any swamp."

"True, but Captain Booth is moderately unhappy. You

see, he only has our word for it that there was a third body or even a Robinson. He couldn't ask Leroy Ainslee because he was inconsiderately killed by a train."

I said, "My wife never saw Kayles, but she did see Robinson. You must have read her evidence." I took a glossy color photograph from my desk drawer. "Meet Mr. Robinson."

Perigord took it from my fingers and examined it critically. "You did better with Kayles," he said. "That was a photograph. This is a photograph of a painting." He dropped it on to the desk. "Not what one would call hard evidence for the existence of Robinson."

"Are you saying you don't believe me—or Debbie?" I demanded.

"No—but I'm dissatisfied. Like Captain Booth I'm moderately unhappy." He then said what Frank Cunningham had said before Billy hit him, but in a way that robbed it of offense. "You seem to have problems with your wives, Mr. Mangan. I was very sorry when the first Mrs. Mangan died because I had a regard for her, and I was equally sorry when I heard what had happened to your present wife. I ask myself if these events are related in any way, and if your problems are going to continue. Too much has happened around you in the last year or so." He leaned forward. "Now let us talk about Robinson."

So we talked about Robinson for a long time. At last I said, "I've been wracking my brains to think of what Kayles overheard between me and Sam Ford, and I can't ask Sam." I told him about that, and added pointedly, "And I don't think that was an accident, either."

Perigord looked grave. "I'll ring Commissioner Deane in Nassau, and we'll have that incident investigated."

"And put a guard on Sam," I said.

He nodded and picked up the picture of Robinson. "How accurate is this?"

"I really don't know," I said candidly. "But it's the best Cassie Cunningham and I could do. She said it's difficult for a painter to depict an image in someone else's mind's eye."

"Very well put." Perigord picked up his hat. "Now, there is just one last matter. You came back from Texas without a passport. Well, that's all right because we know the reason. But you came back with six Americans, two of whom are in your home though not, I suspect, as house guests; three are billeted in the Royal Palm Hotel, and the sixth is sitting in your outer office at this moment. We checked *their* passports very carefully and what did we find on further inquiry? All six are members of the security section of the Cunningham Corporation. Mr. Mangan, if you have fears for your own safety or the safety of your wife you should come to me and not import a private army."

"My wife is dear to me."

"I understand that." He stood up. "But I would like to see Mr. Walker now."

I eyed Perigord with respect; he even had the identification down pat. I called in Walker and introduced them. Perigord said, "Mr. Walker, we encourage Americans to come to our island; you are our bread and butter. But we don't like firearms. Are you armed, sir?"

Walker said, "Uh . . ." He glanced at me.

"Tell him," I said.

"Well . . . er . . . yes, I am."

Perigord held out his hand without saying a word and Walker took a pistol from a holster clipped to his belt and handed it over. Perigord put it into his pocket where it made an unsightly bulge and spoiled the line of his uniform. He picked up his swagger stick. "You and your friends may stay, Mr. Walker, even though I have the power to deport you. But all your firearms must be delivered to my office before midday today." He raised the swagger stick in a semisalute. "Good day, Mr. Mangan. I'll let you know of any developments."

As the door closed Walker said, "A billy club, yet! Is he for real?"

"He had you tagged the moment you got off the JetStar. He knows who you are and what you do. I wouldn't underestimate Perigord."

"What do we do about the guns?"

"You do exactly as he says. What have you got? A pistol each?"

"Yeah. And a couple of Armalite rifles."

"My God! Let Perigord have the lot. You'll get them back when you leave." I had the impression that Walker and his friends would feel stripped naked.

While not neglecting Debbie I buckled down to getting the Theta Corporation back into shape. Not that there was much wrong—I had a good staff—but when the boss takes an enforced vacation things tend to loosen and the system becomes sloppy. So I did the necessary tightening here and there.

One of the things I did was to transfer Jack Fletcher to the Sea Gardens Hotel on New Providence. The manager there had broken his leg and was out of action, and Philips, the assistant manager, was a new boy, so I thought it wise to send Fletcher. I went with him to introduce him to the staff. It was to be a quick trip because I did not want to spend time away from Debbie. Although Cora and Addy had brought over a crowd of kids and were company for Debbie I wanted to get back quickly.

Bobby Bowen flew us to Nassau and Steve Walker came along, too. During this period he was never more than ten feet away from me at any moment, and there would be only one door between us, if that. If Jack Fletcher noticed that Walker stuck closer to me than my shadow he made no comment.

After the round of introductions were over we sat in the manager's office to tidy up a few last details. There were minor differences in running the two hotels and I wanted to be sure that Fletcher knew of them. The manager's office at the Sea Gardens is immediately behind the reception desk in the lobby and one wall is of glass—glass with a difference.

From the customer's point of view when standing in the lobby the wall behind the reception desk is fitted with a big mirror. Mirrors are important in hotel design because they give a sense of space, spurious though it may be. But this mirror is of one-way glass so that the manager, sitting at his desk, can see what is happening in the lobby while being unobserved himself.

So it was that, while chatting with Fletcher, I happened to look out idly at the reception desk and beyond. There was the usual scene, a combination of idleness and bustle. Small groups of tourists stood about chatting, and bellhops were bringing in the baggage of a newly arrived tour group. Philips said they had just come from Italy. Everything was normal. At the cashier's desk there was a short queue of departing visitors doing what the whole business was about—they were paying.

There was something about the third man in the queue that interested me. I thought I knew him but could not recollect ever having met him. He was tall with graying hair and had a neatly trimmed moustache and a short beard. I stood up, went closer to the window, and stared at him. He did what many do—he looked at his reflection in the mirror and straightened his tie. For a moment he stared directly into my eyes; his own were green flecked with yellow, and I had looked into those eyes before when lying helpless in the lobby of the Cunningham Building.

I swung around. "Jack, see that man with the beard? I want him held up—delayed until I can find out who he is."

Fletcher looked surprised. "How?"

"Double his bill. Say it's a computer error and spend a long time rectifying it. But keep him there." Fletcher shot off, and I said to Philips, "Go with him. I want the man's name, room number, home address, where he came from, where he's going, and anything else you can find out about him. But be tactful. And quick."

Walker joined me at the window. "What's the panic?"

"That's one of Robinson's friends," I said grimly. "He had no beard when I last saw him, but there's no disguising those eyes and that big nose. When he leaves I want you to stick close to him." I thought for a moment. "How much money have you got on you?"

"I don't really know. A couple of hundred bucks, maybe."

"You might need more. There's no knowing where he might go." I took a cash voucher from the desk, scribbled a figure and added my signature. "The cashier will honor this."

Walker took the slip and gave a low whistle. "Five thousand dollars!"

"He might be flying to Europe, damn it! Ask for American dollars or you might be stuck with Bahamian."

"If I'm going to tail the guy I'd better not join that line at the desk," he said.

"True. Stay here until Philips comes back. He can get the cash from behind the desk."

We watched the comedy at the cashier's desk. My friend, the phony doctor, moved up to the counter and presented his room key with a smile. There was a bit of dumb show and then the bill was presented. He glanced at it, then frowned, prodded at it with his forefinger, and pushed it back across the counter. The cashier made some chat and called over Jack Fletcher who now came into sight.

Walker said, "If he pays by credit card we can trace him through the number."

I nodded. Fletcher was making voluble apologies with much gesturing. He held up one hand in a placatory manner and disappeared from view. Two minutes later he walked into the office followed by Philips. "His name is Carrasco— Dr. Luis Carrasco."

"So he really is a doctor," I commented. "Nationality?"

"Venezuelan."

"Where is he going?"

"I don't know," said Fletcher. "I've only spoken to him for about three minutes. He said he had a plane to catch and would I make it short."

"I know where he's going," said Philips. "He used our interhotel booking service. He's flying to Freeport and he's staying at the Royal Palm. He's booked in for a week."

"Damned nerve!" I said, and looked at Carrasco. He was standing at the desk wearing a preoccupied expression and tapping restlessly with his fingers.

"He'll probably be flying Bahamasair," said Fletcher, glancing at his watch. "There's a flight in an hour."

"He rented a car to be picked up at Freeport International," said Philips.

"One of ours?"

"Yes."

I looked at Walker. "Can we bug that car? I mean, do we have the facilities handy?"

Walker shook his head. "No, but we can have Rodriguez in Freeport in under four hours."

"Make the phone call, direct to Billy Cunningham. Tell him it's bloody urgent."

Walker picked up the telephone, and Fletcher said curiously, "What's all this about, Tom?"

"Something that Commissioner Perigord will want to know about." I had made one mistake with Perigord and another was unthinkable. "What room did Carrasco have?"

Philips said, "Three-one-six."

"Have it locked and sealed. We can get fingerprints." Walker heard that and nodded vigorously. I picked up the voucher which Walker had laid on the desk and tore it up; he would not need that now.

"How long do we keep Carrasco hanging about?" asked Fletcher.

"You can let him go as soon as Walker has finished his call and got a Bahamasair ticket to Freeport." There was a travel agency in the lobby, so I said to Philips, "Get that now and debit it to hotel expenses."

Carrasco had interrupted a transaction between another client and the cashier; he was obviously arguing and was tapping his wristwatch meaningfully. Walker put down the telephone. "Fixed," he said. "Rodriguez is coming over in the JetStar with a bag of gadgets."

The minutes ticked by and Carrasco was becoming increasingly irritable. When I saw Philips walking across the lobby with an air ticket in his hand I said, "Okay, let him go now. Many apologies, and tell him his taxi fare to the airport is on us as compensation for the trouble we've caused him. Do a grovel."

Fletcher shrugged and left as Philips came in and gave Walker the ticket. "Get a taxi for Mr. Walker and have it standing by," I said, and picked up the telephone to ring Perigord.

As I waited for him to come on the line I saw Jack Fletcher doing his obsequious act in a smarmy manner and I hoped he was not laying it on too thick. He escorted Carrasco to the door and Walker nodded to me and left without saying a word.

I got Perigord and told him what was happening. I said, "I don't want this man alarmed because we haven't got Robinson yet. Carrasco could lead us to him."

"At last you are using the brains you undoubtedly possess," said Perigord, and promised to have a discreet escort awaiting Carrasco at the airport.

I told him that Walker was on the same flight, then said, "One last thing; there'll be an American called Rodriguez coming in on the Cunningham JetStar later today. I don't want the Customs holding him up by taking a too close interest in his bags. Can you arrange that?"

"Not if he's bringing firearms," said Perigord. "You know that."

"No firearms—my guarantee," I promised. "He's an electronics expert—I'll tell you about him later."

Perigord agreed. I told him I'd be flying back immediately, then hung up and sat at Fletcher's desk and pondered. Was I right? I had seen him only for a matter of seconds, and I had been in a drugged condition at the time. But it had been very close up. Was I right in staking that he was Carrasco? Staking everything on the color of a man's eyes and the size of his nose?

I thought I was right. The recent painting session with Cassie Cunningham had clarified my mind and etched that face into my mind's eye. But if I was wrong and Perigord laid on an elaborate operation to no good purpose then he would have an even lower opinion of me than ever.

Fletcher came back, and I asked, "What's Carrasco's credit card number?"

"He paid cash. Just dug out his wallet and paid in hundred-dollar bills, American. It didn't empty the wallet, either."

"How much was the bill?"

"A little over eleven hundred dollars. He used the restaurant a lot and his bar bill wasn't small. Then there was the car rental charge."

I leaned back in the chair. "Jack, you've been in this business quite a time. When was the last time you can remember that a bill like that was paid in cash?"

"It's happened a few times," he said. "Not many, though. Usually when a man has cleaned up at the casino—he gets paid out in cash so he pays his bill in cash. But that's usually in Bahamian dollars."

"I don't think Carrasco is a gambler," I said meditatively. "Not that kind, anyway. I'll take a copy of the bill with me." I felt much more confident and happy.

21

I FLEW back to Freeport and went to see Perigord immediately. He had Inspector Hepburn with him, and he came quickly to the point. "Tell us more about this man Carrasco."

I did not do that. Instead, I looked at Inspector Hepburn, and asked, "Do you still think this is about cocaine?"

Perigord said, "Yes, we do."

"Well, I don't. Both Kayles and Robinson seemed surprised when I brought up the subject."

"They would," said Hepburn. "They were not likely to admit it, were they?"

I said, "To my mind their surprise was genuine. It took them aback."

"But we don't have your mind," said Perigord. "I doubt if you would consider yourself an expert on the way criminals behave when confronted."

I saw I was getting nowhere pursuing that line; their minds were made up. "What do you want to know about Carrasco?"

"Everything," Perigord said succinctly.

"He kidnapped me from the Cunningham Building," I said. "And—"

Perigord held up his hand. "You're sure it's the same man?"

I hesitated. "Not one hundred percent, but near enough. I don't trust people who pay large bills in cash." I told them of what had happened and put a copy of the bill on Perigord's desk.

Perigord, too, found that odd. We thrashed it out a bit, then he said, "Mr. Mangan, can we trust your American friends?"

"In what way?"

"Can we trust them to stick to surveillance, but not to take action in the matter of Carrasco? Our police force is relatively small and I would welcome their help in keeping tabs on Carrasco, but not to the extent of their taking violent action. That I can't permit."

"They'll do exactly as I tell them."

"Very well. I have talked to Mr. Walker and he has Carrasco under observation at this moment, and is to report to my man at your hotel. Why is Rodriguez coming, and what is he carrying?" I told him and he smiled. "Yes, I think we can do with scientific aid."

Hepburn said, "There's something I don't understand. If Carrasco kidnapped you in Houston isn't he taking a risk by walking openly about your hotels? He could bump into you at any time. In fact, you *did* spot him—or so you think." He glanced at Perigord. "To my mind this may be a case of mistaken identification. Mr. Mangan admits he only saw the man in Houston for a few seconds."

"What do you say to that?" asked Perigord.

"It's been puzzling me, too," I said. "But I'm ninety-five percent convinced it's the same man."

"Nineteen chances out of twenty in favor of you being correct," he mused. "Those are odds I can live with. We'll watch Dr. Carrasco."

Driving from the police station to the hotel I thought of what Hepburn had said, and came to the conclusion that it could cut both ways. If Carrasco had been the man in Houston then perhaps he was willing to take the chance of me seeing him *because* I had seen him for only a few seconds. In those circumstances perhaps he thought a beard and moustache were sufficient disguise. As I switched between alternatives my mind felt like a yo-yo.

A good hotel has two circulatory systems, one for the clientele which is luxuriously furnished, and the other for the staff which has a more spartan decor; and in the best hotels the two systems are mutually exclusive because one does not want maintenance traffic to erupt into the public rooms. When I got back to the hotel I stuck to the staff system because I wanted to keep out of the way of Carrasco.

Walker reported on Carrasco and related affairs. "He's holed up in his room; probably unpacking. Rodriguez will be here in about two hours; I'll have a man at the airport to meet him. Perigord has a man here in the hotel, and he assigned another to your house to guard your wife." He scratched the angle of his jaw, and added sourly, "They're both armed."

"They're entitled to be," I said. "You're not." It was good of Perigord to think of Debbie. "You're not to lay a finger on Carrasco. Just watch him and report on who he talks to."

"Can we tap his room telephone?"

"It's probably illegal but we'll do it. I'll have a word with the switchboard operator. Carrasco might speak Spanish; do we have anyone who can cope with that?"

"One—two when Rodriguez comes."

"That should be enough. Any problems, let me know." We knocked it around a bit more, trying to find angles we had forgotten, did not find any and left it at that.

For the next three days nothing happened. Carrasco had no visitors to his room and used his telephone only for room service and for restaurant bookings. Rodriguez bugged his car and his room, and put a tape recorder on the telephone tap so that we had a record of his conversations, but we got little joy out of that. A search of Carrasco's possessions brought nothing; he carried with him just what you would expect of a man on holiday.

Debbie wondered audibly about the muscular young black who had been imported into the house to help Luke Bailey, who did not need it, and who was making good time with Addy Williams. She knew about Walker's crew and I saw no reason to keep from her the knowledge that this addition to the household was one of Perigord's cops. "I'd like you to keep to the house as much as possible," I said.

"How long will we have to live like this?" she said desolately. "Being in a state of siege isn't exactly fun."

I did not know the answer to that, but I said, "It will blow over soon, I expect." I told her about Carrasco. "If we can use him to nail Robinson I think it will be finished."

"And if we can't?"

I had no answer to that, either.

I had not expected to go back to New Providence for some time. Jack Fletcher was an experienced manager and did not need his hand held, which is why I had put him into the Sea Gardens. But when he telephoned four days after I had left him in charge he was in a rare panic. "We've got big trouble, Tom," he said without preamble. "Our guests are keeling over in all directions—dropping like flies. Tony Bosworth has his hands full."

"What is it? Does he know?"

"He's closed down the big air conditioner."

"He thinks it's Legionnaires' disease?" I thought quickly. "But it doesn't work that way—it didn't at the Parkway. Let me talk to him."

"You can't. He's in a conference with officials from the Department of Public Health."

"I'll be right over," I said. "Have a car waiting for me at the airport."

During the flight I was fuming so much that I expect steam was blowing out of my ears. After all the trouble I had taken to ensure the hotels were clean, this had to happen. Surely Tony must be wrong; the symptoms seemed quite different to me. This would be enough to give Jack Cunningham another heart attack.

Fletcher met me at Nassau Airport himself. As we drove to the Sea Gardens I said, "How many people ill?"

His answer appalled me. "A hundred and four—and I'm not feeling too good myself." He coughed.

"My God!" I glanced at him. "Are you really not feeling well, Jack? Or was that just a figure of speech?"

"I'm feeling lousy. I'm running a temperature and I have a hell of a headache."

He was not the only one. I said, "You're going to bed when we get back. I'll have Tony look you over. How many of that figure you gave me are staff?"

"As of this morning we had three on the sick list—four with me now." He coughed again convulsively.

"Stop the car," I said. "I'll drive." I found it puzzling that the number of staff casualties should be so low. As I drove off again I said, "How many registrations have you got?"

"Something over three hundred; I'll let you know when we get to my office."

"Never mind," I said. "I'll ask Philips. You go to bed." What he had told me meant that about one-third of the clientele had gone down sick. "Any deaths?"

"Not yet," he said ominously.

We got to the Sea Gardens and I packed Fletcher off to his staff flat and then went to look for Philips. I found him helping out at the cashier's desk where there was a long line of tourists anxious to leave as quickly as they could—like money bats. The buzz of conversation in the queue was low and venomous as though coming from a disturbed hive of bees. I was in no mood to placate the rats leaving the sinking ship, to mix the metaphor even further, and I hauled him out of there. "Someone else can do that. Jack Fletcher's gone down sick, so you're in charge. Where's Bosworth?"

Philips jerked his thumb toward the ceiling. "Doing his rounds."

"Has he any help?"

"A load of doctors from Nassau and some nursing staff from the hospital."

"Track him down; I want to see him in Fletcher's office five minutes ago."

When I saw Tony Bosworth he looked tired and drawn, his eyes were reddened as though he had not slept, and he swayed a little on his feet. I said, "Sit down before you fall down, and tell me what the hell we've got."

He sighed as he sat down. "The tests aren't through yet, but I'm fairly certain it's legionellosis."

"Damn!" I mopped the sweat from my brow and loosened my tie. It was hot and humid and I realized why. The air conditioning in the public rooms was not working. "It's hitting faster this time, isn't it?"

"It's the Pontiac fever form, I think. It hits sooner and harder, in the sense that more people exposed to it contract the symptoms—ninety-five percent is the usual rate."

"My God!" I said. "Then we still have a long way to go. Did you see what was happening in the lobby as you came through?"

He nodded. "I'm not sure it's wise to allow those people to leave. They could go away and still come down with the bug."

"I don't see how we can stop them. You can't expect people to stay in what they think is a pest house. What's the position of the Public Health Department?"

"They're still making up their minds." Tony's eyes met mine. "I think they'll close you down."

I winced. "How could this happen?" I demanded. "You know the precautions we took."

"Tom, I don't know." He, too, took out a handkerchief and wiped his brow, then ran it around the edge of his collar. "What's puzzling me is the spotty spread. We're not getting an incidence of ninety-five percent—it's more like thirty percent."

"Then perhaps it's not Pontiac fever."

"All the symptoms check." Tony scratched his head. "But *all* the Italians have gone down, seventy-five percent of the Americans, but only twenty-five percent of the British."

I blinked at that. "You mean it's attacking by nationality selectively? That's crazy!" I had a thought. "It's tending to give Bahamians a miss, too. Only four of the staff have gone down."

"Four? Who's the fourth?"

"Jack Fletcher—I've just packed him off to bed. I'd like

you to look at him when you have time. Who are the other three?" He named them, and I said slowly, "They all live here in the hotel." Most of the staff had homes of their own, but a select few of the senior staff, like Fletcher, had staff flats.

It was as though I had goosed Bosworth. He jerked visibly and sat up straight from his slumped position, and I could see the Big Idea bursting from him. Someone has christened it the Eureka Syndrome. He leaned forward and grabbed the telephone. A minute later he was saying, "Nurse, I want you to go to every patient and ask a question—Do you habitually take tub baths or a shower? Make a tabulated list and bring it to the manager's office. Yes, nurse, I'm serious. Get someone to help you; I want it fast."

He put down the telephone, and I said dryly, "I'm not surprised the nurse asked if you were serious. What is this?"

"National habits," he said. "Do you know the Russians don't have plugs in their wash hand basins? They don't like washing their hands in dirty water so they let the taps run."

For a moment I thought Tony had gone completely round the bend. "What the hell have the bloody Russians to do with this?" I said explosively.

He held up both his hands to quiet me. "I once talked with an Italian doctor. He told me the Italians consider the English to be a dirty race because they bathe in their own filth. He said most Italians take showers. Now, every Italian in the hotel has gone down with this bug—every last one of them."

"And seventy-five percent of the Americans, but only twenty-five percent of the English."

"Whereas, if the infection had been coming from the air conditioner as at the Parkway, it should have been ninety-five percent overall. You know what this means, Tom; it's in the water supply, not the air conditioner."

"That's bad." I sat and thought about it. If the water supply was contaminated the hotel was sure to be shut down. I said, "It won't work, Tony. Everybody has been drinking the damn water, and they sure as hell don't drink their shower water."

"But that's the point. You can drink a gallon of water loaded down with this bug and it'll do no harm in the gut. To be infectious it must be inhaled into the lungs. At the Parkway the air in the lobby and on the pavement outside was filled with drift from the air conditioner—an aerosol loaded with *L. pneumophila* which was inhaled. Exactly the same thing happens when you take a shower; the water is broken up into very fine droplets and you inhale some of it."

"Jack Fletcher takes showers," I said. "I was in his apartment once and his wife said he was in the shower. I could hear him; he has a fine bathroom baritone." I blew out my cheeks. "So what do I tell those people out there? That everything is okay as long as they don't take a shower? I really don't think that would work."

"I'm sorry," said Tony. "But I really think you'll have to close if my theory turns out to be right. I'll lay in some sodium hypochlorite to flush out the system."

Three-quarters of an hour later we had the answer; all the patients, without exception, had taken showers. Tony had sent some of the older people to the Princess Margaret Hospital and they were interrogated, too. Same answer. "That does it," he said. "It's in the water supply."

I said, "We have to retrieve something out of this mess, so we'll turn it into a public relations exercise. I'll notify the Department of Public Health that we're closing before they tell me I must." I grinned at Tony and quoted, " 'His cause is just who gets his blow in fust.' Then there are the customers. We'll get them into other hotels, preferably our own, and stand the expense." It would break Jack Cunningham's heart, but would be good business in the long run.

"What about all the people still here and sick?"

"They can stay if you and the other medicos can look after them. My worry is how many of them are going to die here."

"None," said Tony. "No one has been known to die of

Pontiac fever yet. They'll be up and about in a few days—a week at most."

"Thank God for that!" I said fervently. "Now for the big question. I know we can get this bacterium out of the water system. What I want to know is how it got in."

"I'll check into that," said Tony. "I'll need your maintenance engineer, and I think we should have one of the Public Health people along."

"And you'll have me," I said. "I want to know exactly what happened so I can make sure it never happens again."

We began the investigation that night. All afternoon I had been helping Philips and the rest of the managerial staff to organize the future well-being of our departing guests. It took a lot of telephoning around but it got done, and although my competitors were pleased enough to take the business, they did not really like it. We all knew it would be bad for trade in the future.

Then I had to quell a minor revolt on the part of the staff. Word had somehow got around that there was something wrong with the hotel water and I was in danger of losing some of my best people. It took some straight talking on the part of Tony Bosworth, including a demonstration in which he drank a full glass of water straight from the tap—and so did I. I was glad he believed his own theories but I was not so sure, and it took some effort to drink that water without gagging.

Four of us gathered together at eight that evening—myself, Tony Bosworth, Bethel, the hotel maintenance engineer, and Mackay from Public Health. Tony had a dozen sterilized sample bottles. "Where do you want to start?" asked Bethel. "Bottom up or top down?"

"We're nearer to the bottom," said Tony. "Might as well begin there."

So we went down into the basement where the boilers were. A hotel needs a lot of hot water and we had three calorifiers, each of a capacity of three million British Thermal

Units. The huge drums of the calorifiers were connected by a tangle of pipes colored red, blue and green, with arrows neatly stenciled to indicate the direction of the flow. Tony asked questions and I looked about. The place was spotless and dry.

Bethel was explaining something technical to Tony when I broke in. "This place is as dry as a bone, Tony; there have been no leaks recently." I turned to Bethel. "When did you last strip down any of this?"

He frowned. "Must have been eight months ago, Mr. Mangan. A normal maintenance check. This equipment is efficient; hardly ever goes wrong."

"Where does the water come from?"

"Out of the main city supply." He nodded towards Mackay. "Mr. Mackay can tell you more about that."

"Then why should we be the only building hit?" I asked Tony.

"That's not exactly true," said Mackay. "Isn't the city water piped into tanks somewhere at the top of the building?"

"That's right," said Bethel. "Right at the top to give it a good head."

"So it could have been contaminated in the tanks after it left the city mains," I said. "I don't think it could have happened down here. Everything is as tight as a drum."

"Let's go to the top," proposed Tony, so we went up in the service elevator.

The water tanks were on the roof and they were big. "Twenty-five thousand gallons," said Bethel. "Five thousand in each tank." He pointed out the main piping rising up the side of the hotel. "The water comes up there and is distributed by this manifold into the tanks. Each tank has a ball valve to control the water level." He shrugged. "The whole system is just the same as the one you'll have in your own home; it's just that this is bigger."

"I've never seen mine," I said.

Bethel grinned. "I don't come up here too often myself.

The system is automatic." He pointed. "You can see that the tanks are all interconnected by that manifold at the bottom.

That meant that water would flow freely between the tanks. "Why five?" I asked. "Why not one big tank?"

"Well, if something happens—a tank springs a leak, say— we can isolate it and go on using the other four." Bethel was very good at answering stupid questions from a layman.

"And the tanks are sealed?"

"Sure. There's a manhole on the top of each so we can get at a sticky valve if we have to, but the lids are bolted down on a mastic seal."

"Let's take a look," said Tony, and began to climb the steel ladder on the side of the nearest tank.

We all followed him. On top of the tank Bethel squatted on his haunches. "Here's the manhole. I had the tanks re-painted about three months ago and we just painted over the manhole covers, bolts and all. You can see this hasn't been opened since then—the paint seal isn't cracked."

I looked at Mackay. "Then how did the bug get into the system? It *must* be in the city water." Something bright on the roof shot a sun reflection into my eye and I turned slightly to get rid of it.

"Impossible!" said Mackay positively. "Not if this is the only building affected. Look." He unrolled the chart he was carrying which proved to be a water distribution map. "All those houses take the same water. Even the airport is on the same water main."

"People normally don't shower in airports," said Tony.

"They do in houses," retorted Mackay. "It can't be in the city water. Of that I'm certain."

Bethel had wandered away and was standing on the next tank. "Hey!" he called, and again the reflection stabbed my eye as I turned. "This one's been opened." We crossed to the tank and stood around the manhole cover. "The paint has cracked around the bolts."

"Opened sometime in the last three months," said Tony.

"Later than that," said Bethel confidently. He pointed to

where bright metal showed where paint had flaked away. "It hasn't started to rust. I'd say sometime in the last week."

"That adds up," said Tony.

"Who would have opened it?" I asked.

"I didn't," said Bethel. "Harry Crossman might have, but if he did he didn't tell me."

Crossman was Bethel's assistant. "It will be on his work sheets," I said. "I want to see them. I want to see them now."

Bethel stood up. "They're in my office."

"Bring back a wrench," said Tony. "I want to take samples from here."

There was no point in me watching Tony take samples so I went with Bethel. We climbed down on to the roof and walked towards the elevator motor housing, and I kicked something which rolled away and came to a stop with a clink at the edge of a water tank. I stooped and picked it up and found the object that had been sending reflections into my eye.

But it was more than that—much more. It was a cylindrical glass tube broken at one end. The other end was pointed as though it had been sealed in a flame, and I had seen others like it in Jack Kayles's first-aid box on *My Fair Lady*. Suddenly ideas came slamming into my head so hard and so fast that they hurt. Whole areas of mystification suddenly became clear and made sense; a weird and unnatural sense, it is true, but conforming to logic.

I turned and yelled, "Tony, come down here."

He clambered down the ladder. "What's the matter?"

I held out the glass tube. "Could you take a swab from the inside of there and test it for your damned bug?"

He looked surprised. "Sure, but. . . ."

"How long will it take?"

Not long. After the last scare they set up a testing facility in the hospital here. Say, four days."

"I can't wait that long, but take care of it and do your test." I turned and ran for the staircase.

Five minutes later I was talking to Walker at the Royal

Palm on Grand Bahama. He said, "Where are you, Mr. Mangan? I'm supposed to be guarding you."

"I had to leave in a hurry, but never mind that. I want you to send a man on to the roof. No one is to get near the water tanks up there."

"The water tanks!" he echoed. "What the—"

"Never mind arguing, just do it," I said sharply. "And put another man near the air-conditioning cooling tower. Nobody is to get near that, either. Nobody at all."

"Not your maintenance crew?"

"Nobody," I said flatly. I did not know if Carrasco had local assistance or not, but I was taking no chances. "Where's Carrasco?"

"He spent the day sightseeing in West End," said Walker a shade wearily. "Right now he's having dinner at the Buccaneer Club out at Deadman Reef. I have two men with him—Rodriguez and Palmer."

"You'll probably have police to help you at the hotel as soon as I've talked to Perigord. And after that I'm flying back."

As I rang off Bethel came in. "Nothing in Harry's work sheets, Mr. Mangan."

"I know. He didn't do it. Do you know Bobby Bowen, my pilot?" Bethel nodded. "Chase him up, will you? Tell him we'll be flying to Freeport. Oh, and tell Dr. Bosworth he'll be coming with me. Mackay can take the samples to the hospital." Bethel turned to go, and I added, "And thanks. You've been a great help."

When he had gone I rang Perigord. He was not in his office, not entirely unnaturally considering the time of day, but neither was he at home. The telephone was answered by his daughter who told me in a piping voice that Mummy and Daddy were out. Where were they? She was vague about that. They had gone out to dinner. Could be the Stoned Crab or the Captain's Charthouse or possibly the Japanese Steak House in the International Bazaar or the Lobster House in the Mall. Or was it the Lucayan Country Club? I sighed and thanked her, then reached for the Grand Bahama telephone directory.

I found him in none of those places but finally tracked him down in the Mai Tai. It took me some time to convince him of my sanity and even longer to move him to action. I think I ruined his dinner.

22

Tony Bosworth and I walked into the lobby of the Royal Palm and I noticed immediately the two uniformed policemen, one standing by the elevators, the other at the foot of the staircase. I crossed to the desk. "Is Commissioner Perigord here?"

"In the manager's office."

I jerked my head at Tony and we went in. Perigord, in plain clothes, was talking on the telephone, and Walker sat on a settee. Perigord said into the mouthpiece, "I quite agree; I'll check it out thoroughly. I can expect you tomorrow, then." He looked up. "He's here now; I'll have it in more detail by then. Yes, I'll meet you. Goodbye." He put down the telephone. "Now, Mangan, you'll have to explain—"

I cut him short. "First things first. I'd like you to get those coppers out of the lobby and out of sight. I don't want Carrasco scared off."

He leaned forward. "If your story is correct then Carrasco is the most dangerous man in the Bahamas."

"No, he's not," I contradicted. "Robinson is, and he's the joker I want. He's the boss." I pulled up a chair and sat down. "Besides, you can't charge Carrasco with anything. You need hard proof and you've got none. But scare him and he'll skip, and Robinson will send someone else in his place—someone we don't know. Besides, I don't like uniformed policemen cluttering up the public rooms in my hotels. It lowers the tone."

Perigord nodded and stood up. "We may be guarding an empty stable," he said sourly. "Carrasco may not be back. Your men have lost him." He walked out.

I turned on Walker. "For God's sake! Is that true?"

He said heavily, "He went into the john at the Buccaneer

Club and didn't come out. Rodriguez thinks he left by the window. His car is still there but no Carrasco."

I thought for a moment. "Maybe he's in Harry's Bar; that's not far from the Buccaneer."

"No—Palmer checked that out."

I thought of the topography of Deadman Reef. "A boat," I said. "He's meeting a boat. Have your men thought of that?"

Walker said nothing but reached for the telephone as Perigord came back. He glanced at Tony. "Who is this?"

"Dr. Bosworth. He identified the disease and has been of great help."

Perigord nodded briefly and sat down. "Are you really trying to tell me that Carrasco is a maniac—the stereotyped mad doctor of the B movies—who is poisoning the water in hotels in these islands?"

"I don't believe him to be mad, but that's what he's doing. And Robinson is directing him."

"But why?"

"I've had a few thoughts in that direction which I'll come to in a minute. Let's look at the evidence."

"That I'd be pleased to do," said Perigord sardonically.

"I know it's all circumstantial, but so is most evidence of murder. When I found that glass tube it all came together suddenly. One, I'd seen others like it on Kayles's boat. Two, I remembered what Kayles must have heard me saying to Sam Ford."

"Which was?"

"I was blowing my top about the chain of disasters which had hit the Bahamas. Rioting in the streets of Nassau, Legionnaires' disease at the Parkway, the burning of the Fun Palace, even the shredding of the luggage at the airport. Now, I'd knocked Kayles cold and he was just coming to his senses. He must have been fuzzy—dislocated enough in his mind to think I was actually describing Robinson's doings to Sam. So when he escaped he reported to Robinson that I knew all."

I frowned. "And what convinced Robinson was that there

was at least one item on that list that Kayles wasn't privy to. That indicated to Robinson that I did indeed know about his plans—he told me so—and he was as worried as hell because I might have told you."

Perigord said, "Are you telling me that Robinson burned down the Fun Palace? And sabotaged the carousel at the airport?"

"Yes, I think he did—but not personally. Another thing: when Robinson admitted to trying to have me killed in an air crash he made a curious remark. He said the death of the Americans was an unexpected bonus, and he went on to say that Wall Street was a bit rocky about it. The idea seemed to please him."

"Come to the point you are so circuitously making."

"It was all pulled into place by a remark made by Billy Cunningham," I said. "When we put together the Theta Corporation Billy did some research in the course of which he talked to Butler of the Ministry of Tourism. He learned that eighty percent of the economy and two-thirds of the population are supported by tourism. Billy said to me that it was too many eggs in one basket, and it worried him a little. And that's your answer."

"Spell it out," said Perigord.

"Robinson is trying to sabotage the economy of the Bahamas." Perigord regarded me expressionlessly, and I said, "How many tourists have we lost since all this began? Ask Butler, and I guarantee the answer will startle you. And it's not long since Billy Cunningham warned me that if this series of disasters continued the Cunningham Corporation would think seriously of pulling out. The company which runs the Parkway in Nassau is already nearly bankrupt."

"It's all too thin," complained Perigord. "Too speculative. The only hard evidence we have is the glass tube you found, and that won't be evidence if it's clean. How long will it take you to make the tests, Dr. Bosworth?"

"The hospital in Nassau is doing the testing, and it will take four days."

"Not sooner?"

"This bacterium is very elusive," said Tony. "The samples have to go through a guinea pig and then be cultured on an agar medium supplemented by cystein and iron. Then—"

Perigord flapped his hand. "Spare me the technical details," he said irritably. "All right—four days."

"I'll tell you something, Commissioner," said Tony. "If that capsule gives a positive result it means someone has found a way of culturing *Legionella pneumophila* in quantity, and that implies a well-equipped biological laboratory. It's not something you can whip up in a kitchen."

Perigord absorbed that in silence. Walker stirred and said, "There's something you ought to know. This morning one of my guys found Carrasco in a place he shouldn't be—on one of the back stairs used by the cleaning staff. He said he'd got lost; taken a wrong turning and gone through the wrong door."

I slapped the desk with the flat of my hand. "Perigord, what more do you want?" I turned on Walker. "So Carrasco has given you the slip before. I hope to God he didn't doctor the water tanks here."

"No way," said Walker, stung. "And he didn't give us the slip. He dropped out of sight and my guy went looking for him. He wasn't out of sight for more than three minutes."

"I could bear to know a lot about who and why," said Perigord.

"There's a proverb to the effect that fishing is best done in troubled waters," I said. "The CIA know it as destabilization. They've been pretty good at it in the past."

He looked startled. "You're not suggesting the CIA is behind this?"

"I don't know who is behind it—I didn't say it was the CIA. It's not in the American interest to destabilize a sound capitalist economy in this part of the world. Others do come to mind, though."

"Five will get you ten that Carrasco is a Cuban," said Walker. "Venezuelan my ass." The telephone rang and he picked it up. "I'm expecting this." He held a short conversation, his end of it consisting of monosyllables. As he laid down the handset he said, "You were right; Carrasco went out in a boat. He's just come back and he's in the Buccaneer Club now, having a drink. We have a picture of him landing on the beach."

"Taken at night," I said scornfully. "A fat lot of good that will be. And what good is a picture? We already know what he looks like."

"There was another guy in the boat," said Walker reasonably. "We might like to know who he is. As for picture quality, if anyone can come up with something good it's Rodriguez; he has some kind of gismo on his camera. That guy is gadget-happy. He says Carrasco came back in a small boat that's probably a tender to a big yacht. After landing Carrasco, the boat went out to sea again."

"A night rendezvous," said Perigord. "I'll have a police boat take a look at Deadman Reef." He reached for the telephone.

When he had finished we continued to kick the problem around for quite a while. No, Perigord had not investigated the catastrophe of the airport carousel; it had not been considered a police matter at the time. He would look into it next day. The fire at the Fun Palace in Nassau had been investigated for arson, but no firm evidence had come up. It might be possible to borrow a deep-diving submersible from the Americans to look for the remains of Pinder's Navajo in Exuma Sound. Evidence of sabotage would be useful.

"Useful for what?" I asked. "That's in the past and I'm worried about the future. I'm wondering what Robinson's department of dirty tricks will come up with next."

It was agreed that Carrasco was our only lead and that he would be closely watched. I looked hard at Walker. "And don't lose him again."

"I'll assign some of my own men to him," said Perigord. "There are too many whites watching him now. My blacks will blend into the background better." He looked at his watch. "Nearly midnight. I suggest that Dr. Bosworth will sleep better in a bed than in that chair. And I'm for bed, too."

I turned and found Tony asleep. I woke him up. "I'll find you a room. Come on."

We went into the lobby, but Walker stayed behind to wait for the call which would tell us that Carrasco had left the Buccaneer. He would not have long to wait because the Buccaneer closes at midnight. There were quite a few returning revelers in the lobby and I waited at the desk for a few moments while they collected their keys.

Perigord walked towards the entrance, but turned and came back. "I forgot to tell you that I have informed Commissioner Deane in Nassau of these developments, and he is flying across to see me tomorrow. He will certainly want to see you. Shall we say my office at ten tomorrow morning?"

Perigord may have been the top copper on Grand Bahama, but there was a bigger gun in Nassau. I said, "That will be okay."

The man next to me asked for his key. "Room two-three-five."

Carrasco!

I should not have looked at him but I did, in an involuntary movement. He picked up his key and turned toward me. He certainly recognized me because I saw the fractional change in his expression, and he must have seen the recognition in my eyes because he dropped the key, whirled, and ran for the entrance.

"Stop him!" I yelled. "Stop that man!"

Carrasco turned on me and there was a gun in his hand. He leveled it at me and I flung myself sideways as he fired. Then there was another shot from behind me, and another. When I next looked, Carrasco was pitching forward to fall on the floor. I looked back and saw Perigord in the classic stance—legs apart with knees bent, and his arms straight out with both hands clasped on the butt of the revolver he held.

I picked myself up shakily and found I was trembling all

over, and my legs were as limp as sticks of cooked celery and about as much use in holding me up. Perigord came forward and put his hand under my elbow in support. "Are you all right? Did he hit you?"

"I don't think so. I don't feel anything. He threw a bloody scare into me, though."

Somewhere in the middle of all that I had heard a woman scream and now there was a babble of excited voices. Perigord's uniformed men appeared from where he had hidden them, and he motioned them forward to break up the mob which was surrounding Carrasco's body. He raised his voice. "All right, everybody; it's all over. Please clear the lobby and go to your rooms. There's nothing more to see."

I beckoned to the nearest bellboy. "Get something to cover the body—a tablecloth or a blanket." I saw Walker standing in the doorway of the manager's office, and strode over to him. "What the hell happened?" I was as mad as a hornet. "How did he get here without warning?"

Walker was bewildered. "I don't know, but I'll find out. There's Rodriguez." He ran towards the entrance of the lobby where Rodriguez had just appeared.

Perigord was standing over the body and Tony Bosworth was on his knees beside it. Tony looked up and said something and Perigord nodded, then came over to me. "He's dead," he said. "I didn't want to kill him but I had no option. There were too many innocent bystanders around to have bullets flying. Where can we put him?"

"In the office will be best."

The policemen carried the body into the office and we followed. "Where did his bullet go?" I asked. "Anyone hurt?"

"You'll probably find a hole in the reception desk," said Perigord.

"Well, thanks. That was good shooting." Walker returned and I shook my finger under his nose. "What happened? He damn near killed me."

Walker spread his hands. "The damnedest thing. Rodriguez was in the bar watching Carrasco, and Palmer was in the car outside with the engine running. When Carrasco made his move to go, Rodriguez went to the public phone to make his call and found that some drunken joker had cut the cord. It had been working earlier because I'd talked to him about a possible boat. He didn't have much time because Carrasco was already outside, in his car, and on the move. So he made a judgment—he went after Carrasco."

Perigord said, "Perhaps Carrasco knew he was being watched. Perhaps he cut the telephone cord."

"No way," said Walker. "Rodriguez said that Carrasco never went near the public phone when he came back from his sea trip. It was just plain dumb luck."

"There was no reason for Carrasco to cut the cord," I said. "He wasn't going anywhere mysterious; he was coming back here. And now he's dead, and we've lost our lead to Robinson."

"Well, let's have a look at him," said Perigord. He stripped away the tablecloth which covered the body, knelt beside it, and began going through the pockets, starting with the inner breast pocket. "Passport—Venezuelan." He opened it. "Dr. Luis Carrasco." He laid it aside. "Wallet with visiting cards in the name of Dr. Luis Carrasco; address—Avenida Bolivar, 226, Caracas. And money, more than a man should decently carry; there must be four thousand dollars here."

There were several other items: a billfold containing a few dollars in both American and Bahamian currency, coins, a pen knife, a cigar case containing three Havana cigars—all the junk a man usually carries in his pockets.

From a side pocket of the jacket Perigord took a flat aluminum box. He opened it and there, nestling in cotton wool, were three glass ampules filled with a yellowish liquid. He held it up. "Recognize them?"

"They're exactly like those I saw in Kayles's boat," I said. "And like the broken one I found on the roof of the Sea Gardens Hotel. My bet is that he picked them up tonight when he went on his little sea trip. He wouldn't want to carry those about too long, and they weren't in his room when we searched it."

He closed the box and stood up. "I think you're beginning to make your case. Commissioner Deane will definitely want to see you tomorrow morning."

I glanced at the clock. "This morning." I was feeling depressed. Later, when the body was removed on a stretcher, I reflected gloomily that Carrasco had advanced his bloody cause as much in the manner of his death as in life. A shoot-out in the lobby of a hotel could scarcely be called an added attraction.

23

THE MORNING brought news—bad and good.

When I got home I told Debbie what had happened because there was no way of keeping it from her; it was certain to be on the front page of the *Freeport News* and on the radio. She said incredulously, "Shot him!"

"That's right. Perigord shot him right there in the lobby of the Royal Palm. A hell of a way to impress the guests."

"And after he shot at you. Tom, you could have been killed."

"I haven't a scratch on me." I said that lightly enough, but secretly I was pleased by Debbie's solicitude which was more than she had shown after my encounter with Kayles in the Jumentos.

She was pale. "When will all this stop?" Her voice trembled.

"When we've caught up with Robinson. We'll get there." I hoped I put enough conviction into my voice because right then I could not see a snowball's chance in hell of doing it.

So I slept on it, but did not dream up any good ideas. In the morning, while shaving, I switched on the radio to listen to the news. As might have been predicted the big news was of the shooting of an unnamed man in the lobby of the Royal Palm by the gallant and heroic Deputy Commissioner Perigord. It was intelligent of Perigord to keep Carrasco's name out of it, but also futile; if Robinson was around to hear the story he would be shrewd enough to know who had been killed.

The bad news came with the second item on the radio. An oil tanker had blown up in Exuma Sound; an air reconnaissance found an oil slick already twenty miles long, and the betting was even on whether the oil would foul the beaches of Eleuthera or the Exuma cays, depending on which way it drifted.

The Bahamas do not have much going for them. We have no minerals, poor agriculture because of the thin soil, and little industry. But what we do have we have made the most of in building a great tourist industry. We have the sea and sun and beaches with sand as white as snow—so we developed water sports; swimming, scuba diving, sailing—and we needed oiled water and beaches as much as we needed *Legionella pneumophila*.

I could not understand what an oil tanker was doing in Exuma Sound, especially a 30,000-tonner. A ship that size could not possibly put into any port in any of the surrounding islands—she would draw far too much water. I detected the hand of Robinson somewhere; an unfounded notion to be sure, but this was another hammer blow to tourism in the Bahamas.

I dressed and breakfasted, kissed Debbie goodbye, and checked into my office before going on to see Perigord. Walker, my constant companion, had not much to say, being conscious of the fiasco of the previous night, and so he was as morose as I was depressed. At the office I gave him a job to do in order to take his mind off his supposed shortcomings. "Ring the Port Authority and find out all you can about the tanker that blew up last night. Say you're inquiring on my behalf." Then I got down to looking at the morning mail.

At half past nine Billy Cunningham unexpectedly appeared. "What's all this about a shoot-out at the OK Corral?" he demanded without preamble.

"How do you know about it?"

"Steve Walker works for me," he said tersely. "He keeps me informed. Was Debbie involved in any way?"

"Didn't Walker tell you she wasn't?"

"I forgot to ask when he rang last night." Billy blew out his cheeks and sat down. "I haven't told Jack about this, but he's sure to find out. He's not in good shape and bad news won't do him any good. We've got to get this mess cleared up, Tom. What's the pitch?"

"If you've talked to Walker you know as much as I do. We've lost our only lead to Robinson." I held his eye. "Have you flown a thousand miles just to hold my hand?"

He shrugged. "Billy One is worried. He reckons we should get Debbie out of here, both for her own sake and Jack's."

"She's well enough protected," I said.

"Protected!" Billy snorted. "Steve Walker is pissed off with your cops; he tells me they've taken his guns. How can he protect her if his guys are unarmed?"

"Perigord seems to be doing all right," I said. "And there's an armed police officer at the house."

"Oh!" said Billy. "I didn't know that." He was silent for a moment. "How will you find Robinson now?"

"I don't know," I said, and we discussed the problem for a few minutes, then I checked the time. "I have an appointment with Perigord and his boss. Maybe they'll come up with something."

It was then that Rodriguez and the good news came in. "I've got something for you," he said, and skimmed a black-and-white photograph across the desk.

It was a good photograph, a damned good photograph. It showed Carrasco hopping over the bows of a dory which had its prow dug into a sandy beach. The picture was as sharp as a pin and his features showed up clearly. In the stern of the dory, holding on to the tiller bar of an outboard motor, was another man who was equally sharply delineated. I did not know him.

"You took this last night?" Rodriguez nodded. "You were crazy to use a flash. What did Carrasco do?"

"He did nothing. And who said anything about a flash? That crazy I'm not."

I stared at him then looked at the picture. "Then how . . . ?"

He laughed and explained. The "gismo" mentioned by

Walker was a light amplifier, originally developed by the military for gunsights used at night but now much used by naturalists and others who wished to observe animals. "And for security operations," Rodriguez added. "You can take a pretty good picture using only starlight, but last night there was a new moon."

I looked at the photograph again, then handed it to Billy. "All very nice, but it doesn't get us very far. All that shows is Carrasco climbing from a boat onto a beach. We might get somewhere by looking for the man in the stern, but I doubt it. Anyway, I'll give it to Perigord; maybe he can make something of it."

"I took more than one picture," said Rodriguez. "Take a look at this one—especially at the stern." Another photograph skimmed across the desk.

This picture showed the dory again which had turned and was heading out to sea. And it was a jackpot because, lettered across the stern were the words: "Tender to *Capistrano.*"

"Bingo!" I said. "You might have made up for losing Carrasco last night." I looked at Billy. "That's something for you to do while I'm with Perigord. Ring around the marinas and try to trace *Capistrano.*"

Five minutes later I was in Perigord's office. Also present was Commissioner Deane, a big, white Bahamian with a face the color of mahogany, and the authority he radiated was like a blow in the face. I knew him, but not too well. We had been at school together in Nassau, but I had been a new boy when he was in his last year. I had followed him to Cambridge and he had gone on to the Middle Temple. Returning to the Bahamas he had joined the police force, an odd thing for a Bahamian barrister to do, because mostly they enter politics with the House of Assembly as prime target. He was reputed to be tough and abrasive.

Now he said raspily, "This is a very strange business you've come up with, Mangan."

"We'd better discuss it later." I tossed the pictures before Perigord. "Carrasco probably made a rendezvous with a oat called *Capistrano*. Rodriguez took those last night."

A little time was wasted while we discused how Rodriguez ould possibly have taken photographs at night without a ash, then Perigord twitched an eyebrow at Deane. "With our permission?"

"Yes," said Deane. "Get busy. But you have a watching rief, that's all."

Perigord left, and Deane said, "As I started to say, you ave come up with an oddity. You have suggested a crime, r a series of crimes, with no hard evidence—merely a chain f suppositions."

"No evidence! What about the ampules taken from Car-asco?"

"Those won't be evidence until we find what is in them, nd Perigord tells me that will take four days. We flew an mpule to Nassau during the night. So far the whole affair is ery misty. A lot of strange things have been happening round you, and don't think my deputy has not kept me in-ormed. Now, these events are subject to many interpreta-ions, as all subjective evidence is."

"Subjective!" I said incredulously. "My first wife disap-peared and my daughter was found dead; there's nothing loody subjective about that. My second wife and I were idnapped; I suppose we dreamed it up. There have been wo cases of disease in hotels and that's fact, Commissioner, loody hard fact."

"What is subjective is your interpretation of these events," aid Deane. "You have brought in a number of events—the reakdown of a baggage carousel at the airport, a fire, an air rash, and a number of other things, and the only connec-ion you can offer is your interpretation. Just give me one iece of hard evidence, something I can put before a court— hat's all I ask."

"You've got it—the ampules."

"I've got nothing, until four days from now. And what's in he ampules might prove to be a cough cure."

"You can prove it right now," I said. "Just take one of

those ampules, break it, and inhale deeply. But don't ask m
to be in the same room when you do it."

Deane smiled unexpectedly. "You're a stubborn man. N
I won't do that because you may be right. In fact, I think yo
are right." He stood up and began to pace the room. "You
interpretation of events dovetails with a number of mysterie
which have been occupying my mind lately."

I sighed. "I'm glad to hear it."

"A lot of telephoning was done during the night. We nov
know that Dr. Luis Carrasco is unknown at 226 Avenida Be
livar in Caracas."

That was disappointing. "Another lead gone," I said de
jectedly.

"Negative findings can be useful," observed Deane. "I
tells us, for instance, that he was bent, that he had somethin
to hide." He added casually, "Of course, now we know hi
real name all becomes clear."

I sat up. *"You know who he is?"*

"When you sealed his hotel room you did well. We coul
make nothing of the fingerprints so we passed them on to th
Americans, and their report came on that telephone just be
fore you arrived here. Carrasco turns out to be one Serafi
Perez."

That meant nothing to me. "Never heard of him."

"Not many people have," said Deane. "He liked his anc
nymity. Perez is—was—a Cuban, a hardline communist an
Moscow-trained. He was with Che Guevara when Guevar
tried to export the revolution, but he broke with Guevar
because he thought Guevara was mishandling the business
As it turned out Perez proved to be right and Guevar
wrong. Since then he's been busy and a damn sight mor
successful than Che. He's been showing up all over th
place—Grenada, Nicaragua, Martinique, Jamaica. Notic
anything about that list?"

"The hot spots," I said. "Grenada has gone left, so ha
Nicaragua. Jamaica is going, and the French are holding or
to Martinique with their fingertips."

"I believe Perez was here during the riots in Nassau. There was a certain amount of justification for that trouble, but not to the length of riot. Many of the rioters had no direct connection and I smelled a rent-a-mob. Now I know who rented it."

"So much for Carrasco-Perez," I said. "A white ant."

Deane looked puzzled. "What do you mean?"

"When I was at Cambridge I knew a South African. He once said something which had me baffled and I asked him to explain it. He said he had been white-anted; apparently it's a common South African idiom. A white ant is what we would call a termite, Commissioner."

Deane grunted. "Don't talk to me about termites," he said sourly. "I've just discovered that my house is infested. It's going to cost me five thousand dollars—probably more."

I said, "You take a wooden post or a beam in a house. It looks good and solid until you hit it, then it collapses into a heap of powder—the termites have got into it. When the South African said he'd been white-anted he meant he'd been undermined without his knowledge. In his case it was student politics—something to do with the student union. Commissioner, the Bahamas are being white-anted. We're being attacked at our most vulnerable point—tourism."

"A good analogy," said Deane thoughtfully. "It's true that the Ministry of Tourism is perturbed about the fall in the number of visitors lately. So is the Prime Minister—there was a special Cabinet meeting last week. And there's more political unrest. Fewer tourists means more unemployment, and that is being exploited. But we need evidence—the Prime Minister demands it. Any crackdown without evidence would lead to accusations of police interference in political matters. The Prime Minister doesn't want the Bahamas to have the reputation of being a police state—that wouldn't do much for tourism, either."

"Then investigate the sinking of that tanker in Exuma Sound last night. The report mentioned a twenty-mile oil slick only eight hours after she went down. If that's true the oil came out awfully fast. If I were you I'd question the skipper closely—if he's still around. Don't wait for the official inquiry; regard it as a police matter."

"By God!" said Deane. "I hadn't made *that* connection."

"And find Robinson," I said. "What do you know about *him?*"

"Nothing at all. Your Mr. Robinson is an unknown quantity."

Perigord came in. "*Capistrano* just left Running Mon marina, heading east along the coast."

East! "Making for the Grand Lucayan Waterway and the north coast," I said. "Florida next stop."

"What kind of a boat is she?" asked Deane.

"Sixty-foot motor yacht, white hull," said Perigord. "I don't think she's all that fast, she's a displacement type according to the management of Running Mon. She put into the marina during the night with engine trouble. Had it fixed this morning."

I looked at Deane who was sitting immobile. "What are we waiting for? You have a fast police launch, and *Capistrano* is still in Bahamian waters."

"So we put men aboard, search her, and find nothing. Then what?" Deane stood up. "I'll tell you what would happen next. We'd have to let her go—with profuse apologies. If your Mr. Robinson is as clever as you say we would certainly not find anything because there would be nothing to be found."

"But you might find Robinson," I said. "He could be aboard and he's wanted for kidnapping in Texas."

"Not so," contradicted Deane. "A man calling himself Robinson is wanted for questioning concerning a kidnapping in Texas. He cannot possibly be extradited merely for questioning. We would have to let him go. He has committed no crime in the Bahamas for which we have evidence—as yet."

"Robinson might not be on board, anyway," said Perigord.

"Then aren't you going to do *anything?*" I demanded desperately.

"Oh, yes," said Deane blandly. He lifted his eyebrows interrogatively at Perigord. "I hope your contingency planning is working well."

"It is. A fast Customs boat will pass *Capistrano* and enter the Lucayan Waterway ahead of her. There'll be another behind. Once she's in the Waterway she's bottled up. Then we put the Customs officers aboard her."

"But I thought you said. . . ." I was bewildered.

"We might as well try," said Deane smoothly. "Who knows what the Customs officers might find if they search thoroughly enough. Cocaine, perhaps?"

I opened my mouth again, then shut it firmly. If this pair was about to frame Robinson by planting cocaine on his boat they would certainly not admit it to me, but it seemed that Deane was a hard case who was not above providing his own evidence. After all, all he had to do was to keep Robinson in the Bahamas for four days.

"We had better be on hand," Deane said casually. "You'll come, too—you can identify Robinson." He picked up the photograph of Carrasco-Perez. "And I shall certainly want to question those on board about their association with Perez. We rendezvous at the Casuarina Bridge in thirty minutes."

"I'll be there," I said.

Hoping and praying that Robinson would be aboard *Capistrano* I drove the few hundred yards to the Royal Palm knowing that Billy Cunningham would want to be in at the kill. As soon as he saw me he said, "*Capistrano* was in a marina called Running Mon, but she's gone now."

I said, "I know. The police are going to pick her up."

"Is Robinson on board?"

"I hope so. I'm joining Perigord and Deane. They want me to identify Robinson. Want to come along?"

"Try stopping me," he said. "I'm looking forward to meeting that son of a bitch."

I made a decision. "We'll go by boat. Let's go down to the marina."

We found Joe Cartwright in the marina office. I popped my head around the door, and said, "I want the rescue boat, Joe, with a full tank."

Cartwright looked up. "Can't be done, Mr. Mangan. Got the engine out of her. Tuning her up for the BASRA Marathon next month."

"Damn! What else have we got that's fast and seaworthy?"

"What about the inflatable?" he suggested. "She's not bad."

"Get her ready."

Within minutes we were at sea, roaring east along the south coast toward the Lucayan Waterway. Some people feel uncomfortable about being in a blow-up boat but they are very good. They are unsinkable, and the British even use them as lifeboats for inshore rescue. And they are damned fast even if they do tend to skitter a bit on the surface of the water.

I told Billy about the plan of attack, and presently I pointed. "There's the Waterway, and that's the Customs launch just turning in. We've got *Capistrano* trapped."

I slowed as we entered the Waterway. The Casuarina Bridge was nearly two miles ahead, and in the distance I could see the Customs launch lying next to a white-hulled boat. "They've got her." We motored on and drew alongside the Customs launch where I tossed the painter to a seaman and cut the engine. "Let's go aboard."

As we stepped on to *Capistrano*'s deck I was accosted by a Customs officer. "Who are you?"

"Tom Mangan." I looked up at the bridge and saw Perigord and Deane looking down. "I'm with Commissioner Deane." Three men stood on the afterdeck. None of them was Robinson. "That the crew?"

"Yes; skipper, engineer and seaman-cum-cook."

"No one else?"

"We're still looking. I've got men searching below."

One of the three men approached us. "Hell, Captain, this is crazy. We're not carrying anything illegal. We're just on a cruise." He was an American.

"Then you have nothing to worry about," said the Customs man.

"Well, I've gotta get back before the bad weather blows up. Did you hear the weather report? If you don't let me go I'll have to see the American consul here."

"I'll give you his address," said the officer blandly.

Another Customs man emerged from a hatch. "No one below," he reported.

"Are you sure?" I said.

"We opened up every compartment big enough to hold a man."

"It's a bust," said Billy disgustedly.

Deane and Perigord had come down from the bridge and were picking their way along the shore toward us. I looked around the deck of *Capistrano* and stiffened as I noticed that the stern davits were empty. I swung around to face the skipper. "Where's the dory—your tender?"

"Mr. Brown took it."

"Brown? Who's he?"

"The guy who chartered this boat back in Fort Lauderdale."

"When was this?"

"Just as soon as we entered this canal. He said he'd have a final spin and he'd meet us at the other end at the north shore."

"Christ, he's given us the slip." I looked at the Customs man. "You must have been following him too closely and he took fright or an insurance policy. If you weren't going to stop *Capistrano* there'd be no harm done and he'd rejoin her on the north shore. But you did and his insurance has paid off."

"He won't get far. He'll run into the boat at the other end."

"I wouldn't bet on it," said Billy. "This guy plays real cute." He gave an exasperated snort. "Brown, for God's sake!"

The skipper said, "Will someone tell me what the hell's going on?"

I turned and stepped onto the Customs launch. "Come on. Let's go after him." Billy followed me.

We dropped down into the inflatable, and just before I started the engine I heard Deane below, "Mangan, come back!" I ignored him and drowned his voice in a staccato roar as I twisted the throttle. We shot under the bridge and I looked back to see Deane on the deck of *Capistrano*. He was waving frantically.

Billy chuckled. "I guess he's wondering what will happen to Robinson if we get to him first." He suddenly had an automatic pistol in his hand.

"Put that damn thing away," I said. "If Deane knows you have it you're for the chop. And we don't want murder."

"Not murder," said Billy. "Execution." But he put the gun back into its holster.

The Lucayan Waterway stretched ahead of us and there was nothing to be seen on its surface. On either side there were occasional inlets leading to the proposed residential estates on which no houses had yet been built—the water maze. It all went by in a blur as I cranked up to top speed.

"Something ahead—coming this way," said Billy.

It was a small dot in the middle of the Waterway which rapidly grew in size under the influence of our combined speeds. "The dory!" I said.

"And something coming up behind it," said Billy. "The other Customs launch?"

"I hope not," I said.

There was no time to explain why because I was busy trying to ram the approaching boat. I pulled on the tiller but the dory went the other way in an evading maneuver, and as it flashed past I saw the man at the wheel pointing at me. Something hit the side with a thwack and there was the hiss of escaping air.

"Goddamn!" said Billy.

I twisted the boat in the water and cut speed. "This boat is compartmented. One hole won't make much difference." I looked around. There was no sign of the dory.

"I didn't mean that," said Billy. "But if I'm shot at I'm going to shoot back and to hell with Deane." The gun was in his hand again.

I could not argue with that. "It was Robinson; I saw him. Where did he go?"

Billy pointed to an inlet on the port side. "He shot down that rabbit hole."

The boat that had chased Robinson from the north shore was almost upon us. I stood up and waved with both hands, and as it approached it slowed. A Customs officer leaned from the wheelhouse, and I yelled, "Get back to the north shore, you damn fool. Keep the cork in the bloody bottle. If he gets past he can lose you."

"Who are you to give orders?"

"If you want to argue do it with Commissioner Deane. Now, get the hell back and guard that bloody entrance."

The officer withdrew and the launch began to turn in the water. There was a metallic click as Billy put a round into the breech of his pistol. "How to make friends and influence people." He snapped off the safety catch. "What do we do now?"

"I don't know." I wished I had a map. "Winkling him out of there won't be easy, but if we don't he can ditch the dory and make an escape overland. He could lose himself in the pine barrens to the east, and it would take a damned army to find him."

Billy pointed down the Waterway. "A boat's coming. Your friend the Commissioner, no doubt."

I slipped the clutch on the idling engine and we began to move slowly. "We're going in—but easy."

I took the boat into the inlet, the engine putt-putting quietly, and we immediately came to a cross canal. "Which way?" said Billy.

I tossed a mental coin. "To starboard," I said. "It doesn't

really matter." We turned to the right and went on for about a hundred yards and came to another junction. Straight on or turn to the left? This was impossible—worse than Hampton Court Maze—and there were forty-five miles of it.

From behind came the noise of a rapidly accelerating engine, and Billy shouted, "We went the wrong way! Go back!"

I spun the throttle and slammed over the tiller, and I was in time to see Robinson's dory shooting across the canal and into the main artery of the Waterway. As it went Billy popped off a shot and then was thrown back as the boat picked up speed and the bow rose into the air.

We slalomed round the corner and nearly ran into a Customs boat in the Waterway, scooting under its stern and missing by the thickness of a playing card. I twisted the throttle to slow, and kicked over the tiller so as to avoid hitting the opposite bank, then I looked around. The damned dory had disappeared again so I hailed the launch. "Where did he go?"

Deane was on deck. "Mangan, get out of here, and take your friend. This is no place for heroics from civilians."

I repeated, "Where did he go?"

The launch moved so as to be between me and an inlet. "He moved in here—but it's no business of yours. Perigord is organizing reinforcements. *Is* he Robinson?"

"Yes."

"Who's your friend?"

"If you want to know, why don't you ask me?" said Billy. "I'm Billy Cunningham and I want that bastard, Robinson."

"Mr. Cunningham, I see you're holding a gun. You'd better not have it on your person when we meet again. You'd better drop it over the side."

"In a pig's eye," said Billy. He pointed to the hole in the rubber and fabric side of the boat. "Robinson came out shooting."

"Suit yourself," said Deane. "We have excellent jails. Mangan, go away. I want to see you going back down the Waterway."

"Let's go," I said quietly, and turned the boat away.

"Your goddamn cops!" said Billy disgustedly. "You'd think he'd want our help, even thank us for it."

"Be quiet!" I said. "I'm thinking."

Again I wished I had a map. I had used the Waterway many times when I had *Lucayan Girl*, but I had always stuck to the main channel and had not bothered to explore the maze. Now I wished I had. I had a map of Freeport-Lucaya in my office and I tried to visualize the layout of the Waterway.

We went on a mile down the Waterway and came to another inlet on the same side as the one blocked by the Customs launch. I said, "We're going in here."

"Is there a through connection?"

"No."

"Then what's the use?"

I said, "Billy, every section of this water-riddled bit of real estate has but one connection with the main channel, like the one we're in now. Deane knows that and he's sitting there like a terrier outside a rabbit hole waiting for Robinson to come out. Robinson may *not* know that and if he doesn't he'll be looking for another way out. So what happens when he can't find one?"

"He'll leave the boat and take to land."

"Yes. And he's on the town side this time. It wouldn't be too hard for him to steal a car, and he stands a sporting chance of getting away. I think Deane is counting on Robinson wasting enough time looking for an exit to allow Perigord to bring up his reinforcements, and I think he's taking a hell of a chance."

"So?"

"So we're going in to chase him into Deane's arms."

"How in hell are we going to do that if there's no interconnection?"

"Portage," I said. "Now I'm glad we came in this boat and not the other."

I had timed the minutes we had taken to get from one inlet to the other, and had kept a constant speed. Now we were going back, paralleling the Waterway on a minor canal. I reckoned that when we got halfway that would be the place to go overland. Presently I said, "This should be it. We land straight ahead."

I cut the engine and we drifted until the boat nosed the bank. "Keep your voice down," I said. "Robinson could very well be just on the other side of here."

We went ashore and hauled out the inflatable. "We'll take a look across there before carrying the boat over. And keep your head down." We walked over limestone rubble and then over an unused paved road, built for the traffic that had never come. On the other side of the road I dropped into a crouch and then onto my belly as I neared the edge of the next canal.

I peered over the bank and everything was peaceful. A light breeze ruffled the surface of the water and there was no sign of Robinson's dory. I caught a movement out of the corner of my eye and looked to the left. In the middle distance was a half-constructed house, and a man was working on the roof. I returned my attention to the canal. "Okay. Let's bring up the boat."

Billy looked back. "A long haul," he said. "Nearly two hundred yards."

"We'll unship the engine," I said. "And the inflatable has carrying straps."

It was hot and heavy work but we finally made the portage and were sitting in the boat with the engine resecured on the transom. I was about to start up when Billy said, "Listen!"

Someone in the half-built house was using a hammer, but under the rhythmic knocking I heard the faraway growl of an outboard engine. It grew louder, and I said, "He's coming this way. Let's move it."

I started the engine, hoping that Robinson would not hear

it over the noise of his own, and we moved off. I kept the pace slow and, when we had gone about two hundred yards and come to a junction, I killed the engine. Again we heard the sound of another outboard motor, this time distinctly louder. Billy was moving his head from side to side to locate the direction. "To the left," he said, and took out his gun.

I restarted the engine and pushed over the tiller, and we moved to the left and toward the house in the distance. There was a bend ahead and I moved to the inside curve, still traveling slowly because I wanted to keep quiet. Over the sound of our own engine I heard the noise of another.

"There he is," said Billy, and I saw the dory coming toward us on the other side of the canal on the outside of the bend. I twisted the throttle and the boat bucked at the sudden application of power. Then we were on to him and Billy was shooting, but so was Robinson. Even as Billy fired, a bullet impacted inboard close to my hand and again there was the hiss of escaping air. Robinson was too damn good with his shooting; he had fired but two shots and had hit us both times, and although I had told Billy the inflatable was compartmented Robinson had punctured two air chambers out of the five.

Then he was past us and I slammed over the tiller, already feeling the difference in the behavior of the boat; she was slow to come about and not as easily controlled. But Billy shouted, "He's stopped. I hit his engine."

I twisted and looked back. The dory was drifting into the bank and, as it touched, Robinson leaped ashore and began to run. He paused and snapped one shot at us before disappearing behind one of the heaps of gray limestone rubble, the spoil left from the dredging of the canal.

"Let's get after him," urged Billy.

I needed no urging. Already I was heading for the bank and standing, ready to jump. Our feet hit the ground simultaneously, and Billy said, "We'll tackle him from two sides." He gestured with his pistol. "You go that way and keep your head down." He ran in the other direction.

I ran to the nearest heap of limestone and dropped flat

before peering around it cautiously. There was no sign of Robinson. From behind I heard the sound of engines so I looked back to see the Customs launch coming up the canal, fairly boiling along at top speed. Deane must have heard the shots and decided to come in.

I ignored it and turned again to look for Robinson. We were quite close to the house and there were now two men on the roof, and one of them was pointing at something. I followed the direction of his arm, got to my feet, and began to run. Skidding around another heap of rubble I came across Robinson about ten yards away. He had his back to me, and beyond him I saw Billy come into sight.

I was late in the tackle. Before I could get to him Robinson fired and Billy dropped in his tracks. But then I was on to him and I had no mercy. His pistol went flying and it took Deane and two of his men to prize my hands from Robinson's neck.

Deane hauled me to my feet and pushed me away, standing between me and Robinson. "That's enough!" he said curtly.

I heard a car door slam and saw Perigord walking over from a police car near the house. I regained my breath, and said, "Then get the bastard out of my sight before I kill him." I turned and walked toward Billy.

He was sitting up, his hand to his head, and when he took it away it was red with blood. "He creased me!" he said blankly. "Jesus, but it hurts!" There was an unfocused look to his eyes, a sign of concussion. I stooped, picked up his gun, and walked to the water's edge and tossed it into the canal. Then I went back and helped him to his feet.

"You're lucky you're not dead," I said. "Be glad it hurts; it means you'll live."

Already he was looking better. He glanced across at Deane and saw Robinson still prostrate on the ground. "Well, we've got him."

"Yes," I said shortly. Deane would not now need any excuse for holding Robinson. Any man who popped off a gun was automatically his prey—including Billy. Still, Deane had not seen Billy shoot, so, as we walked toward him, I said, "I ditched your gun in the canal."

"Thanks."

Robinson sat up and Deane was addressing him in fast, fluent Spanish. Among the spate of words I heard the name Perez repeated several times. Robinson shook his head and replied in Spanish and then switched into English, with the same plummy accent I had come to know in Texas. "I'm a soldier of the revolution," he said pompously. "And now a prisoner of war. I will answer no questions." He got to his feet.

"Prisoner of war?" said Billy unbelievingly. "The guy's nuts!"

"He's a bloody murderer," I said.

"But that's for a court to decide, Mr. Mangan," said Perigord.

Deane took out handcuffs and then paused, looking at Billy expressionlessly. "Search this man," he said.

Billy grinned widely as Perigord's hands expertly patted his body. "What gun?" he said. "I took your advice. It was good."

It was then that Robinson made his break. He thumped the nearest Customs officer in the gut, sending him to the ground writhing and retching, and took off, running toward the house. He took us all by surprise. Deane dropped the handcuffs and broke into a run, with me at his heels.

The builders at the house had stopped work and were now all on the roof, a good vantage point to view the morning's unexpected entertainment. The sole exception was the driver of a truck which had just arrived. He had got out, leaving the door open and the engine idling, and was calling to the men on the roof. Robinson clouted him in passing and he staggered back to collide with Deane and they both went down in a tangle of arms and legs.

By that time Robinson was in the cab and the engine of the truck roared. I leaped over the sprawled bodies of Deane and the driver and jumped for the cab, but it was too late and the truck was moving. I missed and fell to the ground.

By the time I had picked myself up the truck was speeding up the road.

I saw Perigord getting into his car so I ran and piled in next to him just as he drove off with a squeal of rubber and a lot of wheel spin. He drove with one hand while unhooking the microphone of his radio from its bracket. He began to give brief but precise instructions, and I gathered that he was remarshaling his forces.

The truck was still in sight and we were gaining on it. It turned left on to East Sunrise Highway, and I said, "He'll be going on to Midshipman Road, by the Garden of the Groves."

"Yes," said Perigord, and spoke into the microphone again.

The Garden of the Groves is one of the more sedate of our tourist attractions, the name being a punning one because the one-hundred-acre gardens are dedicated to the memory of Wallace Groves, the founder of Freeport. There were always tourists wandering about that area and chances were that Robinson could kill someone, traveling at the speed he was.

We sped down East Sunrise and turned on to Midshipman, and by then we were within fifty yards of the truck. A car shot out of a side road and hit the truck a glancing blow and Perigord braked hard as it crashed into a palm tree. I fumbled for the door handle as I saw Robinson jump from the cab and run toward the Garden.

Perigord was out before me, and he did something surprising—he threw his swagger stick at Robinson. It flew straight as an arrow and hit Robinson at the nape of the neck and he fell in a tumbled heap in the road.

Perigord was about to go to him but jumped back as a big double-decker London bus came around the corner. The driver swerved to avoid the crashed truck and his brakes squealed, but it was too late. The bus brushed past Perigord but one wheel went over Robinson's head.

EPILOGUE

AFTER THE immediate discussion that followed that incident I did not see Perigord to talk with seriously for nearly a month. He was a very busy man, and so was Commissioner Deane over in Nassau. But he did telephone to tell me that the ampules found on Carrasco-Perez proved to contain a culture of *L. pneumophila,* enough to poison the water in every hotel in the Bahamas.

On the occasion of the annual BASRA Swimming Marathon I invited him and his family back to the house for drinks. Both our daughters had been competitors and Karen, like Sue before her, had won a second prize in her class. Full of pride and ice cream she cavorted in the pool with Ginnie Perigord, and there did not seem to be much difference between a tanned white hide and a natural brown hide.

Debbie laughed and said to Amy Perigord, "Where do they get the energy? You wouldn't think they've just swum two miles. Would you like a drink?"

"I'd rather have tea," said Mrs. Perigord. "I'm not really a drinker."

"We won't bother Luke," said Debbie. "Come into the kitchen and chat while I make it."

I smiled at Perigord as they went away. Because he had attended the Marathon in his official capacity he was in full dress, swagger stick and all. I said, "I propose something stronger. What will you have?"

He sat down and laid his cap and swagger stick by the chair. "Some people think because I'm a black Bahamian that I exist on a liquid diet of rum, but I prefer Scotch."

I went to the poolside bar and held up a bottle of Glenlivet. "This do?"

He grinned. "That will do very well."

I poured two drinks and put a bottle of iced water at his elbow. I said, "Billy Cunningham called me this morning. He says he's growing a streak of white hair where that bullet grazed him. He thinks it makes him look distinguished."

"Did he really lose that pistol in the water?" asked Perigord curiously.

"I'll answer that by asking you a question," I said. "Would Deane really have framed the crew of *Capistrano* by planting cocaine?"

Perigord smiled. "I see." He ignored the water and sipped the Scotch. "Very good," he observed.

"Now, tell me—who was Robinson?"

"We sent his fingerprints to the States and the Americans told us, but we could have found out ourselves once we began to dig. He was an Anglo-Cuban, educated in England. His name was Rojas and he was Perez's brother-in-law."

I contemplated that information which did not mean much to me. "So what happens now? Do we live in a permanent state of siege?"

"I don't think so," said Perigord. "An attempt was made—a covert attack on the Bahamas—and it failed. We have investigated every unusual occurrence since Rojas was killed and have found nothing to indicate that the attack is continuing. In my opinion, an opinion now shared by Commissioner Deane and the Government, the whole idea was conceived, planned and executed by Perez and Rojas. Probably Castro knew nothing about it."

"You think not?"

"I think it was rather like Henry II and Becket. You know the story?"

"Henry said, 'Who will rid me of this turbulent priest?' and the four knights went and slaughtered Becket in the cathedral."

"Henry did penance for it afterward," said Perigord. "I know Fidel Castro is no saint, but I don't think he'd stoop to what that pair did. He's too vulnerable himself. No, there's been bad blood between Cuba and the Bahamas ever since their jet planes shot up our fishery patrol vessel and killed four men, and matters haven't become any easier since. I think Castro wondered aloud how to solve the Bahamian question, and Perez and Rojas decided to take action."

"So you now think we can live like reasonable human beings."

"I would say so." He smiled. "But didn't someone say that eternal vigilance is the price of liberty. It has taught us a lesson from which we have benefited. At a cost."

"I'm not going to relax the security measures in the hotels," I said.

"Very wise. We also have instituted security measures; they are unobtrusive but they are there." He held up his hand. "Don't ask me what they are."

I grinned at him. "I wouldn't dream of it." We sat in silence for a while and Perigord savored his whiskey. I said, "You know the funniest thing in the whole damn business?"

"What?"

"When you threw that swagger stick. You looked so damned silly, but it worked."

"Ah, the swagger stick. Do you know the history of this?"

"No."

"It's the lineal descendant of the ash plant carried by the Roman centurion over two thousand years ago. He used it to discipline his men, but then it became a staff of office. The line split quite early; one way led to the field marshal's baton, the other to the officer's cane. Catch!" He suddenly tossed it to me.

I grabbed it out of the air and nearly dropped it because it was unexpectedly heavy. I had thought it to be merely a cane encased in leather, but this one was loaded with lead at both ends. Perigord said suavely, "Not only a staff of office but a weapon against crime. It has saved my life twice."

I returned the weapon against crime, and he said, "Amy confided in me this afternoon that your wife is expecting a baby. Is that so?"

"Yes—in about six months."

"I'm glad she wasn't permanently harmed by what happened in Texas. In view of what I know about your family history may I offer the hope that it will be a boy?"

And six months later Karen had a brother.

THE PERENNIAL LIBRARY MYSTERY SERIES

Ted Allbeury

THE OTHER SIDE OF SILENCE   P 669, $2.84

"In the best le Carré tradition . . . an ingenious and readable book."

—New York Times Book Review

PALOMINO BLONDE   P 670, $2.84

"Fast-moving, splendidly technocratic intercontinental espionage tale . . . you'll love it."   *—The Times* (London)

SNOWBALL   P 671, $2.84

"A novel of byzantine intrigue. . . ."*—New York Times Book Review*

Delano Ames

CORPSE DIPLOMATIQUE   P 637, $2.84

"Sprightly and intelligent."

—New York Herald Tribune Book Review

FOR OLD CRIME'S SAKE   P 629, $2.84

MURDER, MAESTRO, PLEASE   P 630, $2.84

"If there is a more engaging couple in modern fiction than Jane and Dagobert Brown, we have not met them."   *—Scotsman*

SHE SHALL HAVE MURDER   P 638, $2.84

"Combines the merit of both the English and American schools in the new mystery. It's as breezy as the best of the American ones, and has the sophistication and wit of any top-notch Britisher."

—New York Herald Tribune Book Review

E. C. Bentley

TRENT'S LAST CASE   P 440, $2.50

"One of the three best detective stories ever written."

—Agatha Christie

TRENT'S OWN CASE   P 516, $2.25

"I won't waste time saying that the plot is sound and the detection satisfying. Trent has not altered a scrap and reappears with all his old humor and charm."   *—Dorothy L. Sayers*

Andrew Bergman

THE BIG KISS-OFF OF 1944 P 673, $2.84

"It is without doubt the nearest thing to genuine Chandler I've ever come across. . . . Tough, witty—very witty—and a beautiful eye for period detail. . . ." —*Jack Higgins*

HOLLYWOOD AND LEVINE P 674, $2.84

"Fast-paced private-eye fiction." —*San Francisco Chronicle*

Gavin Black

A DRAGON FOR CHRISTMAS P 473, $1.95

"Potent excitement!" —*New York Herald Tribune*

THE EYES AROUND ME P 485, $1.95

"I stayed up until all hours last night reading *The Eyes Around Me,* which is something I do not do very often, but I was so intrigued by the ingeniousness of Mr. Black's plotting and the witty way in which he spins his mystery. I can only say that I enjoyed the book enormously."
—*F. van Wyck Mason*

YOU WANT TO DIE, JOHNNY? P 472, $1.95

"Gavin Black doesn't just develop a pressure plot in suspense, he adds uninfected wit, character, charm, and sharp knowledge of the Far East to make rereading as keen as the first race-through." —*Book Week*

Nicholas Blake

THE CORPSE IN THE SNOWMAN P 427, $1.95

"If there is a distinction between the novel and the detective story (which we do not admit), then this book deserves a high place in both categories." —*New York Times*

END OF CHAPTER P 397, $1.95

". . . admirably solid . . . an adroit formal detective puzzle backed up by firm characterization and a knowing picture of London publishing."
—*New York Times*

HEAD OF A TRAVELER P 398,. $2.25

"Another grade A detective story of the right old jigsaw persuasion."
—*New York Herald Tribune Book Review*

MINUTE FOR MURDER P 419, $1.95

"An outstanding mystery novel. Mr. Blake's writing is a delight in itself." —*New York Times*

THE MORNING AFTER DEATH P 520, $1.95

"One of Blake's best." —*Rex Warner*

A PENKNIFE IN MY HEART P 521, $2.25
"Style brilliant . . . and suspenseful." —*San Francisco Chronicle*

THE PRIVATE WOUND P 531, $2.25
"[Blake's] best novel in a dozen years . . . . An intensely penetrating study
of sexual passion. . . . A powerful story of murder and its aftermath."
—Anthony Boucher, *New York Times*

A QUESTION OF PROOF P 494, $1.95
"The characters in this story are unusually well drawn, and the suspense
is well sustained." —*New York Times*

THE SAD VARIETY P 495, $2.25
"It is a stunner. I read it instead of eating, instead of sleeping."
—Dorothy Salisbury Davis

THERE'S TROUBLE BREWING P 569, $3.37
"Nigel Strangeways is a puzzling mixture of simplicity and penetration,
but all the more real for that."
—*The Times* (London) *Literary Supplement*

THOU SHELL OF DEATH P 428, $1.95
"It has all the virtues of culture, intelligence and sensibility that the most
exacting connoisseur could ask of detective fiction."
—*The Times* (London) *Literary Supplement*

THE WIDOW'S CRUISE P 399, $2.25
"A stirring suspense. . . . The thrilling tale leaves nothing to be desired."
—*Springfield Republican*

Oliver Bleeck

THE BRASS GO-BETWEEN P 645, $2.84
"Fiction with a flair, well above the norm for thrillers."
—*Associated Press*

THE PROCANE CHRONICLE P 647, $2.84
"Without peer in American suspense." —*Los Angeles Times*

PROTOCOL FOR A KIDNAPPING P 646, $2.84
"The zigzags of plot are electric; the characters sharp; but it is the wit
and irony and touches of plain fun which make the whole a standout."
—*Los Angeles Times*

John & Emery Bonett

A BANNER FOR PEGASUS P 554, $2.40
"A gem! Beautifully plotted and set. . . . Not only is the murder adroit and deserved, and the detection competent, but the love story is charming." —Jacques Barzun and Wendell Hertig Taylor

DEAD LION P 563, $2.40
"A clever plot, authentic background and interesting characters highly recommended this one." —*New Republic*

THE SOUND OF MURDER P 642, $2.84
The suspects are many, the clues few, but the gentle Inspector ferrets out the truth and pursues the case to its bitter and shocking end.

Christianna Brand

GREEN FOR DANGER P 551, $2.50
"You have to reach for the greatest of Great Names (Christie, Carr, Queen . . .) to find Brand's rivals in the devious subtleties of the trade." —Anthony Boucher

TOUR DE FORCE P 572, $2.40
"Complete with traps for the over-ingenious, a double-reverse surprise ending and a key clue planted so fairly and obviously that you completely overlook it. If that's your idea of perfect entertainment, then seize at once upon *Tour de Force.*" —Anthony Boucher, *New York Times*

James Byrom

OR BE HE DEAD P 585, $2.84
"A very original tale . . . Well written and steadily entertaining." —Jacques Barzun and Wendell Hertig Taylor, *A Catalogue of Crime*

Henry Calvin

IT'S DIFFERENT ABROAD P 640, $2.84
"What is remarkable and delightful, Mr. Calvin imparts a flavor of satire to what he renovates and compels us to take straight." —Jacques Barzun

Marjorie Carleton

VANISHED P 559, $2.40
"Exceptional . . . a minor triumph." —Jacques Barzun and Wendell Hertig Taylor, *A Catalogue of Crime*

George Harmon Coxe

MURDER WITH PICTURES P 527, $2.25

"[Coxe] has hit the bull's-eye with his first shot."

—*New York Times*

Edmund Crispin

BURIED FOR PLEASURE P 506, $2.50

"Absolute and unalloyed delight."

—Anthony Boucher, *New York Times*

Lionel Davidson

THE MENORAH MEN P 592, $2.84

"Of his fellow thriller writers, only John Le Carré shows the same instinct for the viscera." —*Chicago Tribune*

NIGHT OF WENCESLAS P 595, $2.84

"A most ingenious thriller, so enriched with style, wit, and a sense of serious comedy that it all but transcends its kind."

—*The New Yorker*

THE ROSE OF TIBET P 593, $2.84

"I hadn't realized how much I missed the genuine Adventure story . . . until I read *The Rose of Tibet*." —Graham Greene

D. M. Devine

MY BROTHER'S KILLER P 558, $2.40

"A most enjoyable crime story which I enjoyed reading down to the last moment." —Agatha Christie

Kenneth Fearing

THE BIG CLOCK P 500, $1.95

"It will be some time before chill-hungry clients meet again so rare a compound of irony, satire, and icy-fingered narrative. *The Big Clock* is . . . a psychothriller you won't put down." —*Weekly Book Review*

Andrew Garve

THE ASHES OF LODA P 430, $1.50

"Garve . . . embellishes a fine fast adventure story with a more credible picture of the U.S.S.R. than is offered in most thrillers."

—*New York Times Book Review*

THE CUCKOO LINE AFFAIR P 451, $1.95

". . . an agreeable and ingenious piece of work." —*The New Yorker*

Andrew Garve (cont'd)

A HERO FOR LEANDA P 429, $1.?
"One can trust Mr. Garve to put a fresh twist to any situation, and the ending is really a lovely surprise." —*Manchester Guardia*

MURDER THROUGH THE LOOKING GLASS P 449, $1.9
". . . refreshingly out-of-the-way and enjoyable . . . highly recommende to all comers." —*Saturday Revie*

NO TEARS FOR HILDA P 441, $1.9
"It starts fine and finishes finer. I got behind on breathing watching Ma get not only his man but his woman, too." —*Rex Sto*

THE RIDDLE OF SAMSON P 450, $1.9
"The story is an excellent one, the people are quite likable, and th writing is superior." —*Springfield Republica*

Michael Gilbert

BLOOD AND JUDGMENT P 446, $1.9
"Gilbert readers need scarcely be told that the characters all come aliv at first sight, and that his surpassing talent for narration enhances an plot. . . . Don't miss." —*San Francisco Chronicl*

THE BODY OF A GIRL P 459, $1.9
"Does what a good mystery should do: open up into all kinds of ramifica tions, with untold menace behind the action. At the end, there is bang-up climax, and it is a pleasure to see how skilfully Gilbert wrap everything up." —*New York Times Book Revie*

FEAR TO TREAD P 458, $1.9
"Merits serious consideration as a work of art." —*New York Time*

Joe Gores

HAMMETT P 631, $2.8
"Joe Gores at his very best. Terse, powerful writing—with the maste Dashiell Hammett, as the protagonist in a novel I think he would hav been proud to call his own." —*Robert Ludlum*

C. W. Grafton

BEYOND A REASONABLE DOUBT P 519, $1.9
"A very ingenious tale of murder . . . a brilliant and gripping narrative." —*Jacques Barzun and Wendell Hertig Taylo*

C. W. Grafton (cont'd)

THE RAT BEGAN TO GNAW THE ROPE   P 639, $2.84
"Fast, humorous story with flashes of brilliance."

—*The New Yorker*

Edward Grierson

THE SECOND MAN   P 528, $2.25
"One of the best trial-testimony books to have come along in quite a while."   —*The New Yorker*

Bruce Hamilton

TOO MUCH OF WATER   P 635, $2.84
"A superb sea mystery. . . . The prose is excellent."
—Jacques Barzun and Wendell Hertig Taylor, *A Catalogue of Crime*

Cyril Hare

DEATH IS NO SPORTSMAN   P 555, $2.40
"You will be thrilled because it succeeds in placing an ingenious story in a new and refreshing setting. . . . The identity of the murderer is really a surprise."   —*Daily Mirror*

DEATH WALKS THE WOODS   P 556, $2.40
"Here is a fine formal detective story, with a technically brilliant solution demanding the attention of all connoisseurs of construction."
    —Anthony Boucher, *New York Times Book Review*

AN ENGLISH MURDER   P 455, $2.50
"By a long shot, the best crime story I have read for a long time. Everything is traditional, but originality does not suffer. The setting is perfect. Full marks to Mr. Hare."   —*Irish Press*

SUICIDE EXCEPTED   P 636, $2.84
"Adroit in its manipulation . . . and distinguished by a plot-twister which I'll wager Christie wishes she'd thought of."   —*New York Times*

TENANT FOR DEATH   P 570, $2.84
"The way in which an air of probability is combined both with clear, terse narrative and with a good deal of subtle suburban atmosphere, proves the extreme skill of the writer."   —*The Spectator*

TRAGEDY AT LAW   P 522, $2.25
"An extremely urbane and well-written detective story."
    —*New York Times*

UNTIMELY DEATH　　　　　　　　　　　　P 514, $2.2.

"The English detective story at its quiet best, meticulously underplayed
rich in perceivings of the droll human animal and ready at the last with
a neat surprise which has been there all the while had we but wits to see
it."　　　　　　　　　　　　—*New York Herald Tribune Book Review*

THE WIND BLOWS DEATH　　　　　　　　　P 589, $2.84

"A plot compounded of musical knowledge, a Dickens allusion, and a
subtle point in law is related with delightfully unobtrusive wit, warmth
and style."　　　　　　　　　　　　　　　　　—*New York Times*

WITH A BARE BODKIN　　　　　　　　　　　P 523, $2.2:

"One of the best detective stories published for a long time."
　　　　　　　　　　　　　　　　　　　　　　—*The Spectator*

Robert Harling

THE ENORMOUS SHADOW　　　　　　　　　　P 545, $2.5(

"In some ways the best spy story of the modern period. . . . The writing
is terse and vivid . . . the ending full of action . . . altogether first-rate."
　　—Jacques Barzun and Wendell Hertig Taylor, *A Catalogue of Crime*

Matthew Head

THE CABINDA AFFAIR　　　　　　　　　　　P 541, $2.25

"An absorbing whodunit and a distinguished novel of atmosphere."
　　　　　　　　　　　　　　—Anthony Boucher, *New York Times*

THE CONGO VENUS　　　　　　　　　　　　P 597, $2.84

"Terrific. The dialogue is just plain wonderful."　　—*Boston Globe*

MURDER AT THE FLEA CLUB　　　　　　　　P 542, $2.5(

"The true delight is in Head's style, its limpid ease combined with humor
and an awesome precision of phrase."　　—*San Francisco Chronicle*

M. V. Heberden

ENGAGED TO MURDER　　　　　　　　　　　P 533, $2.25

"Smooth plotting."　　　　　　　　　　　　　—*New York Times*

James Hilton

WAS IT MURDER?　　　　　　　　　　　　　P 501, $1.95

"The story is well planned and well written."　—*New York Times*

S. B. Hough

DEAR DAUGHTER DEAD   P 661, $2.84

"A highly intelligent and sophisticated story of police detection . . . not to be missed on any account."   —Francis Iles, *The Guardian*

SWEET SISTER SEDUCED   P 662, $2.84

In the course of a nightlong conversation between the Inspector and the suspect, the complex emotions of a very strange marriage are revealed.

P. M. Hubbard

HIGH TIDE   P 571, $2.40

"A smooth elaboration of mounting horror and danger."

      —*Library Journal*

Elspeth Huxley

THE AFRICAN POISON MURDERS   P 540, $2.25

"Obscure venom, manical mutilations, deadly bush fire, thrilling climax compose major opus.... Top-flight."

      —*Saturday Review of Literature*

MURDER ON SAFARI   P 587, $2.84

"Right now we'd call Mrs. Huxley a dangerous rival to Agatha Christie."   —*Books*

Francis Iles

BEFORE THE FACT   P 517, $2.50

"Not many 'serious' novelists have produced character studies to compare with Iles's internally terrifying portrait of the murderer in *Before the Fact,* his masterpiece and a work truly deserving the appellation of unique and beyond price."   —Howard Haycraft

MALICE AFORETHOUGHT   P 532, $1.95

"It is a long time since I have read anything so good as *Malice Aforethought,* with its cynical humour, acute criminology, plausible detail and rapid movement. It makes you hug yourself with pleasure."

      —H. C. Harwood, *Saturday Review*

Michael Innes

APPLEBY ON ARARAT   P 648, $2.84

"Superbly plotted and humorously written."   —*The New Yorker*

APPLEBY'S END   P 649, $2.84

"Most amusing."   —*Boston Globe*

THE CASE OF THE JOURNEYING BOY P 632, $3.12
"I could see no faults in it. There is no one to compare with him."
—*Illustrated London News*

DEATH ON A QUIET DAY P 677, $2.84
"Delightfully witty." —*Chicago Sunday Tribune*

DEATH BY WATER P 574, $2.40
"The amount of ironic social criticism and deft characterization of scenes and people would serve another author for six books."
—*Jacques Barzun and Wendell Hertig Taylor*

HARE SITTING UP P 590, $2.84
"There is hardly anyone (in mysteries or mainstream) more exquisitely literate, allusive and Jamesian—and hardly anyone with a firmer sense of melodramatic plot or a more vigorous gift of storytelling."
—*Anthony Boucher, New York Times*

THE LONG FAREWELL P 575, $2.40
"A model of the deft, classic detective story, told in the most wittily diverting prose." —*New York Times*

THE MAN FROM THE SEA P 591, $2.84
"The pace is brisk, the adventures exciting and excitingly told, and above all he keeps to the very end the interesting ambiguity of the man from the sea." —*New Statesman*

ONE MAN SHOW P 672, $2.84
"Exciting, amusingly written . . . very good enjoyment it is."
—*The Spectator*

THE SECRET VANGUARD P 584, $2.84
"Innes . . . has mastered the art of swift, exciting and well-organized narrative." —*New York Times*

THE WEIGHT OF THE EVIDENCE P 633, $2.84
"First-class puzzle, deftly solved. University background interesting and amusing." —*Saturday Review of Literature*

Mary Kelly

THE SPOILT KILL P 565, $2.40
"Mary Kelly is a new Dorothy Sayers. . . . [An] exciting new novel."
—*Evening News*

Lange Lewis

THE BIRTHDAY MURDER   P 518, $1.95

"Almost perfect in its playlike purity and delightful prose."

—Jacques Barzun and Wendell Hertig Taylor

Allan MacKinnon

HOUSE OF DARKNESS   P 582, $2.84

"His best . . . a perfect compendium."

—Jacques Barzun and Wendell Hertig Taylor, *A Catalogue of Crime*

Frank Parrish

FIRE IN THE BARLEY   P 651, $2.84

"A remarkable and brilliant first novel. . . . entrancing."

—*The Spectator*

SNARE IN THE DARK   P 650, $2.84

The wily English poacher Dan Mallett is framed for murder and has to confront unknown enemies to clear himself.

STING OF THE HONEYBEE   P 652, $2.84

"Terrorism and murder visit a sleepy English village in this witty, offbeat thriller."   —*Chicago Sun-Times*

Austin Ripley

MINUTE MYSTERIES   P 387, $2.50

More than one hundred of the world's shortest detective stories. Only one possible solution to each case!

Thomas Sterling

THE EVIL OF THE DAY   P 529, $2.50

"Prose as witty and subtle as it is sharp and clear. . .characters unconventionally conceived and richly bodied forth . . . . In short, a novel to be treasured."   —Anthony Boucher, *New York Times*

Julian Symons

THE BELTING INHERITANCE   P 468, $1.95

"A superb whodunit in the best tradition of the detective story."

—August Derleth, *Madison Capital Times*

BOGUE'S FORTUNE   P 481, $1.95

"There's a touch of the old sardonic humour, and more than a touch of style."   —*The Spectator*

THE COLOR OF MURDER   P 461, $1.95
"A singularly unostentatious and memorably brilliant detective story."
         —*New York Herald Tribune Book Review*

Dorothy Stockbridge Tillet
(John Stephen Strange)

THE MAN WHO KILLED FORTESCUE   P 536, $2.25
"Better than average."   —*Saturday Review of Literature*

Simon Troy

THE ROAD TO RHUINE   P 583, $2.84
"Unusual and agreeably told."   —*San Francisco Chronicle*

SWIFT TO ITS CLOSE   P 546, $2.40
"A nicely literate British mystery . . . the atmosphere and the plot are exceptionally well wrought, the dialogue excellent."   —*Best Sellers*

Henry Wade

THE DUKE OF YORK'S STEPS   P 588, $2.84
"A classic of the golden age."
  —Jacques Barzun and Wendell Hertig Taylor, *A Catalogue of Crime*

A DYING FALL   P 543, $2.50
"One of those expert British suspense jobs . . . it crackles with undercurrents of blackmail, violent passion and murder. Topnotch in its class."
        —*Time*

THE HANGING CAPTAIN   P 548, $2.50
"This is a detective story for connoisseurs, for those who value clear thinking and good writing above mere ingenuity and easy thrills."
  —*The Times* (London) *Literary Supplement*

Hillary Waugh

LAST SEEN WEARING . . .   P 552, $2.40
"A brilliant tour de force."   —Julian Symons

THE MISSING MAN   P 553, $2.40
"The quiet detailed police work of Chief Fred C. Fellows, Stockford, Conn., is at its best in *The Missing Man* . . . one of the Chief's toughest cases and one of the best handled."
    —Anthony Boucher, *New York Times Book Review*

Henry Kitchell Webster

WHO IS THE NEXT? P 539, $2.25

A double murder, private-plane piloting, a neat impersonation, and a delicate courtship are adroitly combined by a writer who knows how to use the language." —Jacques Barzun and Wendell Hertig Taylor

John Welcome

GO FOR BROKE P 663, $2.84

A rich financier chases Richard Graham half 'round Europe in a desperate attempt to prevent the truth getting out.

RUN FOR COVER P 664, $2.84

I can think of few writers in the international intrigue game with such a gift for fast and vivid storytelling."

—*New York Times Book Review*

STOP AT NOTHING P 665, $2.84

Mr. Welcome is lively, vivid and highly readable."

—*New York Times Book Review*

Anna Mary Wells

MURDERER'S CHOICE P 534, $2.50

Good writing, ample action, and excellent character work."

—*Saturday Review of Literature*

A TALENT FOR MURDER P 535, $2.25

The discovery of the villain is a decided shock." —*Books*

Charles Williams

DEAD CALM P 655, $2.84

A brilliant tour de force of inventive plotting, fine manipulation of a small cast and breathtaking sequences of spectacular navigation."

—*New York Times Book Review*

THE SAILCLOTH SHROUD P 654, $2.84

A fine novel of excitement, spirited, fresh and satisfying."

—*New York Times*

THE WRONG VENUS P 656, $2.84

Swindler Lawrence Colby and the lovely Martine create a story of romance, larceny, and very blunt homicide.

Edward Young

THE FIFTH PASSENGER
"Clever and adroit . . . excellent thriller. . . ."

P 544, $2.2
—Library Journa

If you enjoyed this book you'll want to know about
THE PERENNIAL LIBRARY MYSTERY SERIES
Buy them at your local bookstore or use this coupon for ordering:

Qty	P number	Price
_____	_____	_____
_____	_____	_____
_____	_____	_____
_____	_____	_____
_____	_____	_____
_____	_____	_____
_____	_____	_____
_____	_____	_____
_____	_____	_____
_____	_____	_____
_____	_____	_____
_____	_____	_____
_____	_____	_____
_____	_____	_____
_____	_____	_____
	postage and handling charge	$1.00
	_____ book(s) @ $0.25	_____
	TOTAL	

Prices contained in this coupon are Harper & Row invoice prices only. They are subject to change without notice, and in no way reflect the prices at which these books may be sold by other suppliers.

HARPER & ROW, Mail Order Dept. #PMS, 10 East 53rd St., New York, N.Y. 10022.

Please send me the books I have checked above. I am enclosing $_____ which includes a postage and handling charge of $1.00 for the first book and 25¢ for each additional book. Send check or money order. No cash or C.O.D.s please

Name_____

Address_____

City_____ State_____ Zip_____

Please allow 4 weeks for delivery. USA only. This offer expires 8/31/86. Please add applicable sales tax.